ALMOST GONE

ALMOST GONE

(The Au Pair—Book One)

BLAKE PIERCE

BLAKE PIERCE

Debut author Blake Pierce is author of the psychological suspense series THE AU PAIR, which includes ALMOST GONE (Book #1), ALMOST LOST (Book #2) and ALMOST DEAD (Book #3). Ophelia would love to hear from you, so please visit www.ophelianight.com to receive free ebooks, hear the latest news, and stay in touch.

TABLE OF CONTENTS

CHAPTER ONE

Twenty-three-year-old Cassie Vale sat perched on one of the two plastic chairs in the waiting room of the au pair agency, staring at the posters and maps on the opposite wall. Right above the tacky *Maureen's European Au Pairs* logo was a poster of the Eiffel Tower, and another of the Brandenburg Gate. A coffee shop in a cobbled courtyard, a picturesque village overlooking an azure sea. Scenes to dream about, places she longed to be.

The agency office was cramped and suffocating. The air conditioner rattled uselessly, not a breath of air coming from the vents. Cassie reached up and discretely wiped a drop of sweat, running down her cheek. She didn't know how much longer she could stand it.

The office door suddenly opened and she jumped, grabbing the file of documents on the other chair. But her heart fell to see that it was just another interviewee coming out, this one a tall, slender blonde, exuding all the confidence that Cassie wished she had. She was smiling in satisfaction, holding a sheaf of official-looking forms, and she barely glanced at Cassie as she passed.

Cassie's stomach clenched. She looked down at her documents, wondering if she would also be successful, or if she'd leave disappointed and shamed. She knew her experience was pitifully inadequate, and she had no proper qualifications in childcare. She'd been turned down by the cruise ship agency she'd approached the previous week. They'd said that without experience they couldn't even put her on their books. If it was the same here, she wouldn't stand a chance.

"Cassandra Vale? I'm Maureen. Please come in."

1

Cassie looked up. A dark-suited, gray-haired woman stood waiting in the doorway; clearly she was the owner.

Cassie scrambled to her feet, her carefully organized papers spilling out of the file. Scraping them together, her face ablaze, she hurried into the interview room.

As Maureen paged through them with a frown, Cassie started picking at her cuticles with her fingernails before lacing her hands together, the only way to stop herself from this nervous habit.

She tried deep breathing to calm herself. Told herself that this woman's decision wouldn't be her only ticket out of here. There were other ways to escape and make a fresh start. But right now, this felt like the only one left. The cruise ship company had given her a flat no. Teaching English, her other idea, was impossible without the correct qualifications, and obtaining them was too expensive. She'd need to save for another year to have a hope of getting started and right now, she didn't have the luxury of time. Last week, that choice had been ripped away from her.

"So, Cassandra, you grew up in Millville, New Jersey? Does your family still live there?" Maureen finally asked.

"Please call me Cassie," she replied, "and no, they moved away." Cassie clasped her hands tighter, worried at the direction the interview was taking. She hadn't expected to be questioned about her family in detail, but now she realized that of course they would need background on an applicant's home life, since the au pairs would be living and working in clients' homes. She would have to think fast, because while she didn't want to lie, she feared that the truth would jeopardize her application.

"And your older sister? You say she is working abroad?"

To Cassie's relief, Maureen had moved on to the next section. She'd thought what to say if asked, furthering her own cause in a way that wouldn't require any confirmable details.

"My sister's travels have definitely inspired me to take a job overseas. I've always wanted to live in another country and I love Europe. Particularly France, as I'm fairly fluent in the language."

"You've studied it?"

2

"Yes, for two years, but I was familiar with the language before that. My mother grew up in France and did freelance translation work from time to time when I was younger, so my sister and I grew up with a good understanding of spoken French."

Maureen asked a question in French: "What are you hoping to gain from working as an au pair?"

Cassie was pleased that she was able to reply, fluently, "To learn more about life in another country, and to improve my language skills."

She hoped her answer would impress Maureen, but she remained stern as she finished perusing the paperwork.

"Do you still live at home, Cassie?"

Back to family life again ... did Maureen suspect she was hiding something? She'd need to answer carefully. Moving out at sixteen, as she had done, would raise flags for an interviewer. Why so young? Were there problems at home? She needed to paint a prettier picture that hinted at a normal, happy family life.

"I've been living on my own since I was twenty," she said, feeling her face flush with guilt.

"And working part time. I see you have a reference here from Primi? Is that a restaurant?"

"Yes, I've waitressed there for the past two years." Which was, thankfully, true. Before that there had been various other jobs, and even a stint at a dive bar, as she struggled to afford her shared lodgings as well as her distance education. Primi, her most recent job, had been the most enjoyable. The restaurant team had felt like the family she'd never had, but there was no future there. Her salary was low and tips weren't much better; business in that part of town was tough. She'd been planning to make a move when the time was right, but when her circumstances had changed for the worse, it had become urgent.

"Childcare experience?" Maureen looked over her glasses at Cassie, who felt her stomach twist.

"I—I assisted at a daycare center for three months, before I started with Primi. The reference is in the folder. They gave me basic training on safety and first aid, and I was background checked," she stammered, hoping that it was enough. It had only been a temporary position, filling in for someone on maternity leave. She'd never thought it would be a steppingstone to a future opportunity.

"I've managed children's parties at the restaurant, too. I'm a very friendly person. I mean, I get along with others, and I'm patient…"

Maureen's lips tightened. "What a pity your experience is not more recent. Also you don't have any formal certification in childcare. Most families require qualifications, or at the very least, more experience. It will be difficult to place you with so little."

Cassie stared at her despairingly. She had to do this, no matter what it took. The choice was clear. Get away… or become trapped in a cycle of violence that she thought she'd escaped forever by leaving home.

The bruises on her upper arm had taken a few days to bloom, darkly defined, so she could see each knuckle mark where he'd hit her. Her boyfriend, Zane, who'd promised on their second date that he loved her, and would protect her no matter what.

When the ugly marks had started to appear, she'd remembered, with gooseflesh prickling her spine, that she'd had almost identical bruises in the same place ten years ago. First it had been her arm. Then her neck, and finally her face. Also inflicted by a supposed protector—her father.

He'd started hitting her when she was twelve, after Jacqui, her older sister, had run away. Before that, Jacqui had borne the brunt of his anger. Her presence had protected Cassie from the worst.

The bruises from Zane were still there; it would take a while for them to fade. She was wearing long sleeves to hide them during the interview, and was overly warm in the stuffy office.

"Is there anywhere else you could recommend?" she asked Maureen. "I know this is the best local agency, but would you be able to suggest an online site where I could possibly apply?"

"I can't recommend a website," Maureen said firmly. "Too many candidates have had bad experiences. Some have ended up in a situation where their working hours weren't adhered to, or they were expected to do menial cleaning jobs as well as mind the children. That's unfair on everyone concerned. I've also heard of au pairs being abused in other ways. So, no."

"Please—is there anybody on your books who might consider me? I'm a hard worker and willing to learn, I can easily fit in. Please give me a chance."

Maureen was silent for a moment, then tapped at her keyboard, frowning.

"Your family—how do they feel about you traveling for a year? Do you have a boyfriend, anyone you're leaving behind?"

"I broke up with my boyfriend recently. And I've always been very independent, my family knows that."

Zane had cried and apologized after he'd punched her arm, but she hadn't relented, thinking instead of her sister's warning, given long ago and proven true since then: "No man ever hits a woman once."

She'd packed her bags and moved in with a friend. To avoid him, she'd blocked his calls and changed the timing of her work shifts. She had hoped he would accept her decision and leave her alone, while knowing deep down that he would not. Breaking up should have been his idea, not hers. His ego would not allow for rejection.

He'd already been to the restaurant looking for her. The manager had told him she had taken two weeks' leave and gone to Florida. That had bought her some time ... but she knew he'd be counting the days. A week to go, and he'd be hunting her again.

The US felt too small to escape him. She wanted an ocean—a big one—between them. Because worst of all was the fear that she would weaken, forgive him, and allow him another chance.

Maureen finished checking the paperwork and went on to ask a few standard questions that Cassie found easier. Her hobbies, any chronic medications, dietary requirements or allergies.

"I have no dietary requirements or allergies. And no health problems."

Cassie hoped her anxiety meds didn't count as chronic medication. It would be better not to mention them, she decided, as she was sure they would be a huge red flag.

Maureen scribbled a note on the file.

Then she asked, "What would you do if the children in your care are naughty or disobedient? How would you handle it?"

Cassie drew a deep breath.

"Well, I don't think there's a one-size-fits-all answer. If a child is disobedient because she's running toward a dangerous road, it would require a different approach than if she doesn't want to eat her vegetables. In the first instance it would be safety first and getting the child out of harm's way as quickly as possible. In the second I would reason and negotiate—why don't you like them? Is it the look or the taste? Will you be willing to try a bite? After all, we all go through food phases and usually grow out of them."

Maureen seemed satisfied with that, but the next questions were more difficult.

"What will you do if the children lie to you? For instance, if they tell you they're allowed to do something that the parents have forbidden?"

"I'd say that it's not allowed, and tell them the reason why if I knew it. I'd suggest we speak to the parents together and discuss the rule as a family, to help them understand why it's important." Cassie felt as if she were walking a tightrope, hoping that her answers were acceptable.

"How would you react, Cassie, if you witnessed a domestic fight? Living in a family's home, there will be times when people don't get along."

Cassie closed her eyes for a moment, pushing away the memories triggered by Maureen's words. Screaming, smashing glass, the neighbors shouting angrily. A chair wedged under the rattling handle of her bedroom door, the only flimsy protection she could find.

But just as she was about to say she'd lock herself and the kids in a secure room and call the police immediately, Cassie realized Maureen couldn't be referring to that kind of a fight. Why would she? She was obviously thinking of a spoken argument, a few words snapped in annoyance or shouted in anger; temporary friction rather than terminal destruction.

"I would try to keep the children out of earshot," she said, choosing her words carefully. "And I would respect the parents' privacy and stay well away. After all, fights are part of life and an au pair has no right to take sides or become involved."

Now, finally, she earned a small smile.

"A good answer," Maureen said. She checked her computer again and nodded, as if confirming a decision she'd just made.

"There is only one possibility here that I could offer you. A position with a French family," she said, and Cassie's heart leaped, only to crash-land when Maureen added, "Their last au pair left unexpectedly after a month, and they've had difficulty finding a replacement."

Cassie bit her lip. Whether the au pair had resigned or been fired, she didn't know—but she couldn't afford to have the same happen to her. With the agency fee and the airfare, she'd be plowing all her savings into this venture. Whatever it took, she would have to make it work.

Maureen added, "They are a wealthy family with a beautiful home. Not in town. It's a mansion in the countryside, on a large estate. There's an orchard and a small vineyard—not commercial—and also horses, although equestrian knowledge is not a job requirement. However, you'll have the opportunity to learn to ride when you're there if you like."

"I'd love that," Cassie said. The appeal of the French countryside, and the promise of horses, made the risk seem more worthwhile. And a wealthy family surely meant better job security. Perhaps the last au pair hadn't been willing to try.

Maureen adjusted her glasses before jotting a note on Cassie's form.

"Now, I must emphasize that not all families are easy to work for. Some are very challenging and some are downright difficult. The success of the job will rest on your shoulders."

"I'll do my best to succeed."

"Quitting an assignment before your year is over is not acceptable. It will incur a substantial cancellation fee and you will never work for us again. The details are stipulated in the contract." Maureen tapped her pen on the page.

"I can't see that happening," Cassie replied determinedly.

"Good. Then the final point we need to discuss is the timeframe."

"Yes. How soon will I leave?" Cassie asked, her anxiety flooding back as she wondered how much longer she'd need to duck and dive.

"It usually takes about six weeks, but this family's application is very urgent so we are going to fast-track it. If things move along as expected, you will fly out within a week. Is that acceptable?"

"It—it's perfect," she stammered. "Please, I accept the position. I'll do whatever it takes to make it work, and I won't let you down."

The woman stared back at her long and hard, as if summing her up one last time.

"Don't," she said.

CHAPTER TWO

Airports were all about goodbyes, Cassie thought. Rushed farewells, the impersonal environment robbing you of the words you really wanted to say, and the time to say them properly.

She'd insisted that the girlfriend who'd given her a ride to the airport drop her off rather than come in with her. A hug before jumping out of the car was quick and easy. Better than expensive coffee and awkward conversation, drying up as departure time drew closer. After all, she was traveling alone, leaving everyone she knew behind. It made sense to start that journey sooner, rather than later.

As Cassie wheeled the luggage cart into the terminal, she felt a sense of relief at the goals she'd accomplished so far. She'd gotten the assignment—the most important goal of all. She'd paid the flight and the agency fee, her visa had been fast-tracked, and she was on time for check-in. Her belongings were packed according to the list supplied—she was glad for the bright blue backpack she'd been given with the "Maureen's Au Pairs" logo, because there wouldn't have been room in her suitcase for all her clothes.

From here on until she landed in Paris, she was sure everything would go smoothly.

And then she stopped in her tracks, her heart hammering, as she saw him.

He was standing near the terminal entrance, with his back to the wall, thumbs hooked into the pockets of the leather jacket she'd given him. His height, his dark, spiky hair, and his aggressive jaw made him easy to spot as he scanned the crowds.

Zane.

He must have found out she was leaving at this time. She'd heard from various friends he'd been phoning around, asking where she was and checking up on the Florida story. Zane could be manipulative, and not everyone knew about her situation. Someone must have innocently told him the truth.

Before he could look in her direction, she swiveled the cart round, yanking her tracksuit hood over her head to hide her wavy auburn hair. She rushed the other way, steering the cart behind a pillar and out of his sight.

The Air France check-in desk was at the far end of the terminal. There was no way she could get past without him seeing her.

Think, Cassie, she told herself. In the past, Zane had praised her for her ability to make a fast plan in a tricky situation. "You think on your feet," he'd said. That had been at the beginning of their relationship. By the end, he'd been accusing her bitterly of being sneaky, underhanded, too damn clever for her own good.

Time to be too damn clever, then. She took a deep breath, hoping for ideas. Zane was standing near the terminal entrance. Why? It would have been easier to wait by the check-in desk where he'd be sure of spotting her. So that meant he didn't know which airline she was flying. Whoever he'd gotten the information from either hadn't known, or hadn't said. If she could find another way to the desk, she might be able to check in before he came looking.

Cassie unloaded her luggage, shouldering the heavy backpack and dragging her suitcase behind her. There was an escalator at the building's entrance—she'd passed it on her way in. If she rode it up to the top level she hoped she would find one going down, or an elevator, at the other end.

Abandoning the luggage cart, she hurried back the way she had come and rode the escalator up. The one at the other end was broken, so she climbed down the steep steps, dragging her heavy bag behind her. The Air France check-in desk was a short distance away, but to her dismay, there was already a long and slow-moving line.

Pulling the gray hood further forward, she joined the line, took a paperback from her purse, and began reading. She wasn't taking in the words, and the hood was sweltering. She wanted to rip it away, cool the perspiration on her neck. She couldn't risk it, though, not when her bright hair would be instantly visible. Better to stay in hiding.

But then a firm hand tapped her on her shoulder.

She whirled round, gasping, and found herself staring into the surprised eyes of a tall blonde who was about her own age.

"Sorry to startle you," she said. "I'm Jess. I noticed your backpack and thought I should say hello."

"Oh. Yes. Maureen's Au Pairs."

"Are you flying out on an assignment?" Jess asked.

"I am."

"Me too. Do you want to see if the airline will seat us together? We could request it at check-in."

While Jess chatted about the weather in France, Cassie glanced nervously around the terminal. She knew Zane wouldn't give up easily—not after driving all the way out here. He would want something from her—an apology, a commitment. He would force her to come with him for "a goodbye drink" and pick a fight. He wouldn't care if she arrived in France with fresh bruises…or missed her flight completely.

And then she saw him. He was heading in her direction, a few counters away, scanning each line carefully as he searched.

She turned away quickly, in case he sensed her gaze. With a flicker of hope, she saw they had reached the front of their line.

"Ma'am, you'll need to remove that," the check-in clerk said, pointing to Cassie's hood.

Complying reluctantly, she pushed it back.

"Hey, Cass!" She heard Zane shouting the words.

Cassie froze, knowing a response would mean disaster.

Clumsy with nerves, she dropped her passport and scrabbled for it, her top-heavy backpack tipping over her head.

Another shout, and this time she glanced back.

He had seen her and was pushing his way through the line, elbowing people aside. The passengers were angry; she could hear raised voices. Zane was causing a commotion.

"We'd like to sit together if possible," Jess told the clerk, and Cassie bit her lip at the additional delay.

Zane shouted again, and she realized with a sick feeling that he would reach her in a few moments. He'd turn on the charm and beg her for a chance to talk, reassure Cassie that it would only take a minute for him to say what he needed in private. His aim, she knew from experience, would be to get her away and alone. And then the charm would vanish.

"Who's that guy?" Jess asked curiously. "Is he looking for you?"

"He's my ex-boyfriend," Cassie muttered. "I've been trying to avoid him. I don't want him causing trouble before I leave."

"But he's already causing trouble!" Jess whirled round, irate.

"Security!" she screamed. "Help us! Somebody stop that man!"

Galvanized by Jess's cries, one of the passengers grabbed Zane's jacket as he pushed past. He slipped on the tiles, arms flailing, dragging one of the posts down with him as he fell.

"Hold him," Jess appealed. "Security, quick!"

With a surge of relief, Cassie saw that security had indeed been alerted. Two airport police were rushing over to the line. They were going to reach it in time, before Zane could get to her, or even run away.

"I came to say goodbye to my girlfriend, officers," Zane gabbled, but his attempts at charm were lost on the duo.

"Cassie," he called, as the taller officer grasped his arm. "Au revoir."

Reluctantly she turned to face him.

"Au revoir! It's not goodbye," he shouted, as the officers marched him away. "I'm gonna see you again. Sooner than you think. You better take care."

She recognized the warning in Zane's last words—but for now, they were empty threats.

"Thank you so much," she said to Jess, overwhelmed with gratitude for her gutsy action.

"I also had a toxic boyfriend," Jess sympathized. "I know how possessive they can be, they stick like freaking Velcro. It was a pleasure to be able to stop him."

"Let's go through passport control before he can find a way back in. I owe you a drink. What would you like—coffee, beer, or wine?"

"Wine, for sure," Jess said, as they headed through the gates.

"So, where in France are you headed to?" Cassie asked, after they had ordered the wine.

"This time, I'm going to a family in Versailles. Close to where the palace is, I believe. I hope I'll have a chance to go and see it when I have a day off."

"You said this time? Have you been on an assignment before?"

"I have, but it didn't work out well." Jess dropped an ice cube in her glass. "The family was dreadful. In fact, they put me off using Maureen's Au Pairs ever again. I went with a different agency this time. But don't worry," she added hurriedly, "I'm sure you will be fine. Maureen must have some good clients on her books."

Cassie's mouth felt suddenly dry. She took a big gulp of wine.

"I thought she was reputable. I mean, her slogan is The Premier European Agency."

Jess laughed. "Well, that's just marketing. Other people told me differently."

"What happened to you?" Cassie asked. "Please tell me."

"Well, the assignment sounded OK, although some of Maureen's interview questions worried me. They were so weird that I started wondering if there were problems with the family, because none of my au pair friends were asked similar questions during their interview. And when I arrived—well, the situation wasn't as advertised."

"Why not?" Cassie felt cold inside. She'd found Maureen's questioning strange, too. She'd assumed at the time that every applicant was asked the same questions; that it was a test of your abilities. And maybe it was ... but not for the reasons she'd imagined.

"The family was super-toxic," Jess said. "They were disrespectful and demeaning. The work I had to do was way outside of the scope of my job; they didn't care and refused to change. And when I said I was leaving—that was when it really became a war zone."

Cassie bit her lip. She'd had that experience growing up. She remembered raised voices behind closed doors, muttered arguments in the car, a tightrope sense of tension. She had always wondered what her mother—so quiet, subdued, beaten down—could possibly have found to argue about with her bombastic, aggressive father. It had only been after her mother's death in a car crash that she'd realized the arguments were all about keeping the peace, managing the situation, protecting Cassie and her sister from the aggression that flared unpredictably, and for no good reason. Without her mother's presence, the simmering conflict had boiled over into full-blown war.

She'd imagined one of the benefits of being an au pair would be that she could become part of the happy family she'd never had. Now she feared the opposite would be true. She'd never been able to keep the peace at home. Could she ever manage a volatile situation the same way her mother had done?

"I'm worried about my family," Cassie confessed. "I also had odd questions during the interview, and their previous au pair left early. What will happen if I have to do the same? I don't want to stay around if things are going to turn nasty."

"Don't leave unless it's an emergency," Jess warned. "It causes massive conflict, and you hemorrhage money; you'll be liable for a lot of additional expenses. That nearly put me off trying again. I was very cautious about accepting this assignment. I wouldn't have been able to afford it if my dad hadn't paid for everything this time around."

She put her wine glass down.

"Shall we go to the gate? We're near the back of the plane, so we'll be in the first group to board."

The excitement of boarding the plane distracted Cassie from what Jess had said, and once they were seated, they chatted about other topics. When the plane took off, she felt her spirits lift with it, because she'd done it. She had left the country, she'd escaped Zane, and she was airborne, heading for a new start in a foreign land.

It was only after dinner, when she started thinking harder about the details of her assignment, and the warnings Jess had given her, that her misgivings crept back again.

Every family couldn't be bad, right?

But what if one particular agency had a reputation for accepting difficult families? Well, then, the chances would be greater.

Cassie tried to read for a while, but found she wasn't focusing on the words, and her thoughts were racing as she worried about what lay ahead.

She glanced at Jess. After making sure she was engrossed in watching her movie, Cassie discreetly took the bottle of pills from her purse and swallowed one down with the last of her Diet Coke. If she couldn't read, she might as well try to sleep. She switched off her light and reclined her seat.

Cassie found herself in her drafty upstairs bedroom, huddling under her bed with her back against the rough, cold wall.

Drunken laughter, thumps, and shouts came from downstairs; revelry that would, at any moment, turn violent. Her ears strained, waiting for the smashing of glass. She recognized her father's voice and that of his latest girlfriend, Deena. There were at least four others down there, maybe more.

And then, over the shouts, she heard the creak of the floorboards as heavy footsteps climbed the stairs.

"Hey, little honey," a deep voice whispered, and her twelve-year-old self cringed in terror. "Are you there, girlie?"

She squeezed her eyes shut, telling herself this was just a nightmare, that she was safe in bed and the strangers downstairs were getting ready to leave.

BLAKE PIERCE

The door creaked slowly open and in the spill of moonlight, she saw a heavy boot appear.

The feet trod across the room.

"Hey, girlie." A husky whisper. "I've come to say hello."

She closed her eyes, praying he wouldn't hear her rapid breathing.

The whisper of fabric as he pulled the covers back...and then the grunt of surprise as he saw the pillow and coat that she'd bundled underneath.

"Out and about," he'd muttered. She guessed he was looking at the grimy curtains billowing in the breeze, the drainpipe hinting at a precarious escape route. Next time, she would find the courage to climb down; it couldn't be worse than hiding here.

The boots retreated out of her vision. A burst of music came from below, followed by a shouted argument.

The room was quiet.

She was shivering; if she was going to spend the night hiding, she needed a blanket. She'd better get it now. She eased herself away from the wall.

But as she slid her hand out, a rough hand grabbed it.

"So there you are!"

He yanked her out—she clutched at the bed frame, cold steel scraping her hands, and began to scream. Her terrified cries filled the room, filled the house...

And she woke, sweating, screaming, hearing Jess's worried voice. "Hey, Cassie, are you OK?"

The tendrils of the nightmare still lurked, waiting to draw her back in. She could feel the raw grazes on her arm where the rusty bed frame had cut her. She pressed her fingers there and was relieved to find unbroken skin. Opening her eyes wide, she switched on the overhead light to chase the darkness away.

"I'm fine. Bad dream, that's all."

"Do you want some water? Some tea? I can call the flight attendant."

16

Cassie was going to refuse politely, but then she remembered she should take her meds again. If one tablet didn't work, two would usually stop the nightmares from recurring.

"I'd love some water. Thank you," she said.

She waited until Jess wasn't looking and quickly swallowed another pill.

She didn't try to sleep again.

During the plane's descent, she swapped phone numbers with Jess—and just in case, she took down the name of the family Jess would be working for, and their address. Cassie told herself it was like an insurance policy, that hopefully if she had it, she wouldn't need it. They promised each other that the first chance they got, they would tour Versailles Palace together.

As they taxied into Charles de Gaulle Airport, Jess gave an excited laugh. Quickly, she showed Cassie the selfie her family had taken for her while waiting. The attractive couple and two children were smiling, holding a board with Jess's name on it.

Cassie had received no message—Maureen had just said she would be met at the airport. The walk to passport control seemed endless. She was surrounded by the babble of conversations in a host of different languages. Tuning in to the couple walking alongside her, she realized how little spoken French she was able to understand. Reality was so different from the school classes and language tapes. She felt scared, alone, and sleep deprived, and she was suddenly aware of how crumpled and sweaty her clothes were, compared to the elegantly clad French travelers around her.

As soon as she had her bags, she hurried to the restroom, put on a fresh top, and fixed her hair. She still didn't feel ready to meet her family and had no idea who would be waiting. Maureen had told her the house was over an hour's drive from the airport, so perhaps the children hadn't come along. She shouldn't look out for a big family. Any friendly face would do.

But in the sea of people watching her, she saw no recognition, even though she'd placed her "Maureen's Au Pairs" backpack prominently on the luggage cart. She walked slowly from the gate to the arrivals lounge, looking anxiously for someone to spot her, wave, or call out.

But everyone there seemed to be waiting for someone else.

Grasping the cart's handle with cold hands, Cassie zigzagged around the arrivals hall, searching in vain as the crowds gradually dispersed. Maureen hadn't said what to do if this happened. Should she call someone? Would her phone even work in France?

And then, as she made one final, frantic pass round the floor, she noticed it.

"CASSANDRA VALE."

A small notice board, held by a lean, dark-haired man in a black jacket and jeans.

Standing near the wall, absorbed by his phone, he wasn't even looking for her.

She approached uncertainly.

"Hi—I'm Cassie. Are you …?" she asked, the words trailing off as she realized she had no idea who he could be.

"Yes," he said in strongly accented English. "Come this way."

She was about to introduce herself properly, to speak the words she'd rehearsed about how excited she was to be joining the family, when she saw the laminated card on his jacket. He was just a taxi driver; the card was his official airport pass.

The family hadn't bothered to come and meet her at all.

CHAPTER THREE

The cityscape of Paris unfolded as Cassie watched. Tall apartments and somber industrial blocks gradually gave way to treed suburbia. The afternoon was cold and gray, with patchy, blowing rain.

She craned to see the signboards they passed. They were heading toward Saint Maur, and for a while she thought that might be their destination, but the driver passed the turnoff and continued on the road out of town.

"How much further?" she asked, attempting conversation, but he grunted noncommittally and turned the radio up.

Rain pattered on the windows and the glass felt cold against her cheek. She wished she'd taken her thick jacket from the trunk. And she was starving—she hadn't eaten breakfast and there'd been no opportunity to buy food since.

After more than a half hour, they reached open countryside and drove alongside the Marne River, where brightly painted barges provided a splash of color in the grayness, and a few people, swathed in raincoats, walked under the trees. Some of the trees' branches were already bare, others still clothed in russet-gold leaves.

"It's very cold today, isn't it?" she observed, giving conversation with the driver another try.

His only response was a muttered "Oui"—but at least he turned the heater on, and she could stop shivering. Cocooned in the warmth, she slipped into an uneasy doze as the miles flew past.

Sharp braking and the blare of a horn startled her awake. The driver was forcing his way past a stationary truck, turning off the highway onto a narrow, tree-lined road. The rain had cleared and in the low evening light, the autumn vista was beautiful. Cassie stared out the window, taking in the rolling landscape and the patchwork tapestry of fields interspersed with huge, dark forests. They passed by a vineyard, the neat rows of grapevines curving round the hillside.

Slowing his speed, the driver passed through a village. Pale stone houses with arched windows and steeply sloped, tiled roofs lined the road. Beyond, she saw open fields, and glimpsed a canal lined by weeping willows as they cruised by a stone bridge. The tall church spire drew her gaze and she wondered how old the building was.

This must be close to the chateau, she guessed, perhaps even in its local neighborhood. Then she changed her mind as they left the village behind and wound further into the hills, until she was totally disoriented and had lost sight of that tall spire. She hadn't expected the chateau to be so remote. She heard the GPS give a "Lost Signal" notification and the driver exclaimed with annoyance, picking up his phone and glancing closely at the map while he drove.

And then, a right turn through high gateposts and Cassie sat straighter, staring down the long, gravel driveway. Ahead, tall and elegant, with the setting sun highlighting its stone-clad walls, was the chateau.

Tires crunched on stone as the car stopped outside a high, imposing entrance and she felt a stab of nerves. This home was far bigger than she'd imagined. It was like a palace, topped with tall chimneys and ornate turrets. She counted eighteen windows, with elaborate stonework and detailing, on the two stories of its commanding frontage. The house itself overlooked a formal garden, with immaculately trimmed hedges and paved pathways.

How would she relate to the family inside, who lived in such grandeur, when she had come from nothing?

She realized the driver was tapping his fingers impatiently on the wheel—he clearly wasn't going to help her with her bags. Quickly, she climbed out.

The unforgiving wind chilled her immediately, and she hurried around to the trunk, manhandling her suitcase out, across the gravel, and into the shelter of the porch, where she zipped her jacket up.

There was no doorbell on the heavy wooden door, only a large, iron knocker that felt cold in her hand. The sound was surprisingly loud, and a few moments later Cassie heard light footsteps.

The door opened and she found herself facing a dark-uniformed maid, hair drawn back into a tight ponytail. Beyond her, Cassie glimpsed a large entrance hall with opulent wall coverings and a magnificent wooden staircase at the far end.

The maid glanced around as a door slammed.

Immediately, Cassie sensed the presence of a fight. She could feel it, electric in the air, like an approaching storm. It was in the maid's nervous bearing, in the bang of the door and the chaos of faraway shouts fading to silence. Her insides contracted and she felt an overpowering desire to get away. To run after the departing driver and call him back.

Instead, she stood her ground and forced a smile.

"I'm Cassie, the new au pair. The family is expecting me."

"Today?" The maid looked worried. "Wait a moment." As she hurried into the house, Cassie heard her calling, "Monsieur Dubois, please come quickly."

A minute later, a sturdy man with dark, graying hair strode into the foyer, his face like thunder. When he saw Cassie at the door, he stopped in his tracks.

"You are here already?" he said. "My fiancée said you were arriving tomorrow morning."

He turned to glare at the young, bleached-blonde woman following him. She was wearing an evening gown and her attractive features were taut with tension.

"Yes, Pierre, I printed the email when I was in town. The agency said the flight lands at four in the morning." Turning to the ornate wooden hall table, she shoved a Venetian glass paperweight aside and brandished a page defensively. "Here. See?"

Pierre glanced at the page and sighed.

"It says four p.m. Not four a.m. The driver you booked obviously knew the difference, so here she is." He turned to Cassie and held out his hand. "I am Pierre Dubois. This is my fiancée, Margot."

He didn't introduce the maid. Instead, Margot snapped at her to go and make up the room opposite the children's bedrooms, and the maid hurried away.

"Where are the children? Are they in bed already? They should meet Cassie," Pierre said.

Margot shook her head. "They were having supper."

"So late? Did I not tell you that supper must be early on school nights? Even though they are on holiday, they should be in bed already to stay on schedule."

Margot stared at him and shrugged angrily before walking over to the doorway on the right, stiletto heels clicking.

"Antoinette?" she called. "Ella? Marc?"

She was rewarded by a thunder of feet and loud cries.

A dark-haired boy sprinted into the foyer, clutching a doll by her hair. He was closely pursued by a younger, chubby girl in a flood of tears.

"Give my Barbie back!" she screamed.

Skidding to a stop as he saw the adults, the boy made a dash for the staircase. As he hurtled toward it, his shoulder caught the curved side of a large blue and gold vase.

Cassie clapped her hands over her mouth in horror as the vase teetered on its plinth, then crashed to the floor where it shattered. Shards of colorful glass spilled across the dark wooden boards.

The shocked silence was broken by Pierre's enraged bellow.

"Marc! Give Ella her doll."

Feet dragging, lower lip jutting, Marc shuffled back past the wreckage. Reluctantly he handed the doll to Pierre, who passed it to Ella. Her sobbing subsided as she smoothed the doll's hair.

"That was a Durand art glass vase," Margot hissed at the young boy. "Antique. Irreplaceable. Do you have no respect for your father's possessions?"

A sullen silence was the only response.

"Where is Antoinette?" Pierre asked, sounding frustrated.

Margot glanced up and, following her gaze, Cassie saw a slim, dark-haired girl at the top of the stairs—she looked to be the eldest of the three by a few years. Elegantly dressed in a perfectly ironed frock, she waited with a hand on the balustrade until she had the family's full attention. Then, chin high, she descended.

Anxious to make a good impression, Cassie cleared her throat and attempted a friendly greeting.

"Hello, children. My name's Cassie. I'm so pleased to be here, and happy to be looking after you."

Ella smiled shyly in return. Marc glared unrelentingly at the floor. And Antoinette met her gaze for a long, challenging moment. Then, without a word, she turned her back on her.

"If you will excuse me, Papa," she said to Pierre. "I have homework to finish before bedtime."

"Of course," Pierre said, and Antoinette flounced upstairs again.

Cassie felt her face flame with embarrassment at the deliberate snub. She wondered if she should say something, make light of the situation or try to excuse Antoinette's rude behavior, but she was unable to think of suitable words.

Margot muttered furiously, "I told you, Pierre. The teenage moods are starting already," and Cassie realized that she hadn't been the only one Antoinette had ignored.

"At least she was doing her homework, despite nobody helping her with it," Pierre countered. "Ella, Marc, why don't you both introduce yourselves properly to Cassie?"

There was a short silence. Clearly, introductions weren't going to happen without a fight. But perhaps she could ease the tension with a few questions.

"Well, Marc, I know your name but I'd like to find out how old you are," she said.

"I'm eight," he muttered.

Glancing between him and Pierre, she could see a definite family resemblance. The unruly hair, the strong chin, the bright blue eyes. Even the way they frowned was similar. The other children were also dark, but Ella and Antoinette had more delicate features.

"And Ella, what's your age?"

"I am nearly six," the small girl announced proudly. "My birthday is the day after Christmas."

"That's a good day to have a birthday. I hope it means you get lots of extra presents."

Ella gave a surprised smile, as if this was an advantage she hadn't yet considered.

"Antoinette is the oldest of all of us. She's twelve," she said.

Pierre clapped his hands. "Right, it's bedtime now. Margot, will you show Cassie the house after you've put the children to bed. She will need to know her way around. Make it quick. We must leave by seven."

"I still have to finish getting ready," Margot replied in acid tones. "You can put the children to bed, and call a butler to clear up this mess. I will show Cassie the house."

Pierre drew an angry breath before glancing at Cassie and pressing his lips together. She guessed her presence had made him swallow his words.

"Upstairs and into bed," he said, and the two children followed him reluctantly up the staircase. She was heartened to see that Ella turned and gave her a small wave.

"Come with me, Cassie," Margot ordered.

Cassie followed Margot through the doorway on the left and found herself in a formal lounge with exquisite, showpiece furniture, and tapestries lining the walls. The room was huge and chilly; there was no fire lit in the massive fireplace.

"This lounge is seldom used, and the children are not allowed in here. The main dining room is beyond—the same rules apply."

Cassie wondered how often the massive mahogany dining table was used—it looked pristine and she counted sixteen high-backed chairs. Three more vases, similar to the one Marc had broken earlier, stood on the darkly polished sideboard. She couldn't imagine happy dinner table conversation flowing in this austere and silent space.

What would it feel like growing up in such a house, where whole areas were off limits because of furnishings that could be damaged? She guessed that it might make a child feel as if they were less important than the furniture.

"This we call the Blue Room." It was a smaller lounge, wallpapered in navy, with large French doors. Cassie guessed they opened out onto a patio or courtyard, but it was fully dark, and all she could see were the room's dim lights reflected in the glass. She wished the house had higher-wattage globes—all the rooms were gloomy, with shadows lurking in the corners.

A sculpture caught her eye...the marble statue's stand had been broken, so it lay face up on a table. Its features looked blank and immobile, as if the stone were coating a dead person's face. Its limbs were chunky and rudely carved. Cassie shivered, looking away from the creepy sight.

"That is one of our most valuable pieces," Margot informed her. "Marc knocked it over last week. We will have it repaired soon."

Cassie thought about the young boy's destructive energy and the way he had knocked his shoulder into the vase earlier. Had the action been totally accidental? Or had there been a subliminal desire to shatter the glass, to get himself noticed in a world where possessions seemed to take priority?

Margot led her back the way they had come. "The rooms down that passage are kept locked. The kitchen is this way, to the right, and beyond it are the servants' quarters. There is a small parlor to the left, and a room where we dine as a family."

On the way back they passed a gray-uniformed butler carrying a broom, dustpan, and brush. He stood aside for them but Margot did not acknowledge him at all.

The west wing was a mirror image of the east. Huge, darkened rooms with exquisite furnishings and works of art. Quiet and empty. Cassie shivered, longing for a homey bright light or the familiar sound of a television, if such a thing even existed in this house. She followed Margot up the magnificent staircase to the second floor.

"The guest wing." Three pristine bedrooms, with four-poster beds, were separated by two spacious drawing rooms. The bed-rooms were as neat and formal as hotel rooms, and the bedcovers looked as if they had been ironed flat.

"And the family wing."

Cassie brightened, glad to finally reach the part of the house where people lived.

"The nursery."

To her confusion, this was another empty room, occupied only by a tall crib with high, barred sides.

"And here, the children's bedrooms. Our suite is at the end of the passage, around the corner."

Three closed doors in a row. Margot's voice dropped and Cassie guessed she didn't want to look in on the children—not even to say good night.

"This is Antoinette's bedroom, this is Marc's, and the closest to ours is Ella's. Your room is opposite Antoinette's."

The door was open and two maids were busily making up the bed. The room was enormous and icy cold. It was furnished with two wingback chairs, a table, and a large wooden wardrobe. Heavy red curtains shrouded the window. Her suitcase had been placed at the foot of the bed.

"You will hear the children if they cry or call—please attend to them. Tomorrow morning they need to be dressed and ready by eight. They will be going outdoors, so choose warm clothing."

"I will, but…" Cassie gathered her courage. "Could I please have some supper? I've had nothing to eat since dinner on the plane last night."

Margot stared at her, perplexed, then shook her head.

"The children ate early because we are going out. The kitchen is closed now. Breakfast will be served from seven tomorrow. You can wait till then?"

"I—I suppose so." She felt sick with hunger—the forbidden candy in her bag, intended for the children, suddenly an irresist-ible temptation.

"And I must email the agency and let them know I'm here. Would it be possible to have the Wi-Fi password? My phone has no signal."

Now Margot's stare grew blank. "We have no Wi-Fi, and there is no cell phone signal here. Only a landline telephone in Pierre's study. To send an email, you must go into town."

Without waiting for Cassie's response, she turned away and headed toward the main bedroom.

The maids had gone, leaving Cassie's bed in a state of chilly perfection.

She closed the door.

She'd never dreamed she would feel homesick, but at that moment she longed for a friendly voice, the babble of the television, the clutter of a full refrigerator. Dishes in the sink, toys on the floor, YouTube videos playing on phones. The happy chaos of a normal family—the life she'd expected to become a part of.

Instead, she felt she was already embroiled in a bitter and complicated conflict. She could never have hoped to be instant friends with these children—not with the family dynamics that had played out so far. This place was a battleground—and while she might find an ally in young Ella, she feared she had already made an enemy in Antoinette.

The ceiling light, which had been flickering, suddenly failed. Cassie fumbled in her backpack for her phone and unpacked as best she could in the flashlight's beam, before plugging it into the only visible plug point on the opposite side of the room and shuffling through the darkness to her bed.

Cold, apprehensive, and hungry, she climbed between the chilly sheets and pulled them up to her chin. She'd expected to feel more hopeful and positive after meeting the family, but instead she found herself doubting her ability to cope with them, and dreading what the following day would bring.

CHAPTER FOUR

The statue stood in Cassie's doorway, framed by darkness.

Its lifeless eyes opened and its mouth parted as it moved toward her. The hairline cracks around its lips widened, and then its entire face began to disintegrate. Fragments of marble showered down and rattled on the floor.

"No," Cassie whispered, but found she could not move. She was trapped in bed, her limbs frozen even though her panicked mind implored her to flee.

The statue made its way toward her, arms outstretched, stone chips cascading from its limbs. It began to scream, a high, thin sound, and as it did, she saw what was being exposed under the marble shell.

Her sister's face. Cold, gray, dead.

"No, no, no!" Cassie shouted, and her own cries woke her.

The room was pitch dark; she was curled in a shivering ball. She sat up, panicked, groping for a light switch that wasn't there.

Her worst fear... the one she tried hard to suppress by day, but which found its way into nightmares. It was the fear that Jacqui had died. Because why else would her sister have suddenly stopped communicating? Why had there been no letters, no phone calls, no word from her for years?

Shaking with cold and fear, Cassie realized the clattering stones in her dream had become the sound of rain, gusting in the wind, drumming against the window glass. And above the rain, she heard another sound. One of the children was screaming.

"You will hear the children if they cry or call—please attend to them."

Cassie felt confused and disoriented. She wished she could turn on a bedside light and take a few minutes to calm herself. The dream had been so vivid she still felt locked inside it. But the screaming must have started while she was asleep—it might, in fact, have caused her nightmare. She was needed urgently, and she had to hurry.

She pushed the duvet back, discovering the window hadn't been properly closed. Rain had blown in through the gap, and the lower section of the covers was dripping wet. She stepped out of bed into the blackness and headed across the room in the direction she hoped her phone would be.

A slick of water on the floor had turned the tiles to ice. She skidded, losing her footing and landing with a painful thud on her back. Her head banged against the bedframe and her vision exploded into stars.

"Goddammit," she whispered, easing herself onto her hands and knees and waiting for the pain in her head, and the dizziness, to subside.

She crawled across the tiles and felt around for her phone, hoping it had escaped the floodwater. To her relief, this side of the room was dry. She turned on the flashlight, clambering painfully to her feet. Her head was throbbing and her shirt was drenched. She ripped it off and quickly pulled on the first clothes she could find—a pair of tracksuit bottoms and a gray top. Barefoot, she hurried out of the room.

She shone her flashlight onto the walls but there were no light switches nearby. Carefully, she followed its beam in the direction of the sound, heading toward the Dubois's suites. The room closest to theirs would be Ella's bedroom.

Cassie knocked quickly and went in.

Thankfully, light at last. In the glow of the ceiling lamp she could see the single bed near the window where Ella had kicked off her duvet. Shouting and screaming in her sleep, she was fighting the demons of her dream.

"Ella, wake up!"

Closing the door, Cassie hurried over and sat on the edge of the bed, gently grasping the sleeping girl's shoulders and feeling them hunched and shuddering. Her dark hair was matted, her pajama top bunched up. She'd kicked her blue duvet to the bottom of the bed—she must be cold.

"Wake up, it's OK. You're just having a bad dream."

"They're coming to get me!" Ella sobbed, struggling to get out of her grasp. "They're coming, they're waiting at the door!"

Cassie held her firmly and eased her into a sitting position, dragging a pillow behind her as she smoothed her rumpled top. Ella was shaking with fear. The way she'd referred to "they" made Cassie wonder if it was a recurring nightmare. What was happening in Ella's life to trigger such vivid terror in her dreams? The young girl was completely traumatized, and Cassie had no idea of the best way to soothe her. She had vague memories of Jacqui, her sister, waving a broom at a cupboard to chase off an imaginary monster. But that terror had its roots in reality. The nightmares had started after Cassie had hidden in the cupboard during one of her father's drunken rages.

She wondered whether Ella's fear was also grounded in something that had happened. She'd have to try and find out later, but for now, she needed to convince her that the demons had gone.

"Nobody's coming for you. It's all OK. Take a look. I'm here and the light's on."

Ella's eyes opened wide. Tear-filled, they stared at Cassie for a moment and then her head turned, focusing on something behind her.

Still spooked by her own nightmare and Ella's insistence on seeing "them," Cassie looked quickly round, her heart accelerating as the door banged open.

Margot stood in the doorway, hands on hips. She wore a turquoise silk dressing gown and her blonde hair was tied in a loose braid. Her perfect features were marred only by a residual smudge of mascara.

Fury emanated from her and Cassie felt her insides shrink.

"What took you so long?" Margot snapped. "Ella's crying woke us up, it went on for hours! We had a late night—we are not paying you to have our sleep disturbed!"

Cassie stared at her, confused by the fact that Ella's well-being was seemingly the last thing on Margot's mind.

"I'm sorry," she said. Ella was clinging to her and making it impossible for her to stand and face her employer. "I came as soon as I heard her, but the light in the bedroom had blown, it was completely dark, so it took me a while to get—"

"Yes, it took you too long, and this is now your first warning! Pierre works long hours and he becomes angry when the children wake him."

"But…" With a surge of defiance, the question sprang to Cassie's lips. "Couldn't you have come to Ella if you heard her crying? It's my first night, and I didn't know where anything was in the dark. I'll do better next time, I promise, but I mean, she's your child and she was having a terrible dream."

Margot stepped toward Cassie, her face taut. For a moment Cassie thought she was going to offer a snapped apology and that they would reach a strained truce together.

But that didn't happen.

Instead, Margot's hand whipped out and she struck Cassie hard across the face.

Cassie bit back a scream, blinking tears away as Ella's cries escalated. Her cheek burned from the blow, the bump on her head was throbbing harder, and her mind was reeling in horror from the realization that her new employer was violent.

"Before you were hired, a kitchen maid did your duties. And can do so again, we have many servants. This is your second warning. I do not tolerate laziness, nor staff talking back. Your third offense will mean instant dismissal. Now, stop the child's crying, so we can get some sleep at last."

She marched out of the room, slamming the door behind her.

Frantically, Cassie bundled Ella in her arms, feeling overwhelming relief as her loud sobs subsided.

"It's OK," she whispered. "It's all right, don't worry. Next time I'll come to you sooner, I will be able to find my way better. Would you like me to sleep here the rest of the night? And we could leave your bedside lamp on to be extra safe?"

"Yes, please stay. You can help stop them coming back," Ella whispered. "And leave the light on. I don't think they like it."

The room was furnished in shades of neutral blue, but the bedside lamp, with its pink lampshade, was a bright and comforting item.

Even as she consoled Ella, Cassie felt ready to throw up, and realized her hands were trembling violently. She wriggled under the covers, glad of their warmth because she was freezing cold.

How could she possibly keep working for an employer who verbally and physically abused her in front of the children? It was unthinkable, inexcusable, and it brought back too many of her own memories that she'd managed to forget. First thing in the morning, she should pack up and get out.

But…she'd received no payment yet; she'd have to wait till month's end to have any money at all. There was no way she could afford the taxi ride back to the airport, never mind the expense of changing her flight ticket.

There was also the question of the children.

How could she leave them in the hands of this violent, unpredictable woman? They needed someone to care for them—especially young Ella. She could not sit here, consoling her and promising everything would be all right, only to disappear the very next day.

With a sick feeling, Cassie realized there was no choice. She could not leave at this point. She was financially and morally compelled to stay.

She'd just have to try and balance on the tightrope of Margot's temper, to avoid committing her third and final offense.

CHAPTER FIVE

Cassie opened her eyes, staring at the unfamiliar ceiling in confusion. It took her a few moments to orient herself and to realize where she was—in Ella's bed, with the morning light streaming through a gap in the curtains. Ella was still sleeping soundly, half buried under the duvet. The back of Cassie's head throbbed when she moved, the pain reminding her of everything that had happened last night.

She sat up hurriedly, remembering Margot's words, the stinging slap, and the warnings she'd received. Yes, she had been at fault for not attending to Ella immediately, but nothing that happened after that had been fair. When she'd tried to stand up for herself, she had only been punished further. So perhaps she needed to calmly discuss some house rules with the Dubois family this morning, to make sure this wouldn't happen again.

Why hadn't her alarm gone off yet? She'd set it for six-thirty, hoping this would mean a punctual arrival for breakfast at seven.

Cassie checked her phone and found with a shock that the battery was dead. The constant searching for signal must have drained it faster than usual. Climbing quietly out of bed, she went back to her room, plugged it into the charger, and waited anxiously for it to power up.

She swore under her breath when she saw it was nearly seven-thirty. She'd overslept, and would now have to get everyone up and ready as fast as possible.

Hurrying back to Ella's room, Cassie pulled back the curtain.

"Good morning," she said. "It's a beautiful sunny day, and it's breakfast time."

But Ella didn't want to get up. She must have battled to fall asleep after her bad dream and she'd woken in a mood. Grumpy and tired, she clung tearfully to the duvet when Cassie tried to pull it back. Eventually, remembering the candy she'd brought with her, Cassie resorted to bribery to get her out of bed.

"If you're ready in five minutes, you can have a chocolate."

Even then, further struggles lay ahead. Ella refused to put on the outfit Cassie selected for her.

"I want to wear a dress today," she insisted.

"But Ella, you might be cold if we go outside."

"Don't care. I want to wear a dress."

Cassie finally managed to compromise by choosing the warmest dress she could find—a long-sleeved corduroy frock, with long socks and fleece-lined boots. Ella sat on the bed, legs swinging, lower lip quivering. One child was finally ready, but there were another two still to go.

When she opened Marc's bedroom door, she was relieved to see he was awake and out of bed already. Clad in red pajamas, he was playing with an army of soldiers scattered over the floor. The large steel toy box below his bed was open, surrounded by model cars and an entire herd of farm animals. Cassie had to step carefully to avoid standing on any of them.

"Hello, Marc. Shall we go to breakfast? What do you want to wear?"

"I don't want to wear anything. I want to play," Marc retorted.

"You can carry on playing afterwards, but not now. We're late, and we must hurry."

Marc's response was to burst into noisy tears.

"Please don't cry," Cassie begged him, aware of the precious minutes ticking away. But his tears escalated, as if he were feeding off her panic. He flatly refused to change out of his pajamas and not even the promise of chocolate could change his mind. Eventually, at her wits' end, Cassie wedged a pair of slippers on his feet. Taking his hand in hers and placing a soldier in his pajama pocket, she persuaded him to follow her out.

When she knocked on Antoinette's door, there was no response. The room was empty and the bed neatly made with a pink night-dress folded on the pillow. Hopefully, Antoinette had made her own way to breakfast.

Pierre and Margot were already seated in the informal dining room. Pierre was wearing a business suit, and Margot was also smartly dressed, with her makeup perfectly done and her hair curled over her shoulders. She looked up when they walked in, and Cassie felt her face start to blaze. Quickly, she helped Ella into a chair.

"Sorry we're a little late," she apologized, feeling flustered and as if she was already on the back foot. "Antoinette wasn't in her room. I'm not sure where she is."

"She has finished breakfast, and is practicing her piano piece." Pierre gestured his head in the direction of the music room before pouring more coffee. "Listen. Perhaps you recognize the music— 'The Blue Danube.'"

Faintly, Cassie heard an accurate rendition of a tune that did indeed sound familiar.

"She is very talented," Margot offered, but the sour tone of her comment didn't match the words. Cassie glanced at her nervously. Was she going to say anything about what had happened last night?

But, as Margot stared back in cool silence, Cassie suddenly wondered if she'd misremembered some of it. The back of her head was tender and swollen from where she'd slipped, but when she touched the left side of her face, there was no bruise from the stinging slap. Or maybe it had been the right side? It was frightening that she couldn't remember now. She pressed her fingers into her right cheek, but there was no soreness there, either.

Cassie told herself firmly to stop worrying about the details. She could not possibly have been thinking clearly after a hard bang on the head and possible concussion. Margot had definitely threatened her, but Cassie's own imagination could have conjured up the actual blow. After all, she'd been exhausted, disoriented, and had emerged straight from the throes of a nightmare.

Her thoughts were interrupted by Marc demanding breakfast, and she poured orange juice for the children, serving them food from the breakfast trays. Ella insisted on taking every last piece of ham and cheese, so Cassie made do with a jam croissant and some sliced fruit.

Margot drained her coffee in silence, staring out the window. Pierre paged through a newspaper while he finished his toast. Were breakfasts always so silent? Cassie wondered. Neither parent showed any desire to engage with her, the children, or each other. Was this because she was in trouble?

Perhaps she should start the conversation and straighten things out. She needed to apologize formally for her lateness in reaching Ella, but she didn't think her punishment had been fair.

Cassie composed her words carefully in her head.

"I know I was slow to attend to Ella last night. I didn't hear her crying but next time I'll leave my bedroom door open. However, I don't feel that I was fairly treated. I was threatened and abused, and received two consecutive warnings in as many minutes, so could we please discuss some house rules here?"

No, that wouldn't do. It was too forward. She didn't want to appear antagonistic. She needed a softer approach, and one that would not make more of an enemy out of Margot.

"Isn't it a lovely morning?"

Yes, that would definitely be a good start and bring a positive angle to the conversation. And from there, she could lead into what she really wanted to say.

"I know I was slow to attend to Ella last night. I didn't hear her crying but next time I'll leave my bedroom door open. However, I'd like us to discuss some house rules now, in terms of how we treat each other and when warnings should be given, so that I can make sure I do the best job."

Cassie cleared her throat, feeling nervous, and put down her fork.

But as she was about to speak, Pierre folded his newspaper and he and Margot got up.

"Have a pleasant day, children," Pierre said, as they left the room.

Cassie stared after them, confused. She had no idea what to do now. She'd been told the children were to be ready by eight—but ready for what?

She'd better run after Pierre and check. She headed for the door, but as she reached it, she almost collided with a pleasant-faced woman wearing a staff uniform and carrying a tray of food.

"Ah—oops. There. Saved." She righted the tray and slid the slices of ham back into place. "You are the new au pair, yes? I am Marnie, the head housekeeper."

"Nice to meet you," Cassie said, realizing this was the first smiling face she'd seen all day. After introducing herself she said, "I was on my way to ask Pierre what the children need to do today."

"Too late. He will have gone already; they were heading straight for the car. Did he leave no instructions?"

"No. Nothing."

Marnie set the tray down and Cassie gave Marc more cheese and helped herself hungrily to toast, ham, and a hardboiled egg. Ella was refusing to eat the pile of food on her plate, pushing it around fretfully with her fork.

"Perhaps you can ask the children themselves," Marnie suggested. "Antoinette will know if there is anything arranged. I would advise waiting till she has finished playing the piano, though. She does not like her concentration disturbed."

Was it her imagination or did Marnie roll her eyes at those words? Encouraged, Cassie wondered if they might become friends. She needed an ally in this house.

But there was no time to forge a friendship now. Marnie was clearly in a hurry, collecting empty plates and dirty dishes while she asked Cassie if there were any problems with her room. Cassie quickly explained the issues, and after promising to change the bedcovers and replace the light bulb before lunch, the housekeeper left.

The sound of the piano had stopped, so Cassie headed to the music room near the hallway.

Antoinette was putting the music away. She turned and faced Cassie warily when she walked in. She was immaculately dressed in a royal blue frock. Her hair was tied back in a ponytail and her shoes were perfectly shined.

"You look beautiful, Antoinette, that dress is such a pretty color," Cassie said, hoping compliments would endear her to the hostile girl. "Is there anything you have planned for today? Any activities or other things arranged?"

Antoinette paused thoughtfully before shaking her head.

"Nothing today," she said decisively.

"And Marc and Ella, do they need to go anywhere?"

"No. Tomorrow, Marc has soccer practice." Antoinette closed the piano lid.

"Well, is there anything you would like to do now?" Perhaps allowing Antoinette to choose would help them bond.

"We could go for a walk in the woods. We all enjoy doing that."

"Where are the woods?"

"A mile or two down the road." The dark-haired girl gestured vaguely. "We can leave immediately. I will show you the way. I just have to change my clothes."

Cassie had assumed the woods were within the estate and was taken aback by Antoinette's reply. But a walk in the woods—that sounded like a nice, healthy outdoor activity. Cassie was sure that Pierre would approve.

Twenty minutes later, they were ready to leave. Cassie looked into every room as she escorted the children downstairs, hoping she would see Marnie or one of the other housekeeping staff, so she could tell them where she was going.

She didn't see anybody and had no idea where to start looking. Antoinette was impatient to leave, jumping from foot to foot with excitement, so Cassie decided that humoring her good mood was more important, especially seeing they weren't going to be gone for too long. They headed down the gravel drive and out, with Antoinette leading the way.

Behind a huge oak tree, Cassie saw a block of five stables—she'd noticed them when she arrived the previous day. She walked over to have a closer look and found they were empty and dark, the doors standing open. The field beyond was unoccupied, the wooden railings broken in parts, the gate hanging off its hinges and the grass growing long and wild.

"Do you have horses here?" she asked Antoinette.

"We used to, many years ago, but there have been none for a long time," she replied. "None of us ride anymore."

Cassie stood staring at the deserted stables while she absorbed this bombshell.

Maureen had given her incorrect and seriously outdated information.

The horses had played a part in her decision to come here. They had been an incentive. Hearing about them had made the place sound better, more appealing, more alive. But they were long gone.

During the interview, Maureen had stated that there would be an actual opportunity for her to learn to ride. Why had she misrepresented things, and what else might she have said that wasn't true?

"Come on!" Antoinette tugged her sleeve impatiently. "We need to go!"

As Cassie turned away, it occurred to her that there was no reason for Maureen to falsify information. The rest of her description about the house and the family had been fairly accurate and as an agent, she could only pass on the facts provided.

If so, that meant it must have been Pierre who had lied. And that, she realized, was even more troubling.

Once they had rounded a bend and the chateau was out of sight, Antoinette slowed her pace, none too soon for Ella, who was complaining that her shoes hurt.

"Stop whining," Antoinette advised. "Remember, Papa always says you mustn't whine."

Cassie picked Ella up and carried her, feeling her chubby weight increase with every step. She was already carrying the backpack crammed with everyone's jackets, and her last few euros in the side pocket.

Marc capered ahead, breaking branches from the hedges and throwing them into the road like spears. Cassie had to remind him constantly to keep off the tarmac. He was so inattentive and unaware, he could easily jump into the path of an oncoming car.

"I'm hungry!" Ella complained.

Exasperated, Cassie thought of her untouched plate of breakfast.

"There's a shop around the next corner," Antoinette told her. They sell cold drinks and snacks." She seemed strangely cheerful this morning, although Cassie had no idea why. She was just glad that Antoinette appeared to be warming to her.

She'd hoped the shop might sell cheap watches, because without a phone, she had no means of telling the time. But it proved to be a nursery, stocked with seedlings, baby trees, and fertilizer. The kiosk at the till sold only soft drinks and snacks—the elderly shopkeeper, perched on a barstool next to a gas heater, explained there was nothing else. The prices were freakishly high and she was filled with stress as she counted out her meager stash of money, purchasing chocolate and a can of juice for each child.

While she paid, the three children rushed across the road to take a closer look at a donkey. Cassie shouted for them to come back, but they ignored her.

The gray-haired man shrugged sympathetically. "Children will be children. They look familiar. Do you live nearby?"

"Yes, we do. They are the Dubois children. I'm their new au pair and this is my first day of work," Cassie explained.

She had hoped for some neighborly recognition, but instead, the shopkeeper's eyes widened in alarm.

"That family? You are working for them?"

"Yes." Cassie's fears surged back. "Why? Do you know them?"

He nodded.

"We all know of them here. And Diane, Pierre's wife, used to buy plants from me sometimes."

He saw her puzzled face.

"The children's mother," he elaborated. "She passed away last year."

Cassie stared at him, her mind whirling. She was unable to believe what she'd just heard.

The children's mother had died, and as recently as last year. Why had nobody said anything about this? Maureen hadn't even mentioned it. Cassie had assumed Margot was their mother, but now realized her naivety; Margot was far too young to be the mother of a twelve-year-old.

This was a family that had recently suffered bereavement, been ripped apart by a major tragedy. Maureen should have briefed her on this.

But Maureen hadn't known about the horses being gone, because she hadn't been told. With a stab of fear, Cassie wondered if Maureen had even known about this.

What had happened to Diane? How had her loss affected Pierre, and the children, and the entire family dynamic? How did they feel about Margot's arrival in the home so soon afterward? No wonder she could feel tension, taut as a wire, in just about every interaction within those walls.

"That's—that's really sad," she stammered, realizing that the shopkeeper was regarding her curiously. "I didn't know she'd died so recently. I guess her death must have been traumatic for everyone."

Frowning deeply, the shopkeeper handed her the change, and she put the meager stash of coins away.

"You know the family background, I am sure."

"I don't know much, so I'd really appreciate it if you could explain what happened." Cassie leaned anxiously over the counter.

He shook his head.

"It is not my place to say more. You work for the family."

Why did that make a difference? Cassie wondered. Her fingernail dug into the quick of her cuticle and she realized with a shock that she'd resumed her old stress habit. Well, she felt stressed all right. What the elderly man had told her was worrying enough, but what he was refusing to say was even worse. Perhaps if she was honest with him, he would be more open.

"I don't understand the situation there at all, and I'm scared I've gotten myself in over my head. To be honest with you, I wasn't even told Diane had died. I don't know how it happened, or what things were like before. If I had a better picture, it would really help."

He nodded, looking more sympathetic, but then the phone in the office rang and she knew the opportunity was lost. He walked out to answer it, closing the door behind him.

Disappointed, Cassie turned away from the counter, shouldering her backpack which seemed twice as heavy as before, or perhaps it was the disturbing information the shopkeeper had given her that was weighing her down. As she walked out of the shop, she wondered if she would have a chance to come back on her own and speak to the elderly man. Whatever secrets he knew about the Dubois family, she was desperate to find out.

CHAPTER SIX

A frightened scream from Ella jerked Cassie back to her present situation. Looking across the road, she saw to her horror that Marc had climbed through the split-pole fence and was feeding handfuls of grass to a growing herd that now included five hairy, gray, mud-encrusted donkeys. They flattened their ears and nipped each other as they crowded him.

Ella screamed again as one of the donkeys barged into Marc, knocking him flat on his back.

"Come out!" Cassie shouted, sprinting across the road. She leaned through the fence and grabbed the back of his shirt, dragging him away before he could be trampled. Did the child have a death wish? His shirt was soaked and filthy, and she hadn't brought a spare. Luckily the sun was still shining, although she could see clouds gathering in the west.

When she gave Marc his chocolate, he stuffed the entire bar into his mouth, his cheeks bulging. He laughed, spitting bits of it onto the ground, before racing ahead with Antoinette.

Ella pushed her chocolate away and began crying loudly.

Cassie picked the young girl up again.

"What's wrong? Are you not hungry?" she asked.

"No. I'm missing Mama," she sobbed.

Cassie hugged her tight, feeling Ella's cheek warm against her own.

"I'm sorry, Ella. I'm so sorry. I only just heard about it. You must miss her terribly."

"I wish Papa would tell me where she went," Ella lamented.

"But…" Cassie was at a loss for words. The shopkeeper had clearly said that Diane Dubois had died. Why did Ella think otherwise?

"What did your Papa say to you?" she asked carefully.

"He told me she went away. He wouldn't say where. He just said she left. Why did she go? I want her to come back!" Ella pressed her head into Cassie's shoulder, sobbing her heart out.

Cassie's head was spinning. Ella would have been four at the time, and would surely have understood what death meant. There would have been a chance to mourn, and a funeral service. Or perhaps there hadn't been.

Her mind boggled at the alternative; that Pierre had deliberately lied to Ella about his wife's death.

"Ella, don't be sad," she said, rubbing her shoulders gently. "Sometimes people leave and they don't come back." She thought of Jacqui, wondering again if she would ever find out what had really happened to her. Not knowing was terrible. Death, though tragic, was at least final.

Cassie could only imagine the agony Ella must have endured, believing that her own mother had abandoned her without a word. No wonder she had nightmares. She needed to find out the real story, in case there was more to it. Asking Pierre directly would be too intimidating, and she wouldn't feel comfortable mentioning the subject unless he brought it up himself. Perhaps the other children would tell her their version, if she asked at the right time. That might be the best place to start.

Antoinette and Marc were waiting at a fork in the road. Finally, Cassie saw the woods ahead. Antoinette had underestimated the distance; they must have walked at least three miles, and the nursery was the last building she had seen. The road had become a narrow lane, its paving cracked and broken, the hedges bushy and wild.

"You and Ella can go down that path," Antoinette advised, pointing to an overgrown track. "It's a shortcut."

Grateful for any shorter route, she headed down the narrow path, pushing her way through a profusion of leafy bushes.

Halfway, the skin on her arms started to burn so painfully that she cried out, thinking she'd been stung by a swarm of wasps. Looking down, she saw a swollen rash had broken out all over her skin, wherever the leaves had brushed her. And then Ella screamed.

"My knee is stinging!"

Her skin was swelling into hives, the welts deep red against her soft, pale flesh.

Cassie ducked too late, and a leafy branch lashed across her face. Immediately the stinging spread and she yelled in alarm.

From beyond, she heard Antoinette's shrill, excited laughter.

"Bury your head in my shoulder," Cassie commanded, wrapping her arms tightly around the young girl. Taking a deep breath, she barged along the path, shoving blindly through the stinging leaves until she burst out into a clearing.

Antoinette was screaming in glee, doubled over a fallen tree trunk, and Marc was following suit, infected by her mirth. Neither of them seemed to care about Ella's outraged tears.

"You knew there was poison ivy there!" Cassie accused as she lowered Ella to the ground.

"Stinging nettles," Antoinette corrected her, before bursting into renewed peals of mirth. There was no kindness in the sound—the laughter was utterly cruel. This child was showing her true colors and she was without mercy.

Cassie's surge of rage surprised her. For a moment her only desire was to slap Antoinette's smug, giggling face as hard as she could. The force of her anger was frightening. She actually stepped forward, raising her hand, before sanity prevailed and she lowered it quickly, appalled by what she had nearly done.

She turned away, opened her backpack, and rummaged for the only bottle of water. She rubbed some over Ella's knee and the rest over her own skin, hoping it would soothe the burning, but every time she touched the swelling, it seemed to make it worse. She looked around to see if there was a tap nearby, or a water fountain, where she could run cold water over the painful rash.

But there was nothing. These woods were not the family-friendly destination she'd expected. There were no benches, no notice boards. No garbage cans, no taps or fountains, no well-maintained paths. There was only ancient, dark forest, with massive beech, fir, and spruce trees looming out of tangled undergrowth.

"We need to go home now," she said.

"No," Marc argued. "I want to explore."

"This is not a safe place for exploring. There's not even a proper path. And it's too dark. You should put your jacket on now or you'll catch a cold."

"Catch a cold, catch me!" With a mischievous expression, the boy darted away, weaving swiftly through the trees.

"Damn it!" Cassie plunged after him, gritting her teeth as sharp twigs tore at her inflamed skin. He was smaller and faster than her, and his laughter taunted her as he dove through the undergrowth.

"Marc, come back!" she called.

But her words only seemed to spur him on. She followed doggedly, hoping he would either get tired or decide to abandon the game.

She finally caught up when he stopped to catch his breath, kicking at pine cones. She grasped his arm firmly before he could run again.

"This is not a game. See, there's a ravine ahead." The ground sloped steeply down and she could hear flowing water.

"Let's go back now. It's time to go home."

"I don't want to go home," Marc grumbled, dragging his feet as he followed her.

Nor do I, Cassie thought, feeling sudden sympathy for him.

But when they arrived back in the clearing, Antoinette was the only one there. She was sitting on a folded jacket, braiding her hair over her shoulder.

"Where's your sister?" Cassie asked.

Antoinette glanced up, seemingly unconcerned.

"She saw a bird just after you left, and wanted to have a closer look. I don't know where she went after that."

Cassie stared at Antoinette in horror.

"Why didn't you go with her?"

"You didn't tell me to," Antoinette said, with a cool smile.

Cassie breathed deeply, controlling another surge of rage. Antoinette was right. She should not have abandoned the children without warning them to stay where they were.

"Where did she go? Show me where exactly you last saw her."

Antoinette pointed. "She went that way."

"I'm going to look for her." Cassie kept her voice deliberately calm. "Stay here with Marc. Do not—*do not*—step out of this clearing or let your brother out of your sight. Understand?"

Antoinette nodded absently, combing her fingers through her hair. Cassie could only hope that she would do as she was told. She walked over to where Antoinette had indicated, and cupped her hands around her mouth.

"Ella?" she shouted as loud as she could. "Ella?"

She waited, hoping to hear an answer or approaching footsteps, but there was no response. All she could hear was the faint rustle of leaves in the strengthening wind.

Could Ella really have gone out of earshot in the time she'd been away? Or had something happened to her?

Panic surged inside her as she headed into the woods at a run.

CHAPTER SEVEN

Cassie ran deeper into the forest, weaving through the trees. She yelled Ella's name, praying that she would hear an answer. Ella could be anywhere; there was no clear path for her to have followed. The woods were dark and creepy, the wind was gusting harder, and the trees seemed to muffle her cries. Ella might have fallen into a ravine, or tripped and knocked her head. She could have been snatched by a vagrant. Anything could have happened to her.

Cassie skidded down mossy tracks and stumbled over roots. Her face was scratched in a hundred places and her throat was raw from shouting.

Eventually, she stopped, gasping for breath. Her sweat felt cold and clammy in the breeze. What should she do now? It was starting to get dark. She couldn't spend any more time searching or she'd put them all in danger. The nursery was her closest port of call, if it was still open. She could stop there, tell the shopkeeper what had happened, and ask him to phone the police.

It took her ages, and a few wrong turns, to retrace her steps. She prayed that the others would be waiting safe and sound. And she hoped beyond hope that Ella might have found her way back.

But when she reached the clearing, Antoinette was stringing leaves together in a chain, and Marc was curled up on the jackets, fast asleep.

No Ella.

She imagined the storm of anger on their return. Pierre would be justifiably furious. Margot might simply be vicious. Flashlights would shine into the night as the community hunted for a girl who was lost, injured, or worse, as a result of her own negligence. It was her fault and her failure.

The horror of the situation overwhelmed her. She collapsed against a tree and buried her face in her hands, trying desperately to control her sobs.

And then Antoinette said, in a silvery voice, "Ella? You can come out now!"

Cassie looked up, staring in disbelief as Ella clambered from behind a fallen log, brushing leaves from her skirt.

"What…" Her voice was hoarse and shaky. "Where were you?"

Ella smiled happily.

"Antoinette said we were playing hide and seek, and I mustn't come out when you called, or I would lose. I'm cold now—can I have my jacket?"

Cassie felt bludgeoned by shock. She hadn't believed anyone could dream up such a scenario out of pure malice.

It wasn't just the cruelty, but the calculation in her actions that chilled Cassie. What was driving Antoinette to torment her, and how could she stop it from happening in the future? She could expect no support from the parents. Being nice hadn't worked, and anger would only play right into Antoinette's hands. Antoinette held all the cards and she knew it.

Now they were heading home unforgivably late after telling nobody where they had gone. The children were muddied, hungry, thirsty, and exhausted. She feared that Antoinette had done more than enough for her to be instantly fired.

It was a long, cold, and uncomfortable walk back to the chateau. Ella insisted on being carried the entire way, and Cassie's arms had just about given out by the time they reached home. Marc trailed behind, grumbling, too tired to do more than throw an occasional stone at the birds in the hedgerows. Even Antoinette seemed to be taking no pleasure in her victory and trudged along sullenly.

When Cassie knocked on the imposing front door, it was snatched open immediately. Margot faced her, flushed with rage.

"Pierre!" she shouted. "Finally they are home."

Cassie started to tremble as she heard the angry stomping of feet.

"Where in the name of the devil have you been?" Pierre bellowed. "What irresponsibility is this?"

Cassie swallowed hard.

"Antoinette wanted to go to the woods. So we went for a walk."

"Antoinette—what? For the whole day? Why the hell did you let her do that, and why did you not obey your instructions?"

"What instructions?" Cowering from his wrath, Cassie longed to run and hide, just as she had done when she was ten years old and her father had gotten into one of his rages. Glancing behind her, she saw the children felt exactly the same. Their stricken, terrified faces gave her the courage she needed to keep facing Pierre, even though her legs were shaking.

"I left a note on your bedroom door." With an effort, he spoke in a more normal voice. Perhaps he'd noticed the children's reactions too.

"I didn't find any note." Cassie glanced at Antoinette but her eyes were downcast and her shoulders hunched.

"Antoinette was supposed to perform at a piano recital in Paris. A bus arrived to collect her at eight-thirty but she was nowhere to be found. And Marc had soccer practice in town at twelve."

A cold knot tightened in Cassie's stomach as she realized how serious the consequences of her actions had been. She'd let Pierre, and others, down in the worst possible way. This day should have been a test of her capabilities in organizing the children's schedules. Instead, they'd headed off on an unplanned jaunt into the middle of nowhere and missed important activities. If she had been Pierre, she'd have been livid, too.

"I'm so sorry," she muttered.

She didn't dare tell Pierre outright how the children had tricked her, even though she was sure he suspected it. If she did, they might end up suffering the brunt of his anger.

A gong sounded from the dining room and Pierre glanced at his watch.

"We will talk about this later. Get them ready for supper now. Quickly, or the food will get cold."

Quickly was easier said than done. It took over half an hour, and more tears, before Marc and Ella were bathed and in their pajamas. Thankfully, Antoinette was on her best behavior, and Cassie wondered if she was feeling overwhelmed by the consequences of her actions. As for herself, she was numbed after the catastrophe the day had become. Half drenched from bathing the children, she had no time for a shower. She pulled on a dry top and the welts on her arms flared up again.

They trooped disconsolately downstairs.

Pierre and Margot were waiting in the small lounge next door to the dining room. Margot was sipping a glass of wine while Pierre refilled a brandy and soda.

"Finally we are ready to eat," Margot observed tersely.

Supper was a fish casserole, and Pierre insisted the two older children serve themselves, although he allowed Cassie to help Ella.

"They must learn etiquette at an early age," he said, and proceeded to instruct them on the correct protocol the whole way through dinner.

"Put your serviette in your lap, Marc. Not crumpled on the floor. And your elbows must stay in; Ella does not want to be poked in the side while you are eating."

The stew was rich and delicious and Cassie was starving, but Pierre's haranguing was enough to put anyone off their food. She restricted herself to small, delicate mouthfuls, glancing at Margot to check she was doing things in the correct French way. The children were exhausted, unable to comprehend what their father was saying, and Cassie found herself wishing that Margot would tell Pierre that now was not a good time for nitpicking.

She wondered if dinners had been any different when Diane was alive, and how much the dynamic had changed after Margot's arrival. Her own mother had kept a firm lid on the conflict in her quiet way, but it had erupted uncontrollably when she had gone. Perhaps Diane had played a similar role.

"Some wine?" To her surprise, Pierre filled her glass with white wine before she could refuse. Perhaps this was protocol, too.

The wine was fragrant and fruity, and after just a few sips she felt the alcohol suffuse her bloodstream, filling her with a sense of well-being and a dangerous relaxation. She put her glass down hurriedly, knowing she couldn't afford any slip-ups.

"Ella, what are you doing?" Pierre asked, exasperated.

"I'm scratching my knee," Ella explained.

"Why are you using a spoon?"

"My nails are too short to reach the itch. We walked through nettles," Ella said proudly. "Antoinette showed Cassie a shortcut. I got stung on my knee. Cassie got stung all over her face and arms. She was crying."

Margot banged her wineglass down.

"Antoinette! You did that again?"

Cassie blinked, surprised to learn that she'd done it before.

"I…" Antoinette began defiantly, but Margot was unstoppable.

"You are a vicious little beast. All you want to do is cause trouble. You think you are being clever, but you are just a stupid, mean, childish girl."

Antoinette bit her lip. Margot's words had cracked her cool shell of composure.

"It's not her fault," Cassie found herself saying loudly, wondering too late if the wine had been a bad idea.

"It must be really difficult for her dealing with—" She stopped herself hurriedly, because she'd been about to mention their mother's death, but Ella believed a different version and she had no idea what the true story was. Now was not the time to ask.

"Dealing with so much change," she said. "In any case, Antoinette didn't tell me to take that path. I chose it myself. Ella and I were tired and it looked like a good shortcut."

She didn't dare look at Antoinette while she spoke, in case Margot suspected collusion, but she managed to catch Ella's eye. She gave her a conspiratorial glance, hoping she would understand why Cassie was siding with her sister, and was rewarded with a tiny nod.

Cassie feared that her defense would leave her on even shakier ground, but she had to say something. After all, she knew what it was like growing up in a fractured family where war could erupt at any moment. She understood the importance of an older role model who could offer shelter from the storms. How would she have coped without Jacqui's strength during the bad times? Antoinette had nobody to stand with her.

"So you are choosing to take her side?" Margot hissed. "Trust me, you will regret doing that, just as I have done. You do not know her like I do." She pointed a crimson-manicured finger at Antoinette, who started sobbing. "She is just the same as her—"

"Stop it!" Pierre roared. "I will not have arguments at the dinner table—Margot, shut up now, you have said enough."

Margot leaped to her feet so suddenly her chair overturned with a crash.

"You are telling me to shut up? Then I will go. But don't think I have not tried to warn you. You will get what you deserve, Pierre." She marched to the door but then turned back, staring at Cassie with undisguised hatred.

"You will all get what you deserve."

CHAPTER EIGHT

Cassie held her breath as Margot's angry footsteps retreated down the passage. Glancing around the table, she saw she wasn't the only one shocked into silence by the blonde woman's vicious outburst. Marc's eyes were saucer-wide and his mouth was tightly closed. Ella was sucking her thumb. Antoinette was scowling in wordless fury.

With a muttered oath, Pierre pushed back his chair.

"I'll deal with it," he said, striding to the door. "Put the children to bed."

Relieved to have a job to do, Cassie stood up, glancing at the plates and dishes littering the table. Should she clear the table, or ask the children to help? Tension hung in the air as thick as smoke. She wished for a normal, everyday family activity like washing up to help dissolve it.

Antoinette saw the direction of her gaze.

"Leave everything," she snapped. "Someone clears up later."

Forcing cheerfulness into her tone, Cassie said, "Well, then, it's bedtime."

"I don't want to go to bed," Marc protested, swinging his chair back. As the chair overbalanced he screamed in mock fright, grabbing at the tablecloth. Cassie leaped to his rescue. She was fast enough to stop the chair from falling over, but too late to prevent Marc upsetting two of the glasses and sending a plate crashing to the floor.

"Upstairs," she ordered, trying to sound stern, but her voice was high and unsteady with exhaustion.

"I want to go outside," Marc announced, sprinting toward the French doors. Remembering how he'd outrun her in the forest, Cassie dove after him. He'd already unlocked the door by the time she caught up, but she was able to grab him and stop him from opening it. She saw their reflections in the dark glass. The young boy with his rebellious hair and unrepentant expression—and herself. Her fingers clutching his shoulders, eyes wide and anxious, face sheet-white.

Seeing herself in that unexpected moment made her realize how badly she'd failed in her duties so far. It had been a full day since she'd arrived, and not for one minute had she been in charge. She was fooling herself if she thought otherwise. Her expectations of fitting in with the family and being loved, or at least liked, by the children could not have been more unrealistic. They didn't have a shred of respect for her, and she had no idea how she could change things.

"Bedtime," she repeated wearily. Keeping her left hand firmly on Marc's shoulder, she removed the key from the lock. Noticing a hook high on the wall, she reached up and hung it there. She marched Marc upstairs without letting go. Ella trotted alongside and Antoinette trailed despondently behind, slamming her bedroom door without so much as a good night.

"Do you want me to read you a story?" she asked Marc, but he shook his head.

"All right. Into bed, then. You can get up early tomorrow and play with your soldiers if you go to sleep now."

It was the only incentive she could think of but it seemed to work; or maybe tiredness had finally caught up with the young boy. At any rate, to her relief, he did as she asked. She pulled the duvet up, noticing her hands were trembling from sheer exhaustion. If he made another break for freedom she knew she would burst into tears. She wasn't convinced that he would stay in bed, but for now, at least, her job was done.

"I want a story." Ella tugged her arm. "Will you read me one?"

"Of course." Cassie walked to her bedroom and chose a book from the small selection on the shelf. Ella jumped into bed, bouncing on the mattress with excitement, and Cassie wondered how often she'd been read to in the past, because it didn't seem to be a customary part of her routine. Although, she supposed, there wasn't much about Ella's childhood that had been normal so far.

She read the shortest story she could find, only to have Ella insist on a second one. The words were swimming in front of her eyes by the time she reached the end and closed the book. Looking up, Cassie saw to her relief that the reading had soothed Ella, and she was finally asleep.

She turned off the lamp and closed the door. Walking back down the corridor, she checked on Marc, keeping as quiet as she could. Thankfully, the room was still dark and she could hear soft breathing.

When she opened Antoinette's door, the light was on. Antoinette was sitting up in bed scribbling notes in a pink-covered book.

"You knock before coming in," she chastised Cassie. "It is a rule."

"I'm sorry. I promise I'll do that from now on," Cassie apologized. She dreaded that Antoinette would escalate the broken rule into an argument, but instead she turned back to her notebook, writing a few more words before closing it.

"Are you finishing off homework?" Cassie asked, surprised because Antoinette didn't seem like a person who'd put things off till the last minute. Her room was immaculate. The clothes she'd taken off earlier were folded in the laundry basket, and her school bag, neatly packed, was set under a perfectly tidy white desk.

She wondered whether Antoinette felt as if her life was lacking control, and was trying to exert it in her immediate environment. Or maybe, since the dark-haired girl had made it clear she resented the presence of an au pair, she was trying to prove she didn't need anyone to take care of her.

"My homework is done. I was writing in my personal diary," Antoinette told her.

"Do you do that every night?"

"I do it when I am angry." She placed the lid back on her pen.

"I'm sorry about what happened tonight," Cassie sympathized, feeling as if she were treading on ice that might shatter at any moment.

"Margot hates me and I hate her," Antoinette said, her voice trembling slightly.

"No, I don't think that's true," Cassie protested, but Antoinette shook her head.

"It is true. I hate her. I wish she was dead. She's said things like that before. It makes me so angry I could kill her."

Cassie stared at her in shock.

It wasn't only Antoinette's words, but the calm way she spoke them, that chilled her. She had no idea how she should respond. Was it even normal for a twelve-year-old to have these murderous thoughts? Antoinette should surely be helped to manage this anger by somebody better qualified. A counselor, a psychologist, even a parish priest.

Well, in the absence of anyone competent, she guessed she was the only one available.

Cassie sifted through her own memories, trying to remember what she'd said and done at that age. How she'd reacted and what she'd felt when her own situation had spiraled out of control. Had she ever wanted to kill anybody?

She suddenly remembered one of her dad's girlfriends, Elaine, a blonde with long red fingernails and a high, shrieking laugh. They'd hated each other on sight. During the six months that Elaine had been on the scene, Cassie had loathed her with a vengeance. She couldn't remember wishing her dead, but she'd definitely wished her gone.

Probably this was the same thing. Antoinette was being more outspoken, that was all.

"What Margot said wasn't fair in the least," Cassie agreed, because it hadn't been. "But people say things in anger they don't mean."

Of course, they also came out with the truth when they were angry but she wasn't going to go down that road.

"Oh, she meant it," Antoinette assured her. She was fidgeting with the pen, twisting its lid violently from side to side.

"And Papa always takes her side now. He thinks only of her and never of us. It was different when my mother was alive."

Cassie nodded sympathetically. This, too, was her experience.

"I know," she said.

"How do you know?" Antoinette looked up at her curiously.

"My mother died when I was young. My father also brought new girlfriends—er, I mean a new fiancée—into the house. It caused a lot of clashes and hostilities. They disliked me, I disliked them. Luckily I had an older sister."

Hastily Cassie corrected herself again.

"I have an older sister, Jacqui. She stood up to my dad and helped protect me when there were fights."

Antoinette nodded in agreement.

"You took my side tonight. Nobody has done that before. Thank you for doing that."

She stared at Cassie, her eyes wide and blue, and Cassie felt a lump in her throat at the unexpected gratitude.

"That's what I'm here for," she said.

"I'm sorry I told you to walk through the nettles." She glanced at the welts on Cassie's hands, still swollen and inflamed.

"That's really no problem. I understand it was just a joke." Tears were flooding her eyes now as sympathy welled inside her. She hadn't expected Antoinette to let down her guard. She understood exactly how lonely she must feel, and how vulnerable. It was terrible to think Antoinette had suffered previous verbal abuse from Margot, with nobody there to protect her and her father deliberately siding against her.

Well, she had somebody now—Cassie was in her corner and would support her no matter what it took. The day hadn't been a complete disaster if it meant she'd managed to get closer to this complex and troubled child.

"Try to sleep now. I am sure things will be better in the morning."

"I hope so. Good night, Cassie."

Cassie closed the door, sniffed violently, and wiped her nose on her sleeve. Exhaustion and emotion were getting the better of her. She hurried down the corridor, grabbed her pajamas, and headed for the shower.

When she was standing under the steaming jet of water, she finally allowed her tears to flow.

Although the hot water had soothed her emotions, Cassie soon realized it had caused her skin to flare up again. The nettle stings started itching unbearably. She scrubbed herself hard with her towel in an effort to scratch the itch, but only succeeded in spreading it.

After climbing into bed, she found she was so uncomfortable she couldn't sleep. Her face and arms were throbbing and burning. Scratching offered only temporary relief and actually worsened the pain.

After what seemed like hours of unsuccessfully trying to will herself to sleep, Cassie admitted defeat. She needed something to soothe her skin. The cupboard in the shower room had housed only basic essentials, but she'd seen a large cabinet in the bathroom beyond Ella's bedroom. Perhaps there would be something there that could help.

She walked quietly to the bathroom and opened the wooden cabinet, relieved to see that it was filled with tubes and bottles. There was bound to be something for allergies. She read the labels, struggling with the complicated French, nervous that applying the wrong remedy might make things even worse.

Calamine lotion. She recognized the color and smell even though the label was unfamiliar. This would soothe her skin.

Pouring some into her cupped hand, Cassie slathered it onto the burns. Immediately she felt cool relief. She replaced the bottle and closed the cabinet.

As she turned to leave, she heard a sound and froze.

It was a rough shout, a muffled scream.

It must be Marc. He'd gotten out of bed and was causing trouble with Ella.

She hurried down the corridor but realized after just a few steps that this side of the house was quiet and the children were asleep.

There it was again—a crash and a thud and another scream.

Cassie froze. Was somebody breaking into the house? Her mind raced as she thought of all the treasures it contained. In the States, she would have locked herself in her room and called the police. But there was no cell signal here, so the best she could do would be to alert Pierre. It sounded as if it was coming from that direction anyway.

She would feel braver if she had a weapon. She glanced into her bedroom. Perhaps she should take the steel poker by the fireplace. It wasn't much, but it was something.

Grasping the poker firmly, Cassie tiptoed down the corridor. She rounded the corner and found herself facing a closed wooden door.

This must be the master suite, and the noise was coming from inside.

Cassie leaned the poker against the wall, so she could grab it quickly if she needed to. Then she bent down and peeked through the keyhole.

The lights were on in the bedroom. Her view was limited, but she could see one person—no, two. There was Pierre, his dark hair gleaming in the light. But what was he doing with his hands? They were wrapped round something—he was gripping and shaking it violently. Another plaintive, choking scream reached her, and she drew in her breath sharply as she realized he was grasping a woman's neck.

Cassie's heart pounded as she translated the scene playing out through the tiny hole in the door, where Pierre was murdering Margot.

CHAPTER NINE

Cassie recoiled from the heavy wooden door, adrenaline flooding through her as she replayed the deadly scene in her mind. Heavy hands clamped around a pale neck, those panicked, choking screams. There had been something else as well; a splash of vivid color she couldn't make sense of.

She needed to call for help, and fast.

Who could she call, though? The housekeeper was the only person she knew, and she had no idea where to find her. In any case, if she wasted time looking for her, Margot would die. It was as simple as that.

Instead, Cassie herself would have to intervene.

If she burst into the bedroom, shouting at the top of her voice, it would cause a distraction that would hopefully allow the blonde woman to break free.

Terror overpowered her at the thought, but she told herself it had to be done. Even if her legs turned to water and her voice was no more than a pathetic squeak, she had to try and be brave.

As she reached for the door handle, she heard another sound that stopped her in her tracks.

It was a deep-voiced groan of pleasure.

Hesitantly, Cassie bent and peered through the keyhole once again.

Moving her head from side to side to make the most of her narrow view, Cassie realized the object she'd seen was a brightly colored scarf. Margot's wrists were tightly bound, and the scarf was knotted to a brass rail that must be the headboard.

Cassie gasped as she realized what was happening.

This wasn't murder, but a sexual act—dark, violent, and prolonged. She could see Margot struggling to free herself. This wasn't just kinky experimentation; it looked downright dangerous. And she wasn't at all sure that it was consensual. Margot didn't seem to be a willing partner. Perhaps Pierre was punishing her for her earlier outburst, or using it as an excuse to do what he was doing now.

Cassie told herself firmly that however horrifying the act, it was taking place in private and certainly not her business. If Pierre or Margot found out she'd been watching, she'd be in serious trouble. And if one of the children were to see her peeking through the keyhole, she didn't want to imagine what the consequences would be.

Cassie stepped back, but in the shock of what she'd seen, she forgot all about the poker she'd placed against the wall. She knocked it with her foot and it clattered loudly down onto the marble tiles.

The groans stopped suddenly. After a heartbeat of silence, Pierre called out, his voice sharp.

"What's that? Who's there?"

He'd heard. And the sudden creak of bedsprings and the thud of feet on floorboards told her that he was on his way to see.

Cassie picked up the poker and fled down the corridor, running as fast and silently as she could. She prayed that Pierre might stop to put on a gown or slippers, and that she'd be out of sight by the time he opened the door. Because if he saw her, if he even guessed she'd been there, she had a world of trouble coming her way.

She rounded the corner and skidded on the marble tiles, grabbing desperately at the wall to stop herself from falling. Her finger bent back painfully and she swallowed a cry. From behind her she heard the latch click as the bedroom door swung open. And then she heard the pounding of feet down the corridor. Pierre was pursuing her at speed.

Nightmare scenarios raced through Cassie's mind as she headed for her bedroom. She closed the door as quietly as she could and placed the poker back in the fireplace, trying to stop her hands from shaking so it wouldn't rattle against the grate. A moment later she leaped into bed and yanked the covers up to her chin. With her heart banging in her throat, she waited for Pierre to pass by.

Because of course he would pass by, wouldn't he? There would be no reason for him to knock if he saw her door was closed.

The footsteps stopped outside her door, but Pierre did not knock. Instead, to Cassie's disbelief, he simply opened it. He snapped on the light and stood in the doorway. His face was flushed, he was barefoot, and he was wearing a burgundy dressing gown.

Cassie's first immediate and overriding thought was that this was a complete invasion of privacy. No way was it appropriate for an employer to enter an employee's bedroom alone and after hours without knocking. His presence in her private space was making her feel defensive and vulnerable, triggering old memories that had morphed into nightmares. People in her room. Hiding under the bed. *"Hey, little girlie…"*

Pierre stared at her and then took a look around the room, his gaze resting on her bath towel hung on the hook near the door, and the pile of clothes she'd left folded on the armchair near the fireplace.

Cassie sat up, straightening her pajama top and instinctively crossing her arms over her chest. She wanted to shout at him to get out, to scream that he had no right to enter her room without permission.

But this was not a good time to discuss boundaries—not when she'd been peeking through his bedroom door at his private activities.

"Did you hear anything, Cassie? There was a noise just now."

The loud clattering he'd heard was undeniable evidence that someone had been up and about. It was her job to respond to noises and disturbances at night, so there was no way she could claim she hadn't heard it. She had to offer Pierre a coherent explanation for what had happened.

She saw he was looking at her curiously and suddenly remembered the fresh smears of lotion on her face and arms. And with that, the answer came to her. She breathed deeply, trying to speak as calmly as possible and not to sound breathless.

"That was me. I was in the bathroom down the corridor, getting some lotion for my skin. It was itching so much I couldn't sleep. I knocked over a glass bottle while I was putting the lotion away. It didn't break but it made a terrible noise. Sorry it woke you."

Pierre frowned, then nodded as if that made sense to him.

"Your skin, it is all right now?"

"I think it will be fine. The lotion has stopped the itching. Would you like me to check on the children, in case I disturbed them, too?"

Pierre paused and listened.

"Not necessary. All seems to be quiet. Better to let them be, if they are asleep."

She thought he was going to leave, but he didn't. Instead he walked over to the pile of clothes on the desk, bent down, and retrieved a folded item from the floor.

Cassie's eyes widened in alarm as she saw it was her black bra. She'd left it on top of the pile but must have been knocked it off earlier—probably when she'd rushed past to replace the poker.

Pierre shook it out before placing it carefully on top of the pile.

"You must never fold bras," he reprimanded her. "They should be stored open, stacked together, preferably in a drawer. It is better for them."

He looked down at her clothes and nodded in satisfaction while Cassie shrank against the wall, edging the bedcovers higher up her body. She was sure her panties had been under the bra, and that meant he must have seen them, too. She was too shocked by his behavior to think of any response, but Pierre didn't seem to expect one.

"Good night."

He walked back to her door, switched off the light, and left, closing the door behind him.

Cassie let out a long, deep breath. She uncrossed her arms, noticing her hands were still trembling.

He'd had no right to come in here without knocking. However innocent his motives might have been, it was a complete violation—to open her door, turn on the light, stroll across the floor to examine her underwear and advise her on how to store it. She wished she'd gotten her thoughts in order in time to tell him how out of line his behavior was.

She was starting to realize that Pierre didn't care about boundaries. His actions had revealed a darker side to him—a side that craved and took, no matter the consequences.

There was no key in her bedroom door, and although Marnie might be able to find a key if she asked, she couldn't lock herself in without inviting suspicion and criticism from her employers.

She'd need to find another way of rigging up an alarm. Perhaps she could run a string from the door handle to the chair, so that it would overturn if the door opened. She could say she'd done it so she would wake immediately if the children entered.

She urgently needed a contingency plan in place—because what would she do if Pierre decided to come into her bedroom while she was asleep?

CHAPTER TEN

Cassie woke before her alarm went off. She was sweating, curled in a ball and huddled under the duvet. She guessed she'd roused herself from a nightmare. Looking up, she saw the bedroom door was closed. She remembered it being wide open, but that must have been part of her dream. Pierre had definitely closed it when he left.

Thinking of Pierre brought last night's violent scenario rushing back to her. The way Margot had been trying to scream. And the thudding—what had that been? Had she been struggling to get free from her ties?

Preoccupied with Margot's aggression and the children's willful behavior, she hadn't thought much about Pierre. From his behavior, she'd guessed him to be moody, controlling, somewhat of a perfectionist. She'd never dreamed that he had a darker side that drove him to act out on dangerous sexual desires.

Cassie suddenly wondered if any of the children had spied on him the same way she had. That thought was too disturbing for her to pursue so she pushed it away.

It was five-thirty a.m. Too early to wake the children, but at least she could take some time and look presentable herself.

Cassie showered, washed her hair, and used some of the serum she'd brought to dry her hair smooth and shiny. She applied light makeup—a touch of foundation to brighten the tired pallor of her skin, and pink lipstick. She dressed in jeans, boots, and a turquoise top. Finally she was achieving the neat and professional look she'd hoped for on her first day.

Remembering that boundaries were important to Antoinette—and feeling renewed empathy with her in this regard—she knocked on her door and waited for an answer. She had to knock three times before finally receiving a sullen, "Yes?" in response.

Cassie had hoped that Antoinette would be friendlier toward her after the words they'd shared last night, but Antoinette seemed to have rebuilt her barriers even higher. Sulky and uncooperative, she barely acknowledged Cassie's cheerful "Good morning."

"Leave me to dress," she snapped. "I'll come to breakfast on my own."

Cassie assumed that Marc would be playing with his toys again, surrounded by the same mess she'd seen the previous day. But when she entered his room she was concerned to see him still in bed, his face turned to the wall.

"Marc, are you sick?" she asked. She tried to touch his forehead to see if he felt feverish but he batted her hand impatiently away.

"I do not like today," he grumbled.

"But it's a nice day," Cassie pleaded, drawing the curtains back. The sun wasn't up yet, but the sky was cloudless and the horizon already bright gold.

"I hate this day. I am not getting up now. I want orange juice. Bring me juice."

She had no idea whether he was really sick or just moody, but either way, bringing him juice seemed like a sensible compromise.

Cassie went downstairs, relieved to see Marnie was already setting the breakfast table, taking a stack of plates and place mats from the wooden sideboard.

"Good morning. You are bright and early today," she greeted Cassie.

"Marc wants orange juice. Will it be OK to take a glass up to him? He's woken in a terrible mood. So has Antoinette. I haven't even dared go into Ella's room yet."

Marnie thought for a minute.

"You know today is the first of November?"

Cassie stared at her uncomprehending.

"It is All Saints Day here in France, but also it is the day that Diane passed away. This time last year was when it happened. That is probably why they are sad, remembering the loss of their mother. Being a holiday, the date is easy to recall." She shrugged sympathetically. "Wait a moment while I bring the juice."

Cassie waited uneasily, wishing she knew more about what had happened. Would Marnie think Cassie rude or forward if she asked? She worried that French etiquette might be different. Perhaps it was not acceptable to ask such a direct question. And she most definitely did not want to estrange Marnie.

The housekeeper hurried back into the dining room carrying a brimming jug of orange juice. She placed the jug on a mat and handed Cassie a glass.

"Hopefully this makes Marc feel better. He's such a moody child," she offered, and Cassie nodded agreement. She filled the glass three-quarters full. It was made from heavy, ornate crystal, the facets sharp against her fingers. She would rather have taken a simple plastic cup upstairs for Marc, but that didn't seem to be an option in this house.

"I'll battle to cheer him and Antoinette up today," she said. "Do you know if they have any activities planned? I messed up badly yesterday because I didn't realize what was on the schedule."

Marnie laughed as she set the other glasses out. "Yes, word got around. We all know what happened, or we can guess. Pierre is copying me on all the daily activities and I am to make sure you are informed. He used to leave a note on the bedroom door for the last au pair. But she wasn't here very long." Marnie paused, checking herself as if she'd been about to say something and had then thought better of it.

Cassie was about to ask what happened to her, but Marnie continued, as if she'd gotten herself back on track.

"Anyway, seeing today's a holiday, there are no activities." She turned to the table, smoothing the cloth and setting cutlery out with practiced expertise.

"Oh," Cassie said, crestfallen at the thought of the long, empty hours ahead.

"If you want to take them out, there is a carnival in the village," Marnie continued. "It's two miles down the road—go out of the house, turn right, then first right again will lead you directly to the village square. It is held on the same holiday every year and it's quite fun. At any rate, it might cheer the children up. Why not ask Pierre if they can go?"

"That's a good idea. Thank you," Cassie said gratefully. The opportunity to ask about Diane's death had come and gone and she was still none the wiser. She would have to find out another time.

Marnie placed the coffee and milk jugs on the table and picked up her tray.

"We serve bacon for breakfast on holidays. Why not tell Marc that? He loves bacon."

She winked at Cassie before hurrying out through a side door.

Resolving to use the bacon as bribery, Cassie picked up the glass. She was on her way upstairs when she met Pierre coming down. Today he was casually dressed—jeans, sports shoes, and a polo-necked black shirt with a small designer logo.

"Morning," she mumbled. In the cold light of day, her memories of the previous night seemed even more vivid. Worse still, instead of giving the quick greeting she'd expected, Pierre stopped on the stairway, forcing her to do the same.

"Morning, Cassie."

"I'm taking juice up to Marc. He said he was thirsty," she explained, but realized with a twist of her stomach that Pierre had not even noticed the juice.

Instead, he was looking at her.

Cassie bit her lip as his gaze traveled over her shiny hair, her face, taking in the form-fitting top and the jeans—the trendiest pair she owned. It was as if he were seeing her for the first time. Her disheveled, exhausted appearance over the past two days had provided a camouflage which was now stripped away.

"You look very nice," he complimented her, and she stammered out a polite thank you while cringing inwardly.

He took a step toward her. "Your hair, this is your natural color?" He reached out a hand and she realized he was actually going to touch it.

"Yes," she whispered, her mouth suddenly dry. She was trapped where she stood, unable to step back because the banister was directly behind her. Then, to her relief, the click of heels sounded on the landing above, and Pierre lowered his hand.

"What are you going to do with the children today?" he asked in a more formal voice.

"Marnie said there's a carnival in the village. Could I take them there?"

"Of course. It is some distance, so you should drive. I will show you where the Peugeot's keys are, and you will need spending money." He pulled a wallet from his back pocket and handed her a fifty-euro note.

Cassie put the money in her pocket and then stepped aside to allow Margot to pass. Elegant as always in a cream jumpsuit and brown leather boots, she had a plaid scarf wrapped around her neck. She nodded at Cassie, who noticed she looked paler than usual.

"Good morning," Cassie greeted her.

Margot made an effort to speak but to Cassie's shock, she couldn't utter a word. All that came out was a hoarse, rasping whisper.

Cassie forced herself to think two moves ahead, as if she were playing a game of chess. She knew what had happened to Margot. But if she hadn't known, it would be normal and polite to ask.

"Are you all right?" she said, making sure to sound both surprised and concerned.

"A touch of laryngitis," Pierre explained smoothly.

Cassie nodded. "That's so uncomfortable, Margot, your throat must be very sore. Perhaps Marnie can bring you some lemon and honey? Marc doesn't seem himself today, either. I'm not sure if he's coming down with the same thing—but if he is, I won't take him to the carnival," she added hurriedly.

Wordlessly, Margot continued downstairs, and Cassie went on her way with the juice. As she walked to Marc's room she realized how disturbing Margot's subdued demeanor was. Up until now, the blonde woman had been entitled, bossy, and domineering. Today, she seemed mentally and physically crushed.

Her throat must have been viciously bruised for her to have visible marks, as well as a complete loss of voice. Cassie wondered if she had known when she met Pierre that this would be part of the arrangement. Or had she only found out the first time his hands had closed around her throat? If so, she must have made the choice to live with it.

Maybe it was true love, although Cassie thought cynically that it was more likely the money, the prestige, the massive chateau, and the enormous diamond ring that allowed her to endure it.

Zane hadn't owned so much as a square foot of property; a beat-up Ford had been his only worldly possession. Cassie had loved him for his charm and charisma, realizing too late that they were the same volatile qualities her father had possessed, and were just as prone to instant reversal.

The first time Zane had hurt her, she'd known she had to end it.

As she opened Marc's door she wondered, in a moment of terrifying introspection, whether she might have ended up giving Zane a second chance if he had been as wealthy and powerful as Pierre.

At half past ten, Cassie carefully reversed the Peugeot SUV out of the garage. Antoinette and Marc were still immersed in somber silence. Ella was the only cheerful person in the party, but Cassie remembered that she didn't know their mother had died, only that she had "left."

She guessed Ella hadn't realized the significance of the day, and must have been too young to make the connection. This was something she really needed to question Marnie about, as soon as she felt more confident in their friendship.

Cassie's mood lifted as she drove along the scenic lanes, bathed in morning sunshine, following a line of other cars all heading the same way. The narrow roads were crowded with vehicles that were parked in higgledy-piggledy order, leaving barely enough space for the next to squeeze past. Cassie parked as best she could, burying the car's hood in a hedge. As soon as she opened the door she heard music, and the cheerful sound of the live band seemed to raise everyone's spirits.

"This is fun," Antoinette said, grabbing Marc's hand and skipping down the road. Cassie followed at a more sedate pace with Ella.

"We have to keep together," she yelled, as the two older children burst onto the wide green square, lined with colorful bunting and stalls. And then, thinking more practically, she called, "Let's all go get a pancake."

The chocolate crepes were a success. From that stall, the children visited the face-painting kiosk, before moving to an outdoor theater to watch a puppet show. Standing in the front row, the three screamed with laughter at the puppets' antics. Cassie smiled, delighted and relieved that the day was turning out so well. She felt as if a heavy weight had been lifted from her shoulders.

Although there must have been three or four hundred people thronging the square and enjoying the cool, sunny weather, Cassie noticed that the three Dubois children didn't seem to have many friends. They were not seeking out the company of other children or even interacting with them.

In contrast, Cassie greeted everyone she passed, wondering who were locals and who were neighbors, and if she would see the elderly man she'd met the previous day in the nursery, who'd told her he knew the secrets of the Dubois family.

When she saw a young, red-haired woman shepherding twin boys along, she smiled widely, recognizing a fellow au pair. Sure enough, the woman walked over to say hello.

"I am Sarah, from London," she said. "These young lads belong to the Villiers family, who own a vineyard a few miles north of here."

"It's great to meet you. I'm Cassie and I only arrived two days ago so I'm still settling in."

"I've been here almost a year. In fact, I'm going on my annual holiday next week. Are you enjoying it so far? I guess it's too early to tell. But I'm sure you will." She smiled.

"I think I'll cope," Cassie said carefully. "It's going to be a challenging job, though."

She glanced around at Antoinette, who was still spellbound by the puppet show, holding Marc's and Ella's hands tightly in hers.

"Which family do you work for?" Sarah asked curiously, following her gaze.

"The Dubois family. They live in a chateau two miles away. I'm not sure which direction," Cassie confessed, disoriented from wandering around the stalls.

Sarah frowned. "You work for them?"

"Why? Do you know them?"

Sarah didn't answer immediately. Instead, she turned to the twin boys. "Pierre, Nicolas, do you want to do the lucky dip? It's at that stall over there. Go and join the line, I'll catch up with you in a second."

The two boys raced away and Sarah turned back to Cassie.

"You must be very careful," she warned.

Cassie felt suddenly sick, wishing she hadn't eaten the rich chocolate crepe.

"You're the second person who's told me that. I know the family has huge problems. But I don't know why I keep getting told to be careful. What exactly am I being warned about? Do you know?"

Sarah glanced around before leaning closer to Cassie, who strained to hear her over the babble of voices and music.

"Pierre, the owner of the chateau, has a very bad reputation."

"For what?"

"Infidelity. It's common knowledge he was never faithful to his wife, nor is he to his new fiancée. He's a wealthy, powerful landowner and many women are attracted to him. And what he wants, he takes."

Cassie swallowed, thinking of her bedroom door being opened, the light turned on. Pierre's presence in her private space; the way his attention had suddenly focused on her this morning when he saw her looking good.

"I see," she said in a small voice.

"There are rumors that he has … unusual tastes in bed. Kinky stuff. They say some of the women he's had affairs with have broken off the relationship as a result. But who knows the real story or whether their versions are true at all? After all, if a rich man dumps you, you are going to tell people it was your idea, not his, aren't you?"

Cassie nodded. She might have disbelieved Sarah if she hadn't seen the evidence last night, right before her eyes. She knew the rumors were not simply hearsay or damaging lies, but she couldn't risk sharing her knowledge.

"Thank you for the information," she said. "I will be careful. Where did you hear this from, and is there anything else about the family I should know?"

Sarah pursed her lips, considering Cassie's words.

"My employer spoke about it during a lunch with her friends, and I happened to overhear the conversation for a few minutes." She winked at Cassie, as if confessing she'd eavesdropped.

"I think they did go on to mention other issues with that family; the discussion was becoming quite heated," she continued. "But I only heard snippets, and of course I couldn't ask any questions afterwards, since I wasn't told directly."

"No, that would definitely have gotten you into trouble," Cassie said.

Sarah looked up. "My boys are at the front of the line. I must run—there are prizes to be won. Good luck with your assignment." She squeezed Cassie's hand before running over to the lucky dip kiosk.

The puppet show had ended and the children were dispersing.

"What do you want to do now?" Cassie asked Antoinette, who shrugged.

"Take a look at the rest of the stalls, I suppose," she said.

Walking down the pathway, Cassie started to worry more and more about what she had heard, and the way Sarah had described Pierre.

"What he wants, he takes."

She'd already sensed that entitlement in him, a disregard for personal boundaries, or even a complete lack of awareness of them. What would she do if he made a pass at her? She was sure he'd deny ever having done so, and who would believe her version over his?

The children seemed to sense her distraction, and their mood shifted. In the time it took to walk from the puppet show to the nearby kiosks, she was suddenly dealing with three sullen, uncooperative monsters who were a world away from the happy trio who'd arrived at the pancake stand.

"I'm bored," Marc announced, strutting over to the lucky dip stall and swinging from the guard rope. Cassie pulled him away as the structure teetered sideways, prizes clattering down from the shelves.

"Marc, don't do that! You must respect people's property," Cassie chastised him, suddenly aware that she was sounding a lot like Margot.

"I need something fun to do," Marc complained, kicking at stones on the gravel path and sending them flying into the face of a little girl who was passing by.

Scanning the area for inspiration, Cassie noticed a soccer game was under way in the center of the green.

"Who would like to play?" she asked.

Antoinette shrugged, but Marc rushed off in the direction of the game.

As they followed, Ella started complaining her feet hurt, tugging at Cassie's hand and demanding to be carried. And, on her other side, Antoinette began loudly pestering her with questions.

"Tell me, Cassie, did your dad have a lot of girlfriends?"

What exactly was she supposed to say to that? After her recent conversation with Sarah, she could guess why Antoinette might be raising the topic, but from her tone of voice it was clear that Antoinette was not seeking reassurance, but looking to bait Cassie.

"He had one or two," she replied shortly.

"I meant, while he was still married to your mother," Antoinette elaborated in piercing, saccharine tones. "Did he have any girlfriends then?"

"Not that I know of," Cassie replied, forcing a smile.

Inside she felt herself shrinking in fear. How was it possible that she had become the target of Antoinette's venom again? She'd hoped that after their conversation the previous night, Antoinette would have abandoned her vendetta, but clearly it had been a temporary truce.

"But what if you didn't know, Cassie? Do you think you might not have known?" Antoinette smiled sweetly up at her.

Clamping her lips together, Cassie ignored the question and focused on the soccer game. Marc had charged onto the field, ignoring the referee's whistle and the efforts of the organizer to allocate him to a team. He sped around the grass, pushing other children out of the way, shouting victoriously whenever he kicked the ball.

"My feet are sore," Ella complained loudly.

Gritting her teeth, Cassie picked Ella up. She was impossible to carry, squirming and fidgeting as she tried to view the revelry from her new, higher vantage point. It was only a minute before Cassie had to put her down again.

The soccer game was degenerating into chaos. An irate mother rushed onto the field, picking up her daughter who had been knocked over in the melee. She started shrieking recriminations at the organizers.

"Marc! Come here!" Cassie yelled, but predictably, the dark-haired boy ignored her.

"Do you think your dad missed your mother, Cassie?" Antoinette nudged her arm, loudly demanding attention. "Or do you think he was glad to be able to enjoy his girlfriends without her there?"

Cassie heard a shocked exclamation from the woman beside her, who quickly shepherded her child away. She stared down at Antoinette, feeling her fear crystallize into fury, because what the hell was this all about? She opened her mouth, ready to give a sharp response, but at that moment somebody tapped her shoulder.

She turned to face an irate referee grasping Marc by his arm.

"Madame, are you responsible for this child?"

"Yes, I am." Aware of curious stares from the onlookers, Cassie felt her cheeks turn crimson.

"Please control him. He is not allowed to return to the field. He has been disrupting the game and causing injuries."

The referee let go of Marc's arm and the dark-haired boy immediately tried to bolt back to the field. Expecting this, Cassie was prepared. She managed to grab the hood of his jacket and haul him back.

"This is not the way to behave," she reprimanded them, turning from Marc's rebellious face to Antoinette's smug innocence.

"Let me go!" Marc struggled in her grasp.

Antoinette tugged her arm, asking in a piercing voice, "What do you mean, Cassie? Having girlfriends? Aren't men allowed to have girlfriends? Why do you think it's wrong—can you explain?"

As Cassie turned to her, trying to come up with a measured response to the question even though the words made her want to lash out, she was tugged off balance by Ella. The young girl grabbed Cassie's belt with both hands, leaning all her weight onto it so that the leather dug painfully into the small of her back.

"I need to be picked up. Carry me now," she whined.

Antoinette started giggling and pointing at Cassie. "You're going to fall over! Or else your pants will fall down. Oh, you look so funny!"

Marc's cries escalated to a furious shout, and he pummeled Cassie's arm with his fists.

"Let me go! I want to play soccer with the other boys. I don't care about the rules. I hate you."

As he paused to take a breath, Antoinette's barbed question came again.

"You haven't answered me, Cassie. Don't you know it's very rude to ignore people's questions? Why aren't men allowed girlfriends and did your dad enjoy himself with them?"

The relentless baiting finally pushed Cassie past her limits. Her belt was about to break, her arm was bruised and aching, and Antoinette's taunting words and sugary tone were making her want to slap her.

Instead, she yelled so loudly that even Marc was silenced.

"Stop it now! All of you!" she shrieked. "You cannot behave like this in a public place! There are rules for decent behavior." Cassie was aware more heads were turning her way, but she was so angry she was unable to stop herself.

"You know the rules, and you are deliberately breaking them. It's unfair to me, to the other children, to everyone here who's trying to enjoy their day. I know it's a year today since your mother died, but that does not give you an excuse to do this. This is completely unacceptable."

Cassie breathed hard, her throat rough from shouting. At last, Marc appeared chastised—but Antoinette was smiling even more smugly than before as she surveyed the crowd. As Cassie took in the shocked stares and comments from the onlookers, she realized, too late, the hurtfulness of what she had said.

And then she heard a sob from behind her.

Ella was staring up at her, wide-eyed.

"My mother died?" she asked in a quivering voice. "Does that mean she is never coming back?"

Frozen, Cassie looked down at her, unable to find any words.

Ella drew in a giant breath and let out a shrill scream of pure grief.

As she gathered the hysterical child into her arms, Cassie realized what a terrible mistake she'd made. In her anger, she'd given Ella a different truth from the one her own father had told her.

And she'd done so without consulting Pierre, or finding out the real version of events, or even asking why Ella had never been told.

Pierre would be absolutely furious.

Cold with despair, Cassie wished she could turn back the clock and erase her words. She'd overstepped her boundaries completely with this cruel and angry outburst. When Pierre heard about it—which would happen as soon as they got home—she had no doubt she would be instantly fired.

CHAPTER ELEVEN

Driving back to the chateau, Cassie had to force herself to focus on the road. Her fragmented thoughts were spinning in a hundred different directions. She couldn't stop replaying the scene in her mind. How easy it had been to shout those vicious words to the children while anger boiled inside her. How shocked the onlookers had been, gesturing at her as if she were the evil one.

Their disapproval would be nothing compared to what she could expect when they arrived home.

Ella was huddled silently in the back seat, sucking her thumb. Cassie peered into the rearview mirror, watching her in concern.

"Cassie, stop quick, we're going to crash," Antoinette squeaked, startled out of her usual coolness.

Cassie wrenched her attention back to the road, stomping on the brakes to avoid plowing into the Renault in front of her, which had stopped to let a herd of cattle cross.

Marc laughed excitedly at the squeal of brakes.

"Eeeee ... Crash!" he shouted. "Crash, crash, crash."

He entertained himself the rest of the way home with a shouted accompaniment to her driving.

"Vroom vroom! Faster. Eeeee .... Stop! Crash!"

Cassie's head was throbbing by the time they reached the chateau, and she felt cold with despair. She was a failure. She was totally lacking in the patience and wisdom needed to control these children. This job was beyond her capabilities to perform.

The only thing that gave her a tiny measure of comfort was that she had some change in her wallet from the fifty euros Pierre had given her. She hadn't spent much at the fair; most of the money was still there. It was all the cash she had in the world right now and if she was fired on the spot, she was going to need it. It would be enough, at least, to get a taxi to the airport.

As soon as she'd parked the car, Antoinette and Marc jumped out and ran off.

Alone with Ella, Cassie realized this was her chance to speak to the young girl, and hopefully do some damage control before they faced Pierre's wrath. But as she turned around and gathered her thoughts, Ella climbed out and slammed the door.

Cassie swore violently to herself. She hurried after the children, stress curdling her insides.

Antoinette and Marc had detoured to the orchard and were playing tag among the fruit trees, pelting each other with the few overripe peaches that remained. Cassie went to round them up, breathing in the crisp smell of dry leaves, underscored by a hint of rotting fruit.

"Inside," she ordered wearily, and they abandoned their game and scampered up to the front door.

Her stomach clenched as Pierre opened it. A surge of nausea made her want to throw up and she swallowed hard.

"Please, children, remove your shoes at the door. You have been playing in the orchard; I do not want trodden fruit inside," he warned.

As Antoinette was carefully unbuckling her boots, he asked, "So, did you have a good time?"

Cassie stared down at her own shoes, wondering if she would have the strength to cope with the storm that would follow.

"Yes, Papa," Antoinette said in the sweetest of tones. "We ate chocolate crepes, and see our faces? I am a princess, and Marc is a cat. Ella was a mermaid but she messed her paint."

Unable to believe what she was hearing, Cassie raised her head.

"I played soccer and won!" Marc shouted.

He tossed his shoes into the hallway and ran upstairs, his bare feet thudding on the polished wood.

Realizing that Pierre was looking at her, and that her mouth was hanging open in shock, Cassie hastily forced a smile. Why hadn't they said anything? Perhaps they were waiting until they could speak with their father in private. But they had both sounded genuinely happy and not as if they were holding anything back. Surely they hadn't already forgotten how she'd shouted at them.

Ella trailed in, the last of the party, and removed her pink trainers.

Cassie waited anxiously. Antoinette and Marc might have enjoyed the day, but for Ella it had ended in disaster. She must have been holding in her tearful words ever since Cassie dropped the bombshell. Now, surely, they would burst out.

"Did you enjoy the carnival, Ella?" Pierre asked absently, straightening the frame of the brightly colored oil painting that hung above the hall table. Cassie wondered how he could notice the artwork was a degree off center, but not see how tears had smudged the blue sea horses painted on Ella's cheeks into an unrecognizable blur.

Giving the tiniest hint of a nod, Ella trailed wordlessly upstairs. Pierre didn't even glance after her.

"Overtired, I am sure," he said, stepping back to survey the painting.

"She had a busy morning," Cassie agreed, feeling as if the conversation had entered the surreal. The knot in her stomach had loosened ever so slightly. Although she was more confused than ever, she no longer felt as if she was going to throw up on the spot.

Pierre turned back to Cassie.

"There is a tray of sandwiches in the dining room for lunch, and dinner will be served early tonight. It will be a simple meal, just bread, cheese, and soup, as most of the staff have the afternoon off."

"I'll make sure the children are ready in time," Cassie said. "And that Ella has a nap this afternoon."

She needed a nap herself. The bone-deep exhaustion that had suddenly descended must have been caused by the emotional stress of the day.

"Good," Pierre said absently, his attention already elsewhere. He headed out of the house, jingling his car keys in his hand.

Cassie walked slowly upstairs, forcing her sluggish mind to think about what she should say to the children. Antoinette and Marc might genuinely have forgotten her outburst, and if so it would be better not to mention it again. But she couldn't count on that being the case. While Marc had the attention span of a butterfly and didn't seem to hold grudges, Antoinette was the opposite. More likely, she had stashed the incident away in her memory and was waiting for an opportune moment to triumphantly reveal it.

When Cassie walked into her room and saw the plastic bottle of pills on her bedside table, she realized with a jolt that her tiredness, nausea, and mental fog weren't just due to stress. She'd forgotten to take her meds last night, and now she was starting to suffer the effects she associated with skipping a dose.

She opened the bottle and popped a tablet into her mouth before realizing that there was no water in the glass on her bedside table. Picking up the glass, she headed for the bathroom, but as she reached the corridor, she heard someone calling her name.

"Cassie?"

She turned to see Marnie approaching her, holding a piece of paper.

Instead of her usual gray uniform, the housekeeper was wearing black pants and a crimson duffle jacket. She had makeup on and her hair was down, making her look much younger and prettier than she did when she was working.

Was she bringing instructions from Pierre, Cassie wondered hazily, before remembering she'd just spoken to him and he'd mentioned nothing except that dinner would be early.

"I hoped I would find you before I left. I am going to Paris for the evening," Marnie said.

Cassie nodded. The tablet was starting to dissolve on her tongue, tasting vile and causing her nausea to resurface.

She held up a hand, turned, and rushed to the bathroom. Sloshing water in the glass, she gulped the pill down, drinking some more to wash the taste away.

"Sorry," she said to Marnie, who had followed her and was waiting outside the bathroom door with a concerned expression. "I had a pill in my mouth."

"Oh." Marnie nodded in relief. "I was worried you had eaten something bad at the carnival. You look very pale."

"I have a headache," Cassie said, not wanting to explain that she was on anxiety meds. In any case, it wasn't a lie; her head was pounding.

"I hope it gets better soon. Sorry for disturbing you now, but there is something I want to tell you in private." She said the last words in a low voice.

"What?" Cassie felt her heart sink. Could anything else go wrong today?

"While you were out somebody phoned the chateau's landline. It was a young man, asking to speak to you."

"To me?" Cassie frowned. "Do you know why?"

Her best guess was that someone from the carnival had recognized the children and was calling to reprimand her for the way she'd yelled at them in public.

"He said he was your boyfriend, Zane." Marnie handed her the paper.

"Zane?" Cassie's voice was high with incredulity. "He's not my boyfriend, he's my ex. I never gave him the number—I don't know it myself. The agency wouldn't have given it out to anyone, would they? I can't imagine how he found out I was here."

Marnie shrugged sympathetically.

"I am glad I answered it," she said. "Pierre does not like staff receiving personal calls on the house landline. I told Zane you would phone back when you were in town. It will be better if you to ask him not to call here again. Here is his number, and the message he left for you."

"What message?"

84

She stared down at the page. In Marnie's neat, forward-sloping hand was written, "Cassie—please come home."

That evening, Cassie couldn't stop thinking about Zane's message. How on earth had he found out she was here? She urgently needed to call him back. Now that he knew the number, it was a certainty he'd try to get hold of her again, and next time she might not be as lucky.

Pierre and Margot did not come down to dinner. With Marc in his own world, Ella still not talking to her, and Antoinette reading a book at the table, supper was a quiet affair, but Cassie did her best to seem cheerful.

"Isn't this soup delicious?" she asked the silent trio. It wasn't hard to compliment the food here, which was wonderful—the beef and vegetable soup was rich and full of flavor. It was only her lack of appetite that was preventing her from enjoying the meal to its full.

No wonder she didn't feel hungry when she was stressed to the max. It seemed as if every conscious decision she made here had turned out a disaster, and now other people's decisions, which she had no control over, were going the same way.

Knowing that Antoinette would be on the alert for any sign of vulnerability, Cassie forced herself to eat a full bowl of soup and a chunk of baguette. She served the children a generous helping but although Antoinette and Marc cleaned their plates, Ella barely touched hers.

"Are you ill, Ella?" Antoinette asked sweetly, giving Cassie a sideways look that told her she knew exactly why Ella wasn't eating.

Ella shook her head wordlessly.

"It's been a long day," Cassie said. "I am sure she will feel better after a good sleep. Everything seems better in the morning." She smiled at Antoinette, feeling her face ache with the effort.

"Oh, I'm not so sure," Antoinette countered. "Sometimes things can be much worse in the morning."

Cassie had to use all her self-control to prevent herself snapping furiously at the dark-haired girl. Antoinette knew exactly how to push her buttons. Instead, with a huge effort, she kept her smile glued into place.

"If everyone's finished, let's go upstairs," she said calmly. "It's time for bed—and Ella, you haven't had a bath yet."

Antoinette looked disappointed that she hadn't risen to the bait, and Cassie felt a glow of satisfaction.

Cassie ran Ella a bubble bath to try and cheer her up, but the young girl wouldn't even look at Cassie while she helped her bathe. She stared down at the mass of bubbles in the bathwater, and Cassie could only guess at the turmoil going through her mind.

"I'm so sorry, Ella," she said gently. "What I said upset you and I feel so bad about it. It was a terrible way for you to find out what happened to your mother. You must be feeling very sad. Would you like me to read you a bedtime story to cheer you up?"

Ella shook her head firmly.

Cassie put her to bed, turned off her light, and closed the door, wishing there was something more she could do. This poor innocent girl had already been damaged by her toxic family, and now Cassie had added to her burden. She was sure Ella would never trust her again. Why should she? She'd believed Cassie to be her friend, and on her side, and Cassie had betrayed her in the cruelest possible way.

Back in her room, Cassie noticed to her alarm that she hadn't put her pills away. She'd left them on her bedside table, where anyone could see.

As she looked down at the bottle, she felt a surge of fright.

It wasn't full. There were at least four pills missing. That meant four days—and she'd started the new bottle just before she'd left the States. She must have taken her pill last night, and completely forgotten about it. If so, why had she thought she'd missed a dose? Had her symptoms been triggered by the insane stress she'd experienced?

Thinking it over, Cassie found she genuinely couldn't remember if she'd taken a pill the previous night or not, and attempting to do so only left her more confused. The gap in her memory frightened her, but she told herself that this was what stress did.

She put the medication back into her drawer and got into bed.

Sleep seemed impossible. Her mind was racing. She worried what Zane would do, and how soon he'd call again, and how on earth she could manage to get into town to control the situation in time.

Then there was Pierre to worry about. She hadn't had a chance to set up a warning system for her bedroom door. If she finally managed to sleep out of sheer exhaustion, she wouldn't know if he came into her bedroom again.

Cassie sat up in bed, breathing fast, fighting to control her panic.

This was all too much for her. She'd been assigned to a broken family that was in huge conflict. These children needed an experienced mother figure, and professional help. Instead, all they had was her. And she was carrying her own baggage. She'd only managed to survive her toxic childhood with the help of her older sister, and she hadn't survived it undamaged. She wasn't strong enough, or capable enough, to handle this.

She had to quit.

As soon as this thought came to her, Cassie felt an enormous sense of relief.

She couldn't stick this out any longer. She was the wrong person for the job, it was damaging her emotionally, and in the process, causing worse damage to the children.

Zane's phone call was a timely reminder of what she needed to do.

After all, she'd decided on a fresh start to escape the abusive relationship with him. If her current employment was proving to be equally abusive, she shouldn't hesitate to make the same call.

The only question was how to leave, but she could think about that tomorrow.

❧   ❧   ❧

The early morning was dark and windy, and it looked as if the day would be overcast. The breeze was rattling her window and Cassie decided running would be a warmer option than walking.

She dressed quickly in her running gear and a tracksuit top, put her earphones in, and hooked her phone onto her belt. Then she quietly descended the stairs and went out, pleased to be the first person up and about.

She found a path that wound into the trees and followed it, jogging slowly as she figured out what she should say.

Zane's phone call could surely be used as an excuse. There was a family emergency. Please come home. The only problem was that she didn't want to tell Pierre he'd called the chateau.

Instead, she should be honest and upfront, and explain that the job was proving to be too much for her. That she hadn't realized it would cause so much emotional stress, and that if she couldn't look after herself, she couldn't look after his children.

The thought of making that confession terrified her. Pierre would be predictably furious. Or worse still, he might try to talk her into staying.

Of course, there was always the third option, which was simply to leave. Just pack her bags and walk out, perhaps leaving a note to explain why she was quitting. Walk down the road, find the kind old man in the nursery, make a phone call, and get a cab to the airport.

From there it would be a gamble. She'd have to hope that it wasn't too expensive to change her flight, and that one of her friends would be able to loan her the money to do it. Back in the USA, she'd have to go somewhere different so that Zane wouldn't catch up with her again. She'd always wanted to spend time in Florida or New Orleans. Even in winter, there might be restaurants that were still hiring.

With her mind made up, she began to run with renewed purpose. Her route led her on a looping track that ended up circling the vineyards. These looked to be operational, with well-tended vines, and there was already a truck driving slowly out of a stone barn on the far side. The air was fresh and cool, and she breathed in a trace of wood smoke coming from the barn's chimney.

Cassie realized she'd been out for nearly an hour. She'd better head back so that everyone would be on time for breakfast. She crested the hill and found a path that led directly back to the chateau. Breathless, but feeling at peace with her decision, she walked into the house.

Her bedroom door was ajar, and her first thought was that one of the housemaids was working inside, because she'd left it closed. Then, worrying that Pierre or Margot might have come to find out where she was, she approached more cautiously. She couldn't let them suspect anything was wrong. She had to act completely normal until she found the right moment to leave.

Cassie pushed the door all the way open.

She stood, frozen with shock, as she saw the devastation inside.

While she was out, somebody had trashed her room.

Her clothes had been pulled from the shelves and strewn on the floor. Her suitcase was upended in the middle of the room. Her meds—she drew a sharp breath of horror—had been poured out of their containers and trampled into fragments on the tiles.

Cassie picked her way across the floor, feeling as if she were walking through one of her worst nightmares, and wishing it was just a bad dream. She couldn't believe that somebody could have violated her private space in this way. She'd never guessed that she was so hated.

Her wallet had been thrown onto the bed, her bank cards scattered across the covers. The money inside was gone.

Just as she absorbed this blow, she realized something worse.

She'd stashed her passport in the zipper compartment of her bag, and that compartment was now wide open.

Cassie felt inside with a shaking hand, but the compartment was empty.

Somebody had stolen her passport.

CHAPTER TWELVE

Cassie collapsed onto her bed, trembling all over. She realized she was sitting on the bare mattress, because the covers had been ripped from the bed, the pillows torn out of the pillowcases and tossed onto the floor.

She breathed deeply, trying her hardest not to burst into hysterical tears, knowing she couldn't allow herself to fall to pieces right now. The unknown person who'd trashed her room would be waiting for an extreme reaction. They were probably hoping their actions would push her over the edge. She couldn't let them know how badly this had shaken her. She simply wasn't going to let them win.

Thinking this way helped her to cling to her sanity. After a few minutes, her shock had ebbed and she was calm enough to reason again.

There was a chance her passport could just have been tossed into the mess. Perhaps this mystery person had only taken the money after all.

Cassie stood up and, treading carefully to avoid the fragments of pills, she picked up her bedding, shook it out, and replaced it on the bed. One by one, she retrieved her clothes, folded them, and put them back in the cupboard. She picked up her bag and checked all the pockets again before putting it away.

No passport.

She checked under all the furniture.

No passport. The only thing she found was a single unbroken tablet; the sole survivor of the destruction. Carefully, she retrieved it and replaced it in the container.

The way her room had been trashed looked like an act of pure anger, but the theft of her passport went further. That was deliberate malice, and it couldn't have had worse consequences for her.

Without her passport, she was effectively a prisoner here. Replacing it would be a costly and time-consuming process. Her lack of access to email and cell phones would be a hugely complicating factor.

Cassie felt crushed, as if her freedom had been ripped away from her at the last possible moment.

Who? Who could have done such a thing?

Antoinette was her prime suspect, after dropping that saccharine hint the previous night that things were going to get worse.

It could just as easily have been the strange, impulsive Marc—this senseless destruction was characteristic of him. And Cassie realized this might even have been Margot's doing, prompted by sheer spite.

Ella might have wrecked her room to vent her anger, but why would she have taken the passport? If she had known what it was, she would have left it in place, because she clearly couldn't wait to be rid of Cassie for good.

Cassie needed to find out who was behind this. Confronting the family would have to be her next step.

She showered and changed quickly and then left her room, deciding she wouldn't say exactly what had happened until everybody was together in one place. That would give her a chance to see all their reactions.

Cassie opened Antoinette's bedroom door to find her neatly dressed and ready to go downstairs. She realized as she walked in that she'd forgotten to knock, but Antoinette did not remark on it. Was that a sign?

"Morning," she said. "Will you come down to breakfast now, please? There's something important I need to tell everyone."

She stared hard at the girl and Antoinette returned her gaze for only a moment before looking away.

From the passage she heard the stomping of feet and looked around to see Marc passing by. Surprisingly, he had already dressed himself.

"You're up early, Marc," Cassie called, suspicion surging inside her.

"I'm hungry!" he shouted, heading for the stairs at a run.

When she went into Ella's room, she found her curled up in bed, still in her pajamas. She looked to have been crying again. Quickly, Cassie helped her dress, asking if she'd slept well or had any bad dreams, but Ella remained sullen and unsmiling. She didn't say a word to Cassie.

Pierre and Margot arrived at breakfast at the same time Cassie escorted Ella downstairs. Margot was still covering her throat— today she was wearing a high-necked navy jumper that clung to her perfect figure. Looking closer, Cassie saw something else. The perfect red nail on the index finger of Margot's right hand was broken off, almost at the quick.

It could have happened during her struggles with Pierre. But it could just as easily have occurred while violently throwing Cassie's possessions onto the floor.

"I have something very disturbing to tell you," Cassie announced to Pierre when everyone was seated.

Pierre picked up the coffee jug and turned to her, frowning slightly.

"What is that, Cassie?" he asked.

"I went out for a run this morning and while I was gone, someone went through my bedroom. They threw all my clothes out onto the floor, tipped out my toiletries and medication. They crushed and destroyed my tablets. They took money from my wallet, and they also stole my passport." She felt her voice start to tremble and controlled herself with an effort, wondering what reaction her words would provoke.

Pierre was the most visibly shocked. He slammed the jug on the table with a loud oath, his face turning to thunder.

"You are sure?" he asked Cassie incredulously.

"Well, of course." Her voice was shaking badly now and she had to fight for control. "It happened less than an hour ago."

"Did you take photos? Do you have visual proof of what occurred? We may need it," Pierre interrogated her.

"No, no I didn't. I tidied up while I looked for my passport. That's what's important. Nothing else. I don't even mind about the missing money; it was just the change from what we spent at the carnival."

She tore her gaze away from Pierre's grim, glowering face and looked around at the others.

Antoinette, as usual, gave nothing away as she coolly stared back. Marc was wide-eyed and open-mouthed but she couldn't tell if his shock was real or fake. Ella was still refusing to make eye contact, acting as if she hadn't even heard the words. Looking down at the tablecloth, she seemed to have withdrawn into her own private world.

Margot was twisting a strand of blonde hair between her fingers. Cassie thought she looked upset, but she might just be responding to Pierre's mood.

"A missing passport is very serious," Cassie said. "I'm actually not legal without it as I have no ID. I can't travel, and it's going to take a lot of time and expense to get a new one."

Margot cleared her throat. Her voice was hoarse—she could speak this morning, but with difficulty.

"If money is missing, it was probably one of the staff," she said. "Going through your possessions like that, someone was looking for valuables. I have had jewelry stolen before now."

Pierre nodded agreement, his face grim.

"If you like, we can fire them all," Margot suggested, as casually as if she'd been asking someone to pass the salt, and again Pierre nodded in support.

Cassie was shocked by Margot's words, wondering if this blanket dismissal of household staff was a threat, or if it had actually happened before. Would this family really be prepared to fire their entire personnel after a suspected incident?

"No, no," she said hastily. "Please don't even think of doing that. It would be so unfair to all those who are innocent. I wouldn't want them to lose their jobs for no reason."

She hoped her words might be having an effect on somebody at the table, but now everyone was looking at each other instead of at her, making it more difficult to see.

"Perhaps I can ask Marnie to help," Cassie said. "She knows the staff and could ask them if they saw or heard anything."

"A good idea," Pierre agreed. "Marnie has the day off today, but tomorrow she can assist you."

Cassie hoped that since the friendly Marnie had been elsewhere, she would be out of the firing line.

"We can discuss it again tomorrow," Pierre decided. "Today is a busy day."

Cassie expected him to say more about her passport, but he didn't. Instead, he reached for a pain au chocolat before passing around the tray of pastries, commenting on their fine quality this morning.

She realized that the loss of her passport had shattered her world, but had barely impacted upon Pierre's. She was a disposable asset in this house, and Pierre did not understand or empathize with her plight. Perhaps he had already dismissed it as another piece of drama from a servant.

"What are the children doing today?" she asked, realizing that since the passport was no longer a topic for discussion, this question would be expected.

"Margot and I are taking them out this morning. I have a business meeting with a new client, in his beautiful art gallery near Orly. His wife and children are joining him there, and he suggested I bring my family too. We will be back in time for a late lunch, and then the children have afternoon activities which I will brief you on when we return."

"Thank you. Your outing sounds wonderful," Cassie said automatically, but as she spoke, the implications of his words hit home.

She would be in the chateau, on her own, for the entire morning.

"You should spend some time in the library while we are gone," Pierre said. "There is a magnificent selection of books there, in both English and French."

"Thank you. I'll do that," Cassie agreed, but she knew she wouldn't have a chance. She had other, more important, items on her agenda.

This was the perfect opportunity—and the only one she might have, to search the entire chateau. If she was able to find her wallet in time, she might even be able to move ahead with her plans, and be gone for good before the Dubois family returned.

CHAPTER THIRTEEN

Cassie waited impatiently for the family to depart. It seemed to take forever. Pierre was fussing over details. Ella's outfit was not suitable; she could keep her blue coat on but must wear a smarter dress underneath. Marc's hair had to be smoothed down with water to appear neat, and he was ordered to change into clean shoes.

She did her best to organize them as quickly as possible, but all three were visibly reluctant to go on this outing, and Ella was still not saying a word to her.

Finally, everyone was ready to go. Gravel crunched under the wheels as the big Mercedes wound its way down the driveway. Cassie ran upstairs to her bedroom and watched the car until it was out of sight. She told herself that if she looked away or blinked, her plans wouldn't go the way she needed them to. Her eyes were watering by the time the car disappeared over the hill, but she hadn't blinked, and could only hope it was a good omen.

Fretting with nerves, she waited another five minutes to be safe, in case anyone had forgotten anything.

When she was sure they were not coming back, she began her hunt.

She headed straight for the bedroom of the most likely suspect—Antoinette. As she opened the door, she felt a renewed surge of fighting spirit. She was not going to let this toxic family destroy her. She was going to do whatever it took to retrieve her possessions and escape—even if it meant searching their private spaces.

Antoinette's room was so neat that the girl would notice immediately if anything was moved. Cassie knew she would have to put everything back just the way she found it.

She started with the cupboard, rummaging in jacket pockets, searching through piles of clothing, and looking into Antoinette's pink suitcase and school bag. Then she checked the desk, going through each drawer.

A passport was so damned small, it could be anywhere. She even opened Antoinette's journal to check whether it might be wedged in between the pages. She drew the line at reading what the girl had written in her secret book. That, she was not prepared to do.

Cassie couldn't help noticing though, that the writing in the book was uncharacteristically messy, the words scribbled and disordered. So maybe this journal was Antoinette's outlet in more ways than one. Pressured to keep her room and her life in a state of perfection, this must be the one place she allowed herself to rebel.

Twenty frustrating minutes later, Cassie left the room, closing the door quietly behind her. She'd hoped, had even expected, that this was where she would find it. But she'd searched in every possible hiding place, including under the mattress and inside the pillowcase, and it was nowhere to be found.

Marc's room was next. Luckily, in this messy environment, she didn't have to be so careful. As long as she didn't upset the formation of his battle army on the floor, she doubted if he'd notice or care whether anything had been moved.

As she sorted through the chaos of the toy box, Cassie suddenly wondered whether Marc, in his own way, was also resisting the unreasonable standards of neatness and perfection that his father imposed on him. It would certainly explain his strange behavior and the way he seemed to seek out opportunities to disrupt his environment.

Cassie's methodical search left the room slightly tidier than she had found it, but it yielded no results. Her passport was definitely not there.

She was beginning to feel less hopeful about her chances of being gone before the family returned.

She searched Ella's room just as thoroughly and with as little success. The bathrooms on the upper floor yielded nothing either.

It was possible that the passport could have been hastily hidden elsewhere in the house.

Cassie went downstairs, checking each room first to make sure there were no household staff working in it. A housemaid would certainly wonder why she was shaking curtains, peering into drawers, and even reaching down into the larger vases and amphoras. Cassie suspected that in this house, walls had ears and eyes, and that if anyone saw her they would report back to Pierre immediately.

Trying to remain unobtrusive, she made her way through the downstairs section of the house. She looked around the dining room and the hallway very thoroughly, thinking that somebody might have quickly stashed the passport in one of those places before they left for the morning.

The downstairs search took her a full two hours. By the end she was exhausted, overwhelmed by the scale of the house and the number of rooms, and the sheer volume of hiding places and treasures within them. She wondered how many of these were family heirlooms, or whether Pierre had acquired them himself. From the brief hint he'd given at breakfast about a meeting with an art gallery owner, she guessed he was somehow involved in the business.

She'd left out two of the rooms because staff had been cleaning them, and a whole section of the house was locked—but if it was locked for her, it would surely be locked for everyone else. And in any case, she tried to console herself, why would you hide a document somewhere that a housemaid might innocently find it while cleaning?

No, Cassie decided, if you stole something so important, you would keep it in a safe place, a private place.

That meant there was one more room she had to search.

She felt a stab of apprehension as she walked upstairs and headed to the end of the passage. She'd left this room till last because going inside really did feel as if she was overstepping all her boundaries. She'd hoped she would find the passport before she had to look here, but she hadn't. Now she was worried that she'd wasted too much time, because this was the one place where she couldn't possibly risk being discovered.

She knocked softly on Pierre's bedroom door.

"Hello?" she called, just in case anyone was inside cleaning.

There was no reply. All Cassie could hear was the sound of her own rapid breathing.

This side of the house faced the gardens, not the driveway, so it would be more difficult to hear the car coming back. That was another complicating factor.

With a shiver of nerves, she pushed opened the heavy wooden door.

The room beyond was spacious and exquisite. Light streamed in through enormous French doors that led onto an ornate balcony. The huge four-poster bed was covered by an intricate lace throw, and several large paintings hung on the ivory-papered walls.

She could smell a hint of Margot's perfume in the air.

Cassie tiptoed across the room. She wanted to avoid the bed, after the hellish scene she'd spied playing out on it, but it had to be checked so she decided to get it over with by doing it first.

She felt carefully under the pillows and covers, and then spent some time plumping the pillows and replacing the delicate lace cover just as she had found it. She knew Pierre, with his eye for detail, would spot any imperfection straight away.

The dressing table drawers were filled with makeup and a variety of different perfumes. Glass bottles were crammed shoulder to shoulder—there must have been at least twenty perfumes there, but her passport was not in any of the drawers.

Moving to the desk, she was captivated by the brilliant shine of a Venetian glass paperweight. A bouquet of colorful flowers was encased in the perfectly clear globe. With the sun illuminating the glass, the effect was mesmerizing, and for a long, distracted moment she was too entranced by its beauty to remember the urgency of her search.

Then a bang from outside made her jump and the spell was broken. She gave herself a mental slap. What on earth was she doing, pausing to admire objets d'art when there was so much at stake, and her presence here was so risky? She was appalled that she'd been sidetracked so easily. Was this another sign she'd gotten her meds badly wrong? If Pierre walked in, she could not possibly explain her presence here; it was nothing short of criminal.

She held her breath as she listened, but when she heard nothing else, she pulled herself together and continued her hunt, going faster now.

In the study, to the right of the bedroom, Cassie found a landline phone. It rested on the marble desk, next to a few neatly labeled files. She looked at it longingly, knowing she couldn't possibly use it as Pierre might check the last number dialed. The wooden filing cabinet in the room was locked, but she hoped that meant Margot would not be able to access it either.

To the left of the bedroom was a huge dressing room, the walls lined with cupboards that were filled with clothes. Panicking that she was running out of time, Cassie did the quickest search possible, running her hands over all the shelves and into the pockets as best she could.

She found nothing.

Cassie let out a deep breath. To be honest with herself, she hadn't expected the passport to be hidden here, which was why she'd left this room till last.

For all she knew, whoever took the passport might simply have destroyed it. Thrown it into the fire or tossed it into the overflowing kitchen trash can. She might have been wasting her time from the start.

Instead, she needed to direct all her energy toward devising a plan B, whatever that might be. It would definitely involve contacting the embassy, to find out what she needed to do to get a replacement passport.

But as she was on her way back to the door, she suddenly remembered she hadn't checked a very obvious hiding place—under the bed.

She should have thought to look there immediately. After all, it had been her hiding place of choice in the past, when times had turned bad.

Crouching down on the polished floorboards, Cassie peered under the bed, tensing as she heard a distant thumping from somewhere outside. Telling herself to be calm, and that she couldn't let every small sound distract her now that she was almost finished, she resumed her search.

There was nothing there, but she noticed a long, narrow drawer concealed in the bed frame.

She opened it and stared down at its contents, feeling her spine prickle with dread.

The drawer contained leather gags, vicious-looking whips, ropes and harnesses, and some silk scarves like the one she'd seen through the keyhole. There were a few of those, in various bright colors, neatly folded in a corner. Other items, too. Handcuffs, blindfolds, and shiny metal clamps—she didn't want to think exactly how and where they might be applied.

She lifted out one of the scarves. It was gossamer-light to the touch, deep pink in color. Its softness contrasted with the heavy, tough feel of the harnesses as she moved them aside. The chains attached to them rattled loudly as she moved them and she jumped at the unexpected noise. She felt incredibly vulnerable crouching here. Perhaps it was her own guilt at prying into this hidden drawer, but she was suddenly sure she was being watched.

Cassie replaced the harnesses and the scarf carefully after checking there was nothing hidden under them. Then she closed the drawer carefully and stood up, wishing she had never seen the contents. A glimpse through the keyhole was one thing, but stumbling upon an entire stockpile of bondage equipment was something else again. She could never, ever let Pierre know she'd discovered this secret hiding place.

She walked quietly to the bedroom door, but as she reached it, she heard a louder, more familiar sound that caused her to freeze. She waited, panic blooming inside her, praying that she'd misheard.

Then she heard it again, confirming her worst fears.

It was the unmistakable shout of Marc's voice, reverberating down the passage.

She'd spent too long searching, and now the family had returned, and she was trapped in the master bedroom.

At any moment, Pierre might open the door.

CHAPTER FOURTEEN

A door slammed further down the passage, and Cassie heard Marc shout again. She shrank back into Pierre's bedroom, instinctively wanting to hide, but in this tidy, minimalist space there was nowhere to go.

Pierre and Margot might head straight into the modern bathroom, or the study, or the dressing room, and they would see her immediately if they did. Hiding under the bed would simply invite disaster.

Cassie tried to reassure herself by remembering how Marc loved to run ahead of the others. Hopefully, the rest of the family was still on their way upstairs, in which case it would be better if they found her leaving the room, rather than waiting inside. She had to make a decision now, because they might already be wondering where she was, and expecting her to run and help with the children as soon as they arrived home.

She pulled open the bedroom door, slipped through, and closed it quickly behind her. Then she hurried down the passage and round the corner. Her heart sped up as she heard Pierre's voice coming from Marc's bedroom and she realized what a near miss she'd had. The boy must have called his father into the room as he passed by. Perhaps he'd wanted Pierre to admire his battalion of toy soldiers.

If it hadn't been for Marc, Pierre would certainly have discovered her there—perhaps even walked in as she was peering into that secret drawer, and she didn't want to imagine what the consequences would have been. She couldn't risk such a reckless action again, not even for the sake of finding her missing passport.

Antoinette was not in her room, but Ella's door was open. Looking inside, she saw the young girl had already changed out of her smart dress into one of the corduroy pinafores that seemed to be her favorite. That meant the family had been home for longer than she'd thought.

She waved to Ella and said a friendly hello.

"Do you want to go for a walk in the garden before lunch, Ella?" she asked, but Ella's only response was to turn away.

Cassie trudged dispiritedly back to her bedroom. The day had been a total failure. Her search had ended in near-disaster, her passport was still nowhere to be found, and Ella's silence was unrelenting.

Looking out her window, she saw the day was turning cloudy and gray again. She put on a tracksuit top, tidied the clothes that she'd thrown back into her cupboard earlier, and spent some time picking up the crushed tablets and sweeping the dusty residue away with tissues until the floor was clean.

With everything tidied up, she noticed the bottle with the single unbroken pill was still on her bedside table. She should have put it away this morning, because she didn't want her medication lying around in full view.

Cassie opened the bedside drawer and let out an audible gasp as she looked down.

Her passport was there.

She blinked, unable to believe what she was seeing. There it was, lying neatly in the drawer, its gold-embossed cover undamaged.

"How on earth...?" Cassie said aloud.

She grabbed it out of the drawer, needing to feel its reassuring shape in her hand. Paging through, she saw her visa was still there, and none of the pages were creased or torn. It hadn't been tampered with at all.

The frantic worry that had been consuming her since the morning ebbed away and she felt euphoric with relief. Whatever other problems she might have—and she knew there were plenty—the presence of this small, navy-covered document had given her back the power to make decisions. She was no longer a prisoner in this unfriendly house.

Cassie suddenly wondered if the passport might have been in the drawer all along. When she'd unpacked, she remembered thinking that the bag was not the safest place to leave it, and that she should put it somewhere else.

Perhaps she had done that, and then forgotten about it.

She hadn't checked any of the drawers after she'd found her room trashed, because she'd seen the bag's open zipper compartment and assumed it had been taken from there. Still, here it was, and now Cassie found her relief was tinged with worry, because how could she have put it away and not remembered a thing about it afterward?

Was she genuinely losing her mind?

She rubbed her forehead in confusion, trying to replay exactly what she'd done while unpacking, but her thoughts were interrupted by the rattle of her bedroom door. Looking up, she saw Pierre standing in the doorway.

Cassie felt her face grow hot with embarrassment as she realized she was holding the very passport she'd accused one of the family of having stolen earlier.

"I—I just found it," she said. "It was in my bedside table drawer. The money's still missing, but at least the passport has turned up." She forced a smile.

Pierre stepped inside and closed the door behind him. His imposing presence made the room seem smaller, and although he looked stern, Cassie had no idea what was wrong. Something must have happened if he had come to speak to her in private. Perhaps he'd been told about what she did at the carnival, and had come to fire her.

"I believe you have been looking for the passport, Cassie?" Pierre said.

She swallowed. She hadn't been careful enough; one of the housemaids must have seen her rummaging around in the downstairs rooms.

"Yes," she said, deciding to stick as close to the truth as possible. "I thought I might have dropped it while Margot was showing me round on the night I arrived."

Pierre considered her words for a few moments. His silence was unnerving, and she couldn't read the expression in his narrowed, brown eyes.

"Did you think you had dropped it in my bedroom, Cassie?" he asked, and she visibly started at the words, a clear admission of her guilt.

"I…" she began, but there was nothing more she could say. It hadn't been a genuine question, but rather a statement of fact. Somehow, he must have seen or heard her in there.

"Perhaps you didn't notice everything in that room," he continued. "The drawer where Margot keeps her jewelry, for example. That is in a very well-hidden place."

She couldn't meet Pierre's gaze. She looked down at her hands, watching her fingernail dig into her cuticle so deep she thought she would draw blood.

"No. I didn't notice any jewelry drawer. I just had a very quick look around. I'm so sorry. It was unforgivable of me to go in there. I wanted to—well, I wanted to make sure I'd searched everywhere."

"You might have found another drawer, though," he suggested in a conversational tone, as he sat down on the bed next to her.

She stared at him in panic. How had he guessed she'd looked inside that secret drawer? She was sure the bedroom door hadn't opened. Perhaps he'd left the contents arranged in a certain way. She'd tried her best to put things back as they were, but she'd been shocked and rushed and realizing she was out of time.

If he knew for sure, she'd only make things worse by denying it. So perhaps it was better to say nothing at all and simply brace herself for his wrath to descend.

To her surprise, she saw Pierre's heavy features were not flushed with anger. Instead, he was regarding her with the same expression she'd seen the previous morning when he met her on the stairs.

"Do you think rules are made to be broken, Cassie" he said quietly, as if he didn't want his voice to carry further than her bedroom, or even beyond the bed.

She shook her head in violent denial but he continued.

"I think you do. And so do I. It makes life more interesting."

He reached out a hand and smoothed her hair away from her face, then pinched her cheek gently.

His voice was playful, but his words were not.

"I believe searching through your employer's bedroom is a dismissible offense. It could even be a criminal offense. After all, we have had jewelry go missing in the past. Do you think we took no action against the culprit, or since? The local police would be interested to hear of your wrongdoings. Are you wondering if I have proof of what you did? Perhaps we should inform the police already, so they are aware."

Cassie stared at him, fear blooming inside her as Pierre's softly spoken threats told her what he was capable of.

"Please don't. I'm so sorry. I wasn't aware your room was out of bounds. I didn't know that was a rule. Now that I know, I'll never go in there again."

"Yes, you have broken the rules, no doubt about it. But this time I will be lenient to you. I will believe that you acted in innocence. I will say nothing, and nor will you. I will pretend you were just playing games with me. But a game must be played by two people, not so? So next time, in our game, it is my turn to break the rules. You think you will like what I am going to do?"

"I—no, not really," she stammered. Her face was on fire, and she felt paralyzed by indecision, unsure whether the safest option would be to remain quiet, or scream for help. Keeping quiet seemed the less terrifying alternative, even though she was appalled by what Pierre was implying.

"Oh, but you are wrong, Cassie, because I think you will." His tone was teasing now, his fingers roaming over her face as if it were his property—stroking her jaw, her brow, touching her lips, cupping her neck. Then he lowered his hand and touched her thigh, and Cassie felt every muscle in her body turn to ice.

She decided she was going to scream, no matter how much trouble it got her into. She had to put a stop to this before it went any further.

But as she was gathering the courage to do it, he removed his hand and gave a throaty laugh.

"I am looking forward to next time," he whispered to her.

Then he added, with a wink, "And you need not worry. Just as I can punish, so I can reward. And I will reward you generously for playing the game with me."

He pressed his finger over her lips.

"I can see you understand now how things are." He smiled.

The bed creaked as he got up, and a moment later he walked out and closed the door gently behind him.

Cassie let out a long, shaky breath.

She scrubbed her hands over her face where Pierre's fingers had been, desperate to erase his touch. She understood now why Marnie pulled her hair back and went without makeup at work, and why all the housemaids seemed to blend into the background and remain invisible.

She felt creeped out by the entire encounter, and Pierre's parting comment had left her feeling tainted. As for herself, she couldn't have handled the situation any worse. In her shock, she'd allowed him to have his way and her silence had given him tacit permission to continue.

Too late, Cassie realized she should have screamed.

CHAPTER FIFTEEN

After what had happened in her bedroom, Cassie didn't know how she was going to face Pierre over the lunch table. How on earth could she pretend nothing had happened, and act anywhere close to normal?

To her relief, when she brought Marc and Ella downstairs, she found that Antoinette and Pierre had just finished lunch and were getting ready to go.

"Antoinette has a piano lesson in Nanterre this afternoon. I will take her, as I have a business meeting nearby," Pierre said.

He spoke formally, as if he'd never sat down beside her on her bed and whispered those suggestive words.

"And I have soccer," Marc reminded him.

"Soccer is at the sports club, near the village where the carnival was held," Pierre told Cassie. Taking a notepad from the sideboard, he wrote the address and directions down for her.

"The soccer practice begins at two p.m. and finishes at four. There is no need for you to stay and watch, especially as the weather is turning colder. Ella, I am sure, would prefer to return home."

"That's a good idea," Cassie agreed. "We can do some coloring together, Ella, or maybe you'd like to do some baking in the kitchen?"

Cassie was only making the suggestions to fill the silence. She was sure Ella wouldn't reply to her, and she was right. Fortunately, Pierre seemed not to notice.

"I must fetch some documents from my study," he said to Antoinette. "If you are ready, wait in the car."

They left the room, and Cassie uncovered the serving dish and gave the children slices of quiche Lorraine with a side helping of green salad. While she ate, she mentally finalized her plans for leaving.

She couldn't abandon Ella here on her own, so she would have to wait until Marc was back from soccer practice. Would Pierre and Antoinette have returned by then? She had no idea how far away Nanterre was. She was also uncertain of Margot's whereabouts but decided she had probably gone out again. Surely Pierre would not have risked doing what he had done in her bedroom if Margot had been home?

Marc seemed eager to go to soccer, despite the worsening weather. The afternoon was turning cold and windy, and when she walked with him from the parking lot to the sports grounds, Cassie was relieved she didn't have to sit and wait on one of the wooden benches, with only a flimsy gazebo for shelter.

Ella had refused to get out of the car at all, and they drove back to the chateau in silence. As she parked the car, Cassie resolved that one way or another, she needed to fix things. She had two hours to spend with Ella, probably the last private time she'd ever have with the young girl. She needed to apologize and make her peace before she left.

She followed Ella up to her room, and when Ella sat down on the bed, Cassie pulled up a chair and sat facing her.

"Your teddy bear looks like he wants to hear a story," she tried. "Would you like me to tell him one? Maybe you would enjoy it too."

Ella shook her head.

"I could show you how to cut snowflakes out of cardboard and we could color them in. We could decorate them with glitter and hang them from your lampshade."

Her suggestion was met with silence. Ella swung her feet, kicking the bed frame hard.

Cassie was running out of options. Cooking was the only idea she had left, and she didn't think she'd be able to persuade Ella to go downstairs to try it. In which case, it was time to be honest.

"Ella, I'll apologize as many times as I need to. But it's up to you to decide whether to forgive me," she said gently. "I'd like to be friends with you before I leave. I don't want to have to go while we are fighting."

Now Ella looked directly at her with wide blue eyes.

"Where are you going?" she asked in a small voice.

"I'm going back to the States," Cassie confessed. "I've decided I'm not the right person to look after you. You need someone better, someone who's loving and patient and kind."

Cassie planned to go into more detail about the Mary Poppins–like entity that she hoped would replace her, but she didn't get a chance, because Ella burst into tears.

"Don't leave," she pleaded, sobbing.

"I have to." Cassie scooted over to sit beside her on the bed and hugged her tightly. Guilt flooded her as she realized Ella's body was shuddering with sobs.

"Why must you go?"

"Because I'm not happy here," she replied. "I'm very unhappy, and because of that, I can't take care of you properly." Gently rubbing Ella's back, she stared at the rain-spattered window, feeling her own eyes prickle with tears.

"Are you unhappy because someone messed up your room?"

"Yes, that's part of the reason."

"I'm so sorry," Ella wailed. "That was me. I did it."

"You?" Cassie could hear the incredulity in her own voice. She prized Ella's arms away from her, wanting to see her face. Was she being serious? Had she really done that?

"I was so angry." Ella looked up at her and in her tear-filled eyes, Cassie saw only honesty. "I wanted to do the worst thing I could to you. But afterwards I knew you'd be upset and I was worried you would leave, just like Hannah, the last lady who looked after us. So I took your money and passport and I put them in my coat pocket, and then I got back into bed and pretended to be asleep."

Cassie blinked, her mind suddenly full of questions.

"Why did Hannah leave?" she tried.

"I don't know. One day she showed me her passport and she said she was going to fly back home tomorrow, and then she left. I liked her, too. I missed her. But I like you more."

"It was very clever of you to remember what a passport was, but you upset me a lot by stealing it," Cassie reprimanded her.

"I gave it back to you. Your money is here, too. I kept everything safe in my pocket."

She climbed off the bed, picked up her coat from the back of the chair, and handed Cassie a tightly folded wad of money.

Cassie stared down at the notes, unfolding them slowly with her fingertips.

"It's all my fault. I made you sad, and now you're leaving. Please don't go," Ella begged.

"Ella, I'm not the person you need," she tried, but the young girl shook her dark head determinedly.

"Yes, you are. You're the best," she insisted. "We all like you, except for Antoinette, but she doesn't like anyone. Even Marc told Papa this morning how nice you are."

Cassie put the money into her jeans pocket, feeling at a loss. She hadn't realized that she was so valued, and so needed, by the younger children. Ella, in particular, had far more complex issues than she'd realized. What chance did she have to overcome these challenges, living in such an unstable home? She was still so innocent, and Cassie admired the courage it had taken for her to confess what she'd done. That meant a lot.

If she left now, Ella would blame herself, and it would add more weight to an emotional burden which no five-year-old deserved to carry. Cassie knew all too well what the long-term consequences of that could be. Surely she could survive here just a little longer. If she left in another few days, Ella wouldn't blame herself for it.

That sounded like the fair thing to do.

The only problem was that if she was staying, she urgently needed to replace her tablets. She wouldn't be able to cope without them. There must be a doctor in town who could write her a scrip, but she'd have to go today.

Money was another serious worry. She doubted that the change Ella had given back to her would even cover the cost of the medication, so how was she going to afford the doctor?

Cassie remembered that the restaurant had promised a final salary payment at the beginning of the month, from the odd shifts she'd worked in October. She hoped it would be enough, because she didn't want to beg Pierre for a salary advance without being able to tell him why she needed it.

When she went back to her room, though, she realized she wouldn't need to beg.

Her eyes were drawn immediately to the small brown paper parcel placed neatly on her pillow.

Cassie checked behind her and closed her bedroom door before walking over to the bed and cautiously picking it up.

Inside the carefully folded parcel was an emerald green silk scarf, and two hundred euros in cash.

She picked up the scarf, feeling a sense of unreality. The fabric was gossamer-soft to the touch; an expensive, quality item. The crisp, new banknotes had been placed inside a white manila envelope.

Cassie felt sick with dread as she remembered Pierre's words.

"I will reward you generously for playing the game with me."

There was no way this was a salary advance, or a refund for what she'd already spent, or money for gas, or anything else that could be construed as innocent.

Without a doubt, Pierre had made a down payment for favors he would now be expecting in return.

CHAPTER SIXTEEN

Although Cassie knew Marnie had the day off, she hoped that the housekeeper might have returned from her trip to Paris. After her nightmarish encounter in the bedroom with Pierre and the gift she had found on her pillow, she wasn't taking any chances. She wouldn't risk spending another night here unless she could lock her door.

She headed down to the kitchen, where one of the maids told her that Marnie had arrived back just after lunch.

"Would you mind calling her for me?" Cassie asked. "I know she's not working today, but it's urgent."

A few minutes later, Marnie walked into in the kitchen. Fresh from her outing, the housekeeper was still beautifully made up with her hair curling onto her shoulders, and comparing her appearance with the maid on duty, Cassie could see the differences. Now she understood the unspoken rule about work attire in the chateau.

"I need a key for my bedroom," Cassie said.

Marnie frowned. "Why? That room is usually left open. The children need access and we have to be able to clean it. In fact, the original key is missing and the spare is the only one available."

"I'd feel more comfortable if I could lock it when I need to," Cassie said. "I went for an early run this morning, and while I was out, one of the children played a prank on me by messing up my room."

"Oh, dear," Marnie said, but Cassie could see she thought she was overreacting.

"I am sure it was just innocent fun," she explained, wanting to protect Ella, "but it's taken me the whole day to find my money and passport. I can't risk that happening again. I need to be sure that when I'm out and the children are here, my personal belongings stay where they are." She smiled hopefully.

Marnie nodded slowly. "Yes, I see that could have been serious." She had obviously realized there was more to the story.

"I will give you the spare key, but please keep it safe. Don't leave it in the door, and please don't lock the room unless you go out on your own. That way, the cleaning schedule will not be disrupted."

Cassie wondered if the original key had gone missing after being left in the door, and if so who had taken it.

"I'll keep it with me at all times," she promised. "Thank you so much."

She'd only just gone upstairs when she saw Pierre arriving back. Grabbing her purse and jacket, she locked her bedroom door, pocketed the key, and hurried down to meet him. He'd come home later than she'd expected, and it was already a quarter to five in the afternoon. If she was quick, she might still make it to town in time.

Even though she had made up her mind to stay a few more days, she decided to use the trip to town as an opportunity to do reconnaissance. She could get the numbers of taxi companies, and also check where a phone signal was available. Then, when she was ready to leave, it would hopefully go smoothly.

When Cassie reached the front door, she saw Margot had arrived back, too. Her hair looked a few shades blonder, and was freshly blow dried. She must have spent the afternoon at the hairdresser, and been picked up by Pierre on his way home.

Margot brushed past her without so much as a hello, but Pierre paused when he saw her.

"I have to ask you a favor," Cassie said.

"What is that?" Pierre placed his car keys in the copper bowl on the hall table. Cassie noticed Margot had turned back to them, obviously wanting to listen to their conversation.

"Could I please take a couple of hours off? I need to go into town."

"Now?" Pierre asked, frowning. "This is not a convenient time."

"The children have to eat dinner in an hour," Margot observed pointedly.

This trip couldn't be put off any longer, but with Margot siding against her, Cassie knew that she was on the verge of getting an outright refusal. Without her meds, she'd be in serious trouble by this time tomorrow, but she didn't want Pierre to know this. It would be far better if she could give another reason for needing to go.

"I have to check in with the au pair agency and update them," she explained. "They asked me to do it by today at the latest."

Pierre frowned down at her.

"There is no need to drive to town for that. We have a telephone here," he said.

"No, no," Cassie protested, going deeper into her lie. "The phone call's for my account; I wouldn't want you to be charged for it. I also have to run an important errand. I—er—have to make a payment into one of my clothing accounts. It's already overdue and today's the deadline."

She could see Pierre wasn't buying her flimsy, spur-of-the-moment story.

"Don't let her go now. Surely it can wait till the weekend," Margot advised. With a toss of her shiny hair, she headed upstairs.

"I meant to make the payment before I left the States," Cassie said. "I ran out of time to do certain things because of the rush to get here."

Pierre pressed his lips together thoughtfully. Cassie wondered whether he might be concluding that she'd also run out of money, and was only able to go now because he'd just given her some cash.

At any rate, to her massive relief, he gave a reluctant nod.

"Be quick," he said. "Even if you miss supper, you must return in time to put the children to bed."

"I will definitely be back by then," Cassie promised.

She grabbed the Renault's keys and ran to the garage, wondering how she could find a doctor's office at such short notice, so late in the afternoon.

As she was about to climb in the car, she heard footsteps behind her. Looking round, she saw Pierre had followed her.

Cassie regarded him apprehensively, wishing she could throw his money right back in his face, but knowing she couldn't afford to.

Maybe that was why he'd agreed to the trip, knowing that spending the cash would make her even more beholden to him. Biting her lip, she waited for him to speak, wondering if he was going to try and make another pass at her, and if so how she should handle it this time.

"You are going to call the agency?" he asked.

"Yes. Yes, I am," she lied again.

Pierre adjusted the heavy gold signet ring on his index finger.

"What will you tell them?" he said in a quieter voice.

"Tell them?" she repeated, confused, before realizing the implications of his question. She felt herself turn scarlet.

"I'll tell them I'm happy here, that I'm settling in well. I'll say my accommodations are very comfortable and the food is excellent and that I'm starting to make friends with the children."

She pressed the car keys into her palm, conscious of the minutes ticking away. What time did doctors close up for the day in France?

"That is all you will say?"

"Yes, that's all." She felt uncomfortably complicit repeating the words.

"Privacy is very important to us," Pierre emphasized. "Reputation is essential for me personally, and for my family's business. I have had experiences in the past where people have lied, exaggerated, and tried to do damage. This has always resulted in very serious consequences—for them, not for me. Do you understand this, Cassie?"

This was more than just a warning, it was a threat. She felt cold inside, wondering what had happened to people who had spoken out in the past.

"I understand completely," she whispered.

In a louder voice, Pierre continued.

"Do you have enough money to pay this clothing account in full? Here, I will give you an advance on your salary so you can be sure of a successful trip this afternoon."

To her astonishment, he took a leather wallet out of his pocket, peeled four more fifty-euro notes from a large stack, and handed them to her. Before she could say anything else or try to give them back, he turned and left the garage.

She started the car, realizing her hands were shaking. Pierre's message was clear. Cooperate, keep quiet, play the game—and you will be rewarded.

Cassie didn't want to think about what the alternative would be.

Stressed about being too late to see a doctor, Cassie forgot to check for a cell phone signal until she was almost in the town itself. The small, scenic town was a fifteen-minute drive from the chateau and it was well signposted, so she found her way there without difficulty once she was on the main road.

After driving down the main street and back, she spotted the small "Pharmacie" signpost on a corner. She parked and ran inside, glancing at the opening hours on the door which told her that six p.m. was closing time.

"Where can I find a doctor? I need to get a prescription filled urgently," she asked the pharmacist, who was engrossed in a game of Sudoku on his phone.

"Doctor Lafayette might still be open. His practice is at his home, just outside town. It's not far. Do you have GPS?"

"I don't think I'll be able to access it without a Wi-Fi signal," Cassie said, so he sketched a map for her.

She managed to reach the doctor just before he closed up for the day, and he agreed to see her. The practice was beautiful, set in a picturesque building among exquisite gardens. Dr. Lafayette himself was a tall, fit, middle-aged man with a sympathetic manner. He showed her into his rooms, which were decorated in plush leather with paintings of landscapes on the walls.

"You are on a lot of medication," he said, surprised, when she told him what she needed the prescription for.

Cassie was hugely relieved that she had managed to give the Dubois family an alternative reason for coming into town, rather than having to confess she was on a cocktail of chronic anxiety meds.

"I've had bad panic attacks in the past," she said. "I've just arrived in a new country which is rather stressful, and I don't want to have my anxiety triggered by the change in environment."

He nodded, scribbling on his pad.

"Are you studying or working?" he asked.

"I'm au pairing," Cassie replied.

"Ah. For which family?"

She hesitated, remembering Pierre's warning.

"For the Dubois family," she said carefully, watching to see how the doctor reacted, but he was looking down at his notes and she couldn't read his face.

"Are you aware…" he said suddenly and she tensed, already thinking what she would say if he asked her anything about Pierre. But he was only advising her about the tablets.

"Are you aware this medication causes drowsiness?" he said. "It is better to take these tablets at night."

"Yes, that's when I try and take them." Seeing him raise an eyebrow, she amended, "I mean, that's when I do take them. At night."

"And this other medication—your dosage is very high. Too high, in my opinion. I am going to reduce it to half a tablet per day as a maintenance dose. Take a whole tablet if you are anxious or depressed, but otherwise stick to the lower dosage. The higher dosage can cause psychotic episodes."

"I will," Cassie promised.

"So, how are you finding your au pairing experience?" he asked, tearing the page from the notepad.

Although it was neutrally worded, it felt like a leading question, and Cassie suddenly had an overriding desire to tell the truth. After all, if she had heard rumors about the family from other people, this doctor must have, too. Perhaps he was inviting her to explain what she was going through, and why her anxiety had skyrocketed, and how she was already on the point of giving up.

She could tell the doctor that her employer had violent sexual tendencies, and had made a pass at her and then threatened her with consequences if she disclosed anything, while simultaneously bribing her to silence. How his fiancée had verbally abused the children and physically assaulted her. She could explain that the children might already be irreparably damaged through no fault of their own, and that she strongly felt some kind of professional intervention was required, even if it was just a visit from a social worker.

She'd have to be quick, because it was already a quarter to six and she needed to get her meds today, but this might be her only opportunity to tell someone trustworthy about her fears and concerns.

Cassie took a deep breath.

"I'm not sure where to start, but I'm so relieved you asked me this. I've desperately wanted to speak to somebody, because there's so much I need to explain," she began.

And then, from the reception area, the phone started ringing.

"Excuse me," Dr. Lafayette said. "My receptionist has already left for the day. Would you mind if I answer this?"

"Sure," Cassie said, hoping that the call wouldn't take too long.

The doctor was only out of the room for a minute.

"Thank you again for seeing me after hours," Cassie said when he returned. "I'm so grateful."

She intended to use this as a lead-in to her comments, but the doctor's reply silenced her.

"Pierre Dubois is a close friend of mine. He has done a huge amount to support my practice over the years, and my brother is the cellar manager at his estate's vineyard. I am always glad to assist any of his family or staff. So, Cassie, you were going to tell me how you are finding your stay here?"

She was at a loss for words, lightheaded with shock at what he'd just said. The reply she'd formulated so carefully froze on her lips.

The silence stretched between them, quickly becoming uneasy, and she guessed he must have guessed she had intended to speak badly of her employer, and now had nothing to say.

"Regarding the amount of medication you are on, did you disclose it to the agency or your employer?" the doctor asked.

"They didn't ask," Cassie said in a small voice.

Another long silence followed.

Then Dr. Lafayette got up and handed her the scrip.

"If that is all, we can settle up now," he said, formally. "The consultation will be eighty euros."

Cassie had hoped that she'd be able to pay with her credit card, but it wouldn't go through, and she had no idea whether it was due to insufficient funds in her account or some other reason.

That meant she had to dip into Pierre's money. Now she truly was beholden to him, because she couldn't give it all back.

She left feeling sick with anxiety. Trustingly, she had told Dr. Lafayette too much, and she had no idea whether his question about the medications was a veiled threat. Would he disclose those details to Pierre? Did friendship and business alliances take priority over patient confidentiality in this town?

From now on, Cassie realized she would have to keep the family's secrets to herself, because she had no idea how far their influence, or power, extended.

CHAPTER SEVENTEEN

It was a minute after six by the time Cassie got back to the pharmacy, but the pharmacist had kindly waited for her and he was able to give her a month's supply of all the tablets she needed.

Cassie was still reeling from the encounter she'd had with Dr. Lafayette. She'd come so close to innocently dropping a bombshell that would have landed her in the worst possible trouble. Even her first hint that there were difficulties with the family could still have consequences. She could only pray that the doctor's close personal friendship with Pierre would not override patient confidentiality, especially given his shock at the amount of meds she was on.

"This prescription is on a three-month repeat," the pharmacist told her. "You can visit any time from the first of December for your next month's supply."

To her relief, he was able to substitute more affordable generics for two of her medications, and even though the meds cost slightly more than the doctor's visit had, her card finally cooperated and she was able to use it.

The pharmacist let her connect to his Wi-Fi while she waited, and logging into her banking, she saw that a small payment had come through from the restaurant. It had been immediately swallowed by the pharmacy charge, so she was down to near-zero again.

She researched local cabs and looked up what it would cost to change her flight. There was so much conflicting information online that she couldn't be sure, but she thought she could probably afford it with her remaining cash, if she didn't spend any more.

However, she had to make one final purchase, which she was able to do at the pharmacy—buying a large voucher for prepaid minutes.

With her minutes loaded and her Wi-Fi operational, Cassie saw a flood of messages and emails come in. There were several missed calls from her friends back home, and a text from Jess, the au pair she'd met on the airplane, asking how things were going and if she wanted to meet up on her day off.

Cassie didn't have enough time, or money, to answer all the messages now. They would have to wait, because she needed to conserve her minutes. However, there was one urgent call that she had to make immediately.

She headed back to the car and dialed the number as soon as she climbed inside, doing mental arithmetic to work out what the time difference was back home.

It was early afternoon, which mean on a weekday, Zane would be on shift at the factory where he worked. Even so, he answered her call in three rings.

"Hang on, baby, I'm just clocking out for a break," he said, and she had to wait for a few endless, expensive minutes while listening to him leaving the factory floor. She imagined him, dressed in his jeans and work jacket, striding across the concrete paving, heading for the side entrance where the smoking area was.

The clangs in the background were replaced by the rush of wind, telling her he'd reached it.

"OK," he said. "I got ten minutes. Let's talk."

Cassie hoped the conversation wouldn't take ten minutes. She wanted to get this resolved as quickly as possible, without bleeding her precious minutes away.

"Zane, how did you find out where I was? I didn't tell you my employer's phone number. I didn't give it out to anyone."

"It took some detective work," Zane explained in self-congratulatory tones. "You see, I noticed that agency name on your bag. So I called them up and pretended I'd lost your number. The first time I tried, I spoke to a lady who wouldn't tell me. She said she could only give you a message. But the second time some other guy answered and he looked it up for me."

"Please don't call there again."

"Why not, baby? Don't you want to speak to me at all?"

"It's not that." How could she explain without making Zane even more determined to keep calling the chateau? She didn't want him thinking he needed to come to her rescue.

"They're a very private family," she said. "They don't allow staff to receive any personal calls in the house. Normally they don't even pass on messages. You were just lucky that the housekeeper happened to answer."

Hopefully that would convince Zane it was pointless trying again.

"So, when are you coming home?" He sounded daunted, but not defeated, by what she'd said.

Cassie checked the car clock. It was already half past six. She needed to hurry back, but she couldn't start driving until she'd dealt with this, as she had no idea how long the signal would last.

"I'm going to be overseas for at least a year," she told him, and heard his exclamation of outrage.

"Do you really think it was fair to me, to leave for such a long time without at least saying a proper goodbye?"

"Zane, we'd broken up by the time I left." Exasperated, Cassie realized the conversation was going around in circles. She started the car and turned up the heater, hoping that she'd be able to find her way back to the chateau in the dark.

"No. You walked out on me. We never broke up. I came back one day and found you'd packed your things and gone."

"There was a reason for that, and you know what it was." Cassie could hear the edge in her own voice. She hadn't forgiven him for what he'd done.

"I have no idea, baby, and I really mean it. No clue at all."

He was lying. He must be.

"Zane, you got angry with me when we fought. You lost your temper and grabbed me so hard you nearly yanked me off my feet.

Then you punched my arm. The bruises took weeks to heal. You meant to hurt me. As I told you at the time, I'm not putting up with that and I'm not willing to give you a second chance."

There was a short silence.

"I really don't know what you're talking about. Do you mean when I pulled you out of the way of that car? Baby, we were arguing in a parking lot, and you were upset, you weren't looking, you were literally going to run right into the path of some SUV. I just wanted to keep you safe."

It hadn't happened that way. Not at all. His version was miles away from the truth. Listening to him was only making Cassie more determined to stay away from him forever. She knew that if she'd been there, watching how he spread his arms innocently as he talked, and raised his eyebrows, looking almost comically defenseless, she would have wanted to buy into his story. Part of her would have longed to believe that he'd been right and she'd misinterpreted the situation.

"I'm not fighting with you any more, Zane, but I'm not coming back."

"Please, Cassie. You don't understand how much I miss you. All our friends are asking where you are. Oh, and I wanted to tell you, there's a job opening at the factory. Not on the floor, in the offices. They're looking for an assistant to the marketing team. It's a good salary and really good prospects. I said I'd tell you. Do you want me to send the details? Applications have to be in by Monday."

Cassie tried to close her ears to his words. Zane had a knack for guessing exactly what it would take to change her mind, and right now she had to admit that a job with prospects was a serious lifeline.

She told herself that the marketing job probably didn't even exist, and if it did exist the applications had probably closed already, and even if the job was still open, why would they give it to her?

It wasn't like Zane, a factory floor worker, could do anything to influence the outcome.

"Not right now, thanks. I'm committed to staying here so I can't come home."

"But baby, you don't sound happy. I can hear it in your voice. You sound stressed out of your mind. You don't want to stay there if it's not right for you."

Cassie gritted her teeth.

"I'm stressed because I'm running late. I have to go now. Please don't call me again. I won't answer and I won't speak to you. Goodbye, Zane."

She stabbed the disconnect button, cutting off his shouted protests.

Then she turned her phone off and drove out of the parking lot, seething with frustration over the pointless conversation, and how weak she ended up being with Zane. Why was it so hard for her to stand up to him? Even when she'd finally gathered the strength to hang up on him, she'd said please don't call me again. Please! Like she was asking him for a favor. She kept putting all the power into his hands. No wonder he believed there could be another chance with her.

At any rate, thanks to that conversation, she was going to be even later getting back. She might not even be in time to put Ella to bed, and she knew she would have to explain why she'd spent so long in town.

While racking her brains for a valid excuse, she ended up missing the turning to the chateau. It all looked so different in darkness. Although the way to town had been well signposted, she hadn't thought to notice any signage going the opposite way. Now she realized her mistake. Town was clearly signposted, the chateau was not. She was disoriented, and had no idea which direction she should be heading. She pulled over and tried to connect to GPS, but to her frustration, she couldn't get a signal.

When she realized a few miles later that she'd definitely gone too far, she tried to turn back, but instead of turning right to drive round the block, she ended up taking a highway on-ramp by mistake. She found herself on the auto-route heading to Strasbourg.

"Shit, shit, shit," she whispered, realizing the extent of the mistake she'd made. On this highway, which was more like a raceway, she couldn't go slowly and try to get her bearings. Traffic was flying along, and she had to accelerate just to avoid causing an accident.

Grasping the steering wheel tightly, Cassie realized she might be forced to drive for miles along this hellish route—the road was as light and bright as the country roads had been dark, but it was speeding her along in entirely the wrong direction. Would she ever find the chateau again? And if she did, how would she explain her unforgivable lateness, after she'd been expressly told to come back in time to put the children to bed?

After what seemed like an endless drive, Cassie managed to find an exit where she could turn around and retrace her route, but after the mistake she'd made, and the stress of the drive, she found her sense of direction was completely thrown out. She missed the off-ramp going the other way and had to start the whole process of turning around again, this time while heading to Paris.

When she finally managed to take what she thought had to be the correct exit, she couldn't remember any of the turns she'd made to reach the highway, and with a sense of doom, she realized she had gone completely wrong.

Cassie felt as if she was stuck in an endless nightmare, turning down each of the quiet, dark country roads she came to, desperately peering into the darkness, hoping to find some sort of a landmark that she could use to orient herself. But the minutes ticked by, and no landmarks appeared.

The houses in this area were set well back from the road, and only a few had doorbells or gate intercoms. In desperation, she tried ringing a few of those that did, but two weren't answered at all, one person told her to go in a direction that led back to the highway, and the last person she tried, an elderly lady, eventually admitted after an exquisitely frustrating back and forth conversation that she had no idea where the chateau was.

Eventually, through sheer luck, Cassie stumbled upon a road she thought she recognized. She couldn't believe it when she realized she was approaching the chateau from a completely different direction, passing by the small village where the carnival had been held. By then, Cassie had given up all hope, because it was too late to redeem herself or even to properly explain herself. How could any normal person get so completely, impossibly lost as she had done?

She'd stopped looking at the car clock while she searched, as it was only making her panic worse, but now Cassie glanced at it while she drove up the winding driveway. It was nearly eight o'clock, and she braced herself for a storm of criticism from Pierre. He would demand to know where she'd been, and she didn't know how she would convince him she had been driving around the area for more than an hour.

When she opened the front door, she was unprepared for the chaos she found inside.

A decorative plate lay in smithereens near the staircase, and somebody—Marc, she guessed—was tunelessly bashing the piano keys in the music room. Ella was sitting at the top of the stairs crying, and further away, she could hear Margot and Antoinette screaming at each other from the dining room.

"Sorry I'm so late. Is everything all right?" Cassie called, anxiety erupting inside her. Where was Pierre? What had happened? She doubted the children would be running amok like this if he was home.

A brief silence followed her shout.

And then Margot shrieked back, her voice high, shrill, and furious.

"Come here immediately, Cassie! How dare you leave me alone with the children for the entire night! Where the hell have you been?"

Margot didn't wait for Cassie to reach the dining room. She confronted her in the corridor, her face flushed with anger, her beautiful blonde hair tousled.

"You explain everything to me, right now," she screamed, and Cassie could smell the alcohol on her breath—something stronger than wine; she reeked of spirits.

"And you'd better tell the truth this time, you lying whore!"

CHAPTER EIGHTEEN

Cassie stared at Margot in shock. She was horrified that the blonde woman was screaming these insults within earshot of the children, and she had no idea how she could defuse the situation when it had already escalated so badly.

Margot had obviously been drinking heavily, and Cassie guessed she hadn't coped with managing the children alone, and had quickly lost control. Now she was venting her rage on Cassie for having gone out and leaving her in this predicament. Perhaps that was partly why she was so angry—because she felt powerless.

"I'm sorry I'm back so late," she said, doing her best to speak calmly. "I went the wrong way coming back from town, and got myself totally lost. Shall I put the children to bed now?"

"Oh, you went the wrong way? Is that the real reason you're so late?" Margot jeered. She stepped forward, leaning into Cassie's space, so close that Cassie could see the intricate embroidery on her expensive-looking turquoise coat.

"Don't you want the children to know that their au pair is nothing better than a common, lying slut?"

Cassie recoiled as she realized that Margot wasn't just flinging random insults, but had jumped to entirely the wrong conclusion. Or maybe, she told herself with a pang of guilt, remembering the whispered threats and promises Pierre had made in her bedroom earlier, not quite as wrong as Cassie would have liked her to be.

Looking past Margot, Cassie saw Antoinette peeking out of the dining room. For once, Antoinette's usual poise had deserted her. Her face was pale and set, and Cassie guessed she had been crying.

"Please, can we discuss this in private?" she begged Margot. "You have misunderstood the situation completely. I'll explain everything to you but I don't think it's right for the children to overhear this."

Margot ignored her pleas and continued with her angry tirade.

"You leave, Pierre leaves immediately afterwards! And then you return more than three hours later? He is still not back. You think I am stupid? I know what you have been doing! I have seen the way he looks at you."

"I don't know where Pierre went," Cassie insisted, aware how weak this sounded and what a coincidence it was that he had left immediately after her—he hadn't even mentioned that he was heading out.

"Show me your wallet. Go on, get it out of your purse and show me!" Margot pointed a crimson-tipped finger at Cassie's shoulder bag.

"My wallet?"

What was Margot hoping to find? Cassie wondered. A hotel key card? A handwritten note? There was nothing like that in her possession. Confused, she opened her purse and handed it over, hoping it would prove her innocence, worrying too late that Margot might rip the entire wallet apart in her anger.

Margot snatched it from her and yanked it open.

"You see," she said triumphantly, pulling a sheaf of orange fifty-euro notes out and flinging them onto the floor. Cassie watched the notes flutter down, and her stomach plummeted with them, because she realized Margot's instinct had been right.

"What a lot of money for someone who was complaining this morning that all their cash had been stolen," Margot taunted her. "Are you going to pretend you drew all this out of your bank account in 'town'? I thought you were going to pay a bill, not get paid. But someone gave you money, didn't they? I wonder who that could have been."

"Pierre gave me an advance on my salary," Cassie said.

"Oh, no, he didn't. You got the money out of him another way, you whore!"

Cassie stifled a cry as Margot grabbed her shoulder, shoving her backward. She stumbled, and her bag slipped off her shoulder. The contents spilled to the floor—Chapstick, lipstick, hair clips, pens, scattering down onto the marble tiles.

She glanced down, and as she did, Margot's hand lashed across her face in a stinging slap. This time Cassie did cry out.

Cassie's first instinct was to slap the blonde woman right back again. The sheer force of her own anger scared her. She controlled herself with a huge effort, telling herself that she must be the better, stronger person here and not stoop to Margot's level. She had to try and resolve this peacefully—especially seeing Antoinette was watching.

"Margot, please! Calm down. What I've said is the truth."

Margot pushed her again and Cassie stood on her lipstick, almost falling over as it rolled under her foot. She heard a crack as the tube broke.

She was beginning to feel strangely dissociated. The way Margot was leaning into her, the taunts, the stink of alcohol on her breath, was dredging up memories that she'd forgotten long ago. Other places, other times. When she'd been much younger, and scared to death, and confronting another drunk, angry woman who had been taunting her.

Elaine, the one she'd hated the most out of all her father's girlfriends.

Cassie remembered now that she hadn't just wished her gone. She really had wished her dead. And she'd said so—shouting out the words while she attacked the woman with her fists—hitting her, kicking her, curling her fingers to try and gouge out her eyes.

"I wish you were dead," she'd screamed at Elaine. *"Get into your car and crash it. Go upstairs and jump out the window!"*

And Elaine had shouted back, attacking her with far more strength.

"Get lost, you stupid, skinny bitch. Why don't you go dive under a truck? Or find your daddy's gun and play with it. You think anyone wants you here?"

Her words had carved a giant chasm in Cassie's heart, because she'd known deep down that the truth was nobody wanted her there. Not her father, nor Elaine, nor any of their drunken friends. She was an expense, a responsibility, an inconvenience. And perhaps, just looking at her, her father had been reminded too much of her mother, and of the person he used to be.

Now, as she fought for control, she remembered how she'd lost it that time. She and Elaine had hurt each other badly. Elaine had ripped out a chunk of her hair, causing Cassie's scalp to bleed, and Cassie had dislocated Elaine's finger so that she'd screamed in agony and finally let go of her. Elaine had to go to the emergency room for treatment, and they'd ended up calling an ambulance because when her dad had come back half an hour later, he'd already been too drunk to drive her there.

In Margot now, she saw the same anger, the same loss of control. The same hatred.

The blonde woman snarled in rage as she grabbed at Cassie. Her nails raked Cassie's skin, tearing at her clothing, her knuckles battering her face.

"Stop it," Cassie screamed.

She dropped her purse and abandoned her own good advice to herself. She wasn't prepared to tolerate this abuse for a moment longer. She'd given Margot more than enough time to calm down and see reason, and she hadn't. Margot was beyond reason or words—she was on the attack, and Cassie was ready.

As Margot lunged toward Cassie, she clawed at the blonde woman's face, feeling her nails rake her skin and hearing Margot gasp. But one of Margot's lime green stiletto heels plunged into Cassie's foot, stabbing through the thin canvas of her trainer. Cassie staggered back, screaming in pain, but with her foot trapped, she overbalanced and fell, her hip and shoulder banging onto the slippery marble floor.

She heard a frightened cry from behind her and knew that Ella had come to see what was happening.

"Ella, go back upstairs," she shouted.

There was nothing she could do if Ella ignored her. The children would be affected by this regardless and the only choice she had was whether they would see her defeated by Margot or whether they would see her win.

Cassie fought back as hard as she could. She grabbed for Margot's ankles, hoping to unbalance her, but Margot began stamping and kicking so that Cassie had to writhe out of the way to avoid her lethal heels.

Cassie kicked back and connected with Margot's shin, so that she screeched in pain. Encouraged, Cassie kicked her again and Margot stepped back, swearing violently.

Then, behind Margot, Cassie saw Antoinette had entered the fray. With her eyes narrowed, she aimed carefully before punching the blonde woman in the back of her knee with all her might.

Margot's leg buckled under her and, shrieking, she toppled off her heels. She made a grab for a shelf to stop her fall, and ripped one side of it from its hinges. Copper birds clanged to the ground around her, but Margot snatched up a tall African mask before it fell.

"Bitch! You hurt me!" Using the heavy mask as a bat, she swung it at Cassie, who jackknifed out of the way as the wooden head crashed to the floor where her arm had been. With Margot temporarily off balance, she grabbed the other end of the mask, trying to jerk it out of Margot's grasp.

Margot leaned toward her, screaming threats and obscenities as she tried to kick Cassie away.

"Bitch! Slut!"

Fighting her off with one hand, keeping a death grip on the mask with the other, Cassie managed to scramble to her feet. Then she pushed as hard as she could on the mask, shoving it backward toward Margot, so that she sprawled onto the floor.

Cassie threw the mask at Margot, feeling a thrill of triumph as it cracked down on her forehead.

Then she turned and ran. Enough was enough. She was going to lock herself in her bedroom until Margot had regained her sanity.

Thankfully, Ella was nowhere to be seen, and Cassie hoped she'd left when she was told to, and hadn't stayed to watch the entire fight.

As she sprinted around the corner, Cassie collided with Pierre.

She saw him at the last minute, and even though she tried to slow down, she still slammed into him with some force.

Pierre grasped her tightly as they both staggered back.

"What is happening here?" he shouted, as Margot rounded the corner, and Cassie struggled out of Pierre's embrace as she saw the venom in Margot's face.

"Take your hands off her," Margot spat.

Cassie saw her cheek was bleeding—her clawing nails had cut through Margot's porcelain skin, and she was limping, but she seemed to be unaware of either injury, still as furious as ever.

"What are you implying?" Pierre asked. His voice was quieter, but the tone made Cassie deeply uneasy.

"You and her!" Margot stabbed a finger at each of them to emphasize her words. "You were together. Don't try to deny it. I know what you were doing."

Pierre sighed heavily.

"Margot, you are wrong. I went into Paris to assess a sculpture that is going for auction next week. Your behavior is completely out of line. As is yours." He turned to Cassie, his heavy brow creased in a frown.

Before Cassie had a chance to explain she'd acted in self-defense against the madwoman that Margot had become, he continued.

"Go to your room immediately, Cassie, I do not require you to work anymore tonight. I will deal with the children now. We can discuss this situation tomorrow."

"But…" she tried.

"Go," Pierre insisted.

Despite his thunderous expression and the finality of his tone, Cassie found the courage to stand her ground. She couldn't allow herself to walk away without explaining what had happened.

"Please will you hear me out? This wasn't my fault," she insisted.

"It was," Margot hissed from behind her.

"Margot attacked me. I was only defending myself."

"You were not! See how my face is scratched," Margot argued.

Pierre looked back and forth, between her and Margot. For a hopeful moment Cassie believed he would at least accept what she'd said. But then his face darkened.

"Margot is my fiancée and I will listen to her side of the story first. In any case, I believe you arrived back unacceptably late. If you had been on time, none of this would have happened. We will discuss it further tomorrow."

Frustrated that Pierre was refusing to hear her, but knowing she couldn't push the situation any further, Cassie turned away. She picked up her scattered belongings and put them back in her bag. One of the banknotes was torn, and the crushed lipstick was beyond repair. As she walked away she felt ashamed, as if Pierre's dismissive words had already decided her guilt.

The piano music had stopped. Cassie guessed Pierre had detoured into the music room as he passed, because Marc was nowhere to be seen. As she reached the staircase, Marnie hurried through from the kitchen with a dustpan and brush, to sweep up the fragments of plate.

"I believe you have just had a horrible fight with Margot," she whispered.

Cassie nodded.

"I'll talk to you later," Marnie said, before turning away and bending down to sweep up the mess on the floor.

Ella was still at the top of the stairs, crying harder.

"Are you going to put me to bed now?" she sobbed. "Margot was so nasty to us tonight."

"Your father is going to put you to bed," Cassie said. "Perhaps he'll read you a story if you ask him nicely."

She ruffled Ella's hair as she passed by.

After she tried three times to get her key into the lock, she realized how badly she had started to shake. By the time she walked into her bedroom, she was on the point of tears. She felt utterly traumatized by the recent fight, and furious over Margot's accusations.

She wished she'd thrown that mask hard enough to knock her out. No, hard enough to cause permanent damage to her selfish, cruel brain.

Scenes from the melee kept replaying in her mind. The stink of spirits on Margot's breath and the insults she'd shrieked at Cassie. How she'd had to writhe away from that sharp, spiked, lime-green heel as Margot tried to trample her. The way her vision had exploded into stars as she'd hit the tiles. The look on Antoinette's face—utterly distraught, as if she'd had enough of Margot's bullying ways.

The whiff of perfume that she'd smelled unexpectedly; a delicate, feminine scent that had been shocking to her for some reason.

Cassie frowned, trying to place it. She hadn't noticed it when Margot attacked her. Her eyes widened as she realized when she'd picked it up. It had been just after she'd cannoned into Pierre. She'd smelled it lingering on his skin.

Suddenly Cassie wondered if Pierre had indeed been out on a romantic assignation with someone else.

Well, whether he had or hadn't, Margot's attack had been completely unjustified, and Pierre had been deaf to her side of the story. He hadn't cared. He hadn't stood up for her and he would do nothing to stop this from happening again.

As for Margot, she was a devil straight from hell.

Rage surged in Cassie as she thought about the way she'd been treated. It was completely out of line. This household was stuck in the dark ages in more ways than one. There was no cell phone connectivity, no internet, no TV, and the owner's fiancée felt entitled to abuse staff as if they were her possessions, and not even human beings.

The more she thought about it, the angrier she became. Rage at the unjust treatment boiled inside her. She felt like marching into Pierre's bedroom right now and slapping Margot as hard as she could. That would show her.

A soft tap on her bedroom door yanked Cassie away from her vengeful thoughts.

"Come in," she said.

Marnie entered, closing the door quickly behind her. She was holding a covered plate.

"I'm so sorry about what happened," she said in a low voice, as she put the plate on the desk. "I don't know if you've eaten tonight, but I brought you some cheese and biscuits in case you were hungry."

"Thanks," Cassie said. She wasn't in the least hungry, but Marnie's gesture was so kind that she couldn't possibly refuse the food. She uncovered the plate and took a biscuit, but her mouth was so dry she struggled to chew it. She coughed, and reached for the glass of water on her bedside table.

"I'm sorry this has happened," Marnie sympathized. "Things have been very difficult for all of us since Margot arrived."

"I can imagine."

"The first time I told her that a food delivery would be late and we would have to change the planned menu for a dinner party, she slapped me."

"Really? You too? That's awful. What did you do?"

Marnie's face hardened. "I was so surprised at the time, I did nothing," she said. "Then afterwards, I felt so furious I could have killed her. Never, ever have I had an employer treat me that way. But I didn't complain, because she fired three of the household staff after a piece of jewelry went 'missing.' I don't think it went missing at all. I think she sold it and Pierre noticed it was gone."

"Really?"

"Oh, yes. Pierre controls the money and what she spends. If they fight, the purse strings are closed. Or at any rate, that is what I understand, from the loud arguments I have overheard."

"How do you feel about being in this situation?" Cassie asked, eating a piece of cheese. The conversation was strangely comforting. At least she didn't feel like Margot's only enemy anymore.

"Everyone working here hates her, and none of us want to stay. I'm looking for another job," Marnie confessed. "I already have one offer, from a guesthouse in a neighboring village. At the end of the month I will decide where to go and hand in my notice."

"I don't blame you. I feel the same way, and I've only been here three days. I also want to quit, and I think I'm going to."

Marnie nodded in sympathy. "It's not easy here. Nobody can blame you for leaving. The au pair who worked here before you walked out after a month for the same reasons. And now I had better leave you to get some sleep. Let's forget we had this conversation and not mention it again, or it will not go well for either of us in this household."

She gave Cassie a conspiratorial smile as she left.

Cassie decided that Marnie's words had cemented her own decision. She was not prepared to stay in a home where this level of violence could, and would, happen regularly. She was an emotional and physical wreck already, and she'd now found out her only friend would be leaving at the end of the month.

Cassie resolved that for her own sanity, she would have to quit in the morning.

She spent an hour carefully packing her bags. She didn't care about Ella's pleas, or Pierre's threats. She wasn't going to think about the career implications of this decision. She was going to take care of herself and her own well-being, and she could only hope the rest would fall into place.

When everything was packed and ready to go, Cassie climbed into bed but found she couldn't sleep. Her back was bruised and aching, she'd wrenched a shoulder muscle during the tussle with Margot, and those were just the physical injuries.

Since she left home, she'd gone out of her way to avoid a repeat of what she'd had to suffer as a child.

She'd actively shunned conflict. She'd broken up with Zane the first time he'd raised a hand in anger. She'd chosen friends who were gentle people, who lived the way she aspired to, and she'd tried to choose jobs where she'd have the minimum of friction in her workplace.

Now it felt as if a Pandora's box of memories had been opened. She remembered the times her father had hit her. That had started as the occasional push and slap, and escalated to full-on beatings, as if he couldn't control his inner rage at the sorry turn his life had taken, and so he let it all out on her.

Cassie recalled, now, that there had been other fights with Elaine. And she vividly remembered the time she'd caught one of Elaine's friends in her bedroom, rummaging through her drawers. Her only weapon had been the house keys she'd been holding. She'd attacked the short, middle-aged man with them, and he'd ended up running out of the room with a cut on his face.

But he had come back, later at night.

"Hey, little honey. Are you there, girlie?"

Cassie shivered. She remembered the choking panic she'd felt hiding away from him, knowing that if he found her there, he wasn't just looking to get payback for the hurt she'd caused him— but planning to do something worse.

With shaking hands, she opened the packs of tablets she'd gotten from the pharmacy. This was not a time for half-doses; she took one of each. She had just enough water left in her glass to swallow them down.

Then she huddled onto her pillows, aching and traumatized, waiting for the pills to work so that she could finally fall asleep.

But as she waited, Cassie realized she could hear a noise coming from the other side of her bedroom door.

Cassie climbed out of bed, tiptoeing over to the door as soundlessly as she could. She listened carefully, waiting for a lull in the gusty breeze that was rattling her window.

Then she heard it unmistakably—the soft, continuous sound of breathing.

Someone was standing outside her room.

CHAPTER NINETEEN

Cassie's hand shook as she turned the key in the bedroom door. She tried to do it quietly, but it made an audible click, and then jammed. She could hear footsteps swiftly walking away.

Cassie wrestled with the lock and finally it turned. She flung the door open and stared down the corridor.

There was nobody in sight.

Who had been outside her room? Pierre? Margot?

Righteous anger led her feet of their own accord down the corridor to Pierre's bedroom. As soon as she rounded the corner, she could hear raised voices and realized they were arguing behind the closed bedroom door. So it couldn't have been either of them. It sounded like a heated and acrimonious debate and she wondered if Margot, too, had smelled the perfume on Pierre's skin, or whether they were still fighting over the way she'd behaved to Cassie earlier.

Cassie was curious to know, but the words weren't clearly audible from the other side of the door. She felt nervous about going near that bedroom again. She'd been there twice and both times it had ended badly. She didn't want to risk being discovered a third time—although in the back of her mind, she fantasized about busting open the door and walking in on their argument and demanding that they hear her side.

At least she would have had her say before she left.

As she stood undecided in the corridor, the voices stopped abruptly, and Cassie hurried back to her room.

She turned out her light and, to calm herself, took another of the tablets from the blister pack and swallowed it without any water at all. If drowsiness was a side effect, she was happy to take double the recommended dose. It was the only way she would be able to get to sleep after the trauma of the day.

As she was on the brink of sleep, she heard a scream from down the corridor that jolted her wide awake again.

Cassie sat up and turned on her bedside light, listening anxiously, wondering what was happening, and if she had remembered to lock her door when she'd returned to her room. When she heard the scream a second time, she recognized Ella's voice. The young girl must be having another nightmare, and regardless of Pierre's order to stay in her room, Cassie needed to go and comfort her.

She rummaged in her suitcase for her dressing gown, in case she ended up spending some time with Ella, and then hurried to her bedroom.

"Ella, it's me. You're OK, don't worry. I'm here."

Quickly Cassie switched on the light and closed the door in case Ella's cries alerted Margot. The last thing she needed was another late night confrontation with the deranged blonde.

"Were you having a bad dream?"

Ella was still in the throes of her nightmare. Her small fists battered Cassie and she cried out in her sleep.

"Stop it! Stop hurting me!"

Concerned about what might have caused this nightmare, Cassie gently prodded her awake.

"Everything's all right," she soothed her. "Look, here's your teddy. Do you want to sit up for a while so you can be sure you won't go back into the dream?"

Ella was boiling hot, and her back felt damp with sweat. She'd been almost buried under the covers, which would have been enough to overheat her, but Cassie hoped she wasn't running a fever too.

"Are you feeling ill?" she asked in concern.

"I had an awful dream," Ella sobbed. "I couldn't breathe, Cassie. Someone was choking me. It was horrible. I thought I was going to die!"

"Oh, Ella, that must have been so scary. I'm sorry you had that dream. But it didn't happen. Look, you're all right now. I think you might have been battling to breathe under all the covers. I don't like sleeping with covers over my head, either. Shall I open your window to let in some air?"

When Ella nodded in assent, Cassie went over to the window and opened it just a sliver, so that a breath of cool air filtered in from outside.

Standing up made her feel dizzy and disoriented, as if she were watching herself open the window from somewhere distant. She guessed it was due to the aftermath of stress.

"I'll stay with you till you fall asleep," she promised, smoothing out Ella's pillow and then helping her get comfortable again.

"What about tomorrow?" Ella asked plaintively. "Will you be here tomorrow? Or will you be gone by the time I wake up?"

Cassie wondered if Ella had been the one standing outside her room. She could have been able to see through the keyhole if she stood on tiptoes. Or perhaps she had simply been waiting outside, and heard Cassie put her suitcase on the floor followed by the sounds of packing. Either way, her guess was disconcertingly accurate and Cassie knew she would have to tell a soothing lie.

"Of course I'll still be here," she reassured the young girl, knowing guiltily that she planned to leave as soon as it was light.

The least she could do was wait until Ella had fallen into an untroubled sleep, so Cassie read her a story, choosing the one Ella said was her favorite. After the story, Ella seemed much calmer and Cassie hoped she'd forgotten her earlier dream.

Cassie sat on the edge of Ella's bed and waited until she was sure she was deeply asleep. She brushed a lock of hair away from her face, in case it fell over her mouth and made her dream that she was choking again.

Then she frowned, peering down. Was that a shadow on her neck, or something else?

Looking closely, Cassie saw the faint but unmistakable outline of a developing bruise.

Anger filled her as she stared at it. Somebody—and she could guess exactly who—had done this to Ella, perhaps only a few hours ago.

She could imagine the confrontation, how Margot might have screamed at Ella to shut up and start listening to her. When she hadn't listened or obeyed, the blonde woman must have grabbed her neck.

Perhaps she'd already been drinking by then. It seemed she was only too quick to get physical when she was angry.

Ella must have been completely traumatized by the experience. No wonder she'd been crying when Cassie had come home. She had probably erased the incident from her mind but in sleep, her subconscious had remembered, and tried to cast out the demons.

Cassie felt a surge of rage so powerful it frightened her.

As the youngest child, Ella was by far the most vulnerable to this type of abuse, and it would leave the deepest scars.

Cassie resolved that before she left France, she was going to report the family to the relevant authorities. Hopefully, Margot's abuse could be investigated and stopped. It would be the last thing she could do to help Ella, before she turned her back on the Dubois family forever.

Cassie returned to her room, still feeling as if she were having an out-of-body experience, and unable to rid herself of the anger still smoldering inside her. She didn't think she could get to sleep in this state, but knew that she'd need all her wits about her if she was going to manage to leave first thing. A sleepless night would do her no good.

She wondered if she should take a third tablet, seeing the second one had only succeeded in making her feel dizzy. Before she could think too hard about it, she took it out of the pack and dry-swallowed it. She guessed she would feel groggy in the morning but at least, for now, she could calm down and get some rest.

After what felt like an hour of uncomfortable shifting on the mattress and feeling sleep would never come, Cassie slipped straight into a nightmare.

She was following her older sister, Jacqui, through the woods. The trees were very dark, their gnarled trunks growing close together and no clear path in sight. The day—or it felt more like evening—was damp and cold, and Cassie wanted to turn back, because she had a strong sense that wherever they were heading was worse than what they were leaving behind.

"Don't be silly," Jacqui told her. "Of course we must keep going. You don't want to go back and live with Dad again, do you? Remember what happened to you there."

"But this place is dangerous," Cassie begged her sister. "We can't live in these woods. It's cold and dark, we haven't packed any clothes, there's nothing to eat. It feels scary here."

Jacqui just turned and raised an eyebrow, the way she liked to do when she was right and Cassie was wrong.

"I'm not staying there so that those people can hurt me. You can go back if you want."

"But now I'm lost. I don't know which way is out."

Cassie stared around her in panic because the trees were closing in, their cold, dark branches forming a cage around her.

"Please help me, Jacqui. Let's go back together."

And then, to her dismay, Jacqui began to taunt her.

"Poor little scared girl. Look at you. You can't stand up for yourself at all. You're weak, and you deserve to be left here on your own. I'll keep going, I'm not afraid. You stay here and see how you like it."

Jacqui started laughing, an unpleasant, high, silvery sound, and Cassie ran at her in a rage.

The trees opened up to reveal a deep ravine behind her. Cassie could have stopped, but she didn't. She shoved Jacqui with all her might and watched her hair fly out, her limbs flailing, as she tumbled to the bottom.

Staring into the gloomy depths of the ravine, Cassie saw her sister's body lying there, unmoving.

She woke, stifling a scream.

Where was she? She wasn't in bed.

Disoriented, Cassie stared around her. It was almost completely dark, but there was a sliver of light shining from under the door. She hadn't sleepwalked for years, but then again, she hadn't been so stressed for ages. She'd done it periodically during difficult times, when she was younger. It had always left her feeling completely disoriented, as if she'd been dumped back into life after being snatched out of it, and had missed out on something important along the way.

She had never been able to shake this feeling even after the doctor explained to her that her conscious mind was inactive during sleepwalking, as it occurred during the deepest part of her sleep.

She reached out, confused by the object gleaming ahead of her, and found herself grasping a shiny brass doorknob.

Cassie snatched her hand away from the cold metal, suddenly realizing where she was. She'd sleepwalked the whole way to Pierre's bedroom door. Perhaps, in her dream, she had been trying to take her longed-for revenge on Margot. It would have gone so badly for her if she'd opened the door. She could imagine the scene Margot would have made if she'd walked into the bedroom.

Quickly she turned away, finding it weird to retrace a route she'd walked in sleep and had no memory of. She realized that with Marnie's late night visit and everything that had happened that evening, she'd been too preoccupied to lock her bedroom door and that was why she had been able to leave the room so easily. If she had remembered to lock the door, and put the key on her bedside table, she was sure she would never have walked this far.

Her dream had felt so real. She remembered how the smugness on Jacqui's face had morphed to terror as she realized what Cassie was about to do. And Cassie hadn't stopped. It hadn't even crossed her mind to show compassion and give Jacqui a chance.

She felt deeply ashamed, as if she'd tapped into a seam of evil inside herself that she hadn't realized was there.

Back in her bedroom she turned the light on and, with the comfort of its glow to break the darkness, managed to sleep again eventually. She thought she had other dreams, but her sleep was too deep to remember what they were.

The chorus of birdsong told her that dawn was approaching, even though the sun was no more than a faint orange glow on the horizon. Cassie checked the time on her phone and saw, with a thrill of nerves, that it was nearly seven a.m. She needed to go. She wasn't sure if Pierre would be up yet, but if he wasn't she would wake him.

She tied her hair back and packed her cosmetics bag away after deciding not to put on any makeup for her confrontation with Pierre, even though she looked very pale. There was a visible bruise on her cheek from the struggle with Margot, and a deep graze on her wrist that was stinging badly. She stared at it, puzzled, realizing she hadn't even noticed it last night. When had that happened?

"I am leaving," she said to herself in the mirror. She tried again, this time with more resolve.

"Pierre, I am leaving. I'm not prepared to work another day in this household. I'd like to use the phone in your study to call a cab, please."

If he said no, she would simply take her bags and march out— she knew where the nursery down the road was, and she was capable of wheeling her suitcase that distance. Pierre wasn't going to stop her. She wouldn't let him.

She'd make sure to be gone before Ella woke, which would probably be in about half an hour's time. That meant it was time to act now.

She put her passport in her jacket pocket, ready to go.

She felt slightly nauseous and very thirsty, but told herself that was probably due to the triple dose of medication she'd taken. Surprisingly, the higher dosage hadn't helped with sleep. As she packed her tablets away—the last items she had to put into her bag—she realized why.

Confused by the unfamiliar packaging, she'd reached for the wrong set of pills. Instead of taking the tablets that caused drowsiness, she'd taken three of the ones the doctor had warned her about, cautioning her to take just half a tablet daily, because more than that could cause psychotic episodes.

No wonder she felt queasy this morning. With any luck, she'd slept through the worst of the effects, and the nausea would now wear off. Hoping that a drink of water would help, she went to the bathroom and drank two full glasses.

Then Cassie lifted her chin, summoned her resolve, and marched down the corridor toward Pierre's bedroom, suppressing a shiver as she approached the closed wooden door.

Raising her hand, she gave a firm knock.

"Pierre?" she called, pleased that her voice sounded steady and strong.

She waited, but heard no reply.

"Pierre, it's Cassie. I need to speak to you urgently. Are you awake?"

Still no reply. She was certain that her knocking would have woken Pierre or Margot if they had been asleep. It would be just her luck if today of all days they had left early to go out.

Well, if that was the case, she would leave a note in his study and call for a cab to come and fetch her. If Pierre wasn't there, she wouldn't let it derail her plans. In fact, it would make leaving easier.

Cassie opened the door, trying not to think about the "third time unlucky" mantra that was ringing through her head as she touched the cold metal handle.

The bedroom was empty and she saw, to her surprise, that the bed was made, even though the coverlet was mussed, as if someone had sat on it. The room was freezing, because the big French door was wide open. The lace curtains were blowing in, wafted by the icy morning air. From the open study door she heard papers rustling and she paused, wondering if Pierre was in there, but realized it must be the wind.

Cassie closed the door behind her, which settled the draft slightly.

She shivered. This felt spooky. She'd really wanted to give her notice formally, and not scurry away behind their backs, but they clearly weren't here, so she had no choice.

She'd just have to make sure the note left no room for doubt or misinterpretation. Spoken words were one thing, written words were another.

The study was in chaos; the wind had blown a pile of papers off the desk and they were lying in disorder on the floor. As she watched, another page fluttered off the mahogany surface.

Cassie hurried back into the bedroom and went to close the French doors.

The sun was rising now and it was already light. The day was perfectly clear, though breezy, and she looked out over the exquisite tapestry of the countryside, visible for miles from this high vantage point. The rolling hills, the majestic forests—though from here, they looked small—the colorful checkerboard of fields and vineyards. She wished she'd had more time to experience the beauty of this area, and in a more pleasant way. If only things could have been different.

But they hadn't been.

One of the wrought iron chairs next to the balcony rail had fallen over. Cassie stepped outside, bracing herself as a chilly gust sliced through her, blowing stray strands from her ponytail.

She bent down to pick up the chair and as she did, something caught her attention, far below. It was a bright splash of turquoise, vivid against the ornate paving stones. Puzzled, she leaned over and looked down.

Clutching the balcony, her hands slippery with sudden sweat, Cassie realized what she was seeing.

That beautiful, expensive coat, those sprawled limbs, a single lime green shoe lying on its own, dislodged during the fall.

"Oh my God," Cassie whispered. She stared down at the appalling sight for endless seconds as her brain fought to accept the reality of what was there.

Then, as her stomach churned harder, she turned and staggered inside on cotton-wool legs. She only just made it to the opulent bathroom before she was violently sick.

CHAPTER TWENTY

Hot, sour vomit burned Cassie's throat. She retched into the white porcelain toilet, vividly recalling the horror she'd seen outside.

Margot's body had been sprawled on the paving stones, unmoving. One of her legs had been bent at a hideous angle.

Margot must surely be dead … but perhaps, by some miracle, she was still alive, but unconscious or comatose.

Cassie spat into the toilet bowl and wiped her mouth. Despite the coldness of the room, clammy sweat had broken out on her forehead and armpits. She felt even dizzier than before, and when she left the bathroom she headed toward the balcony again, disoriented, before turning the other way and hurrying, on shaky legs, to the bedroom door.

"Pierre?" she shouted, as she ran down the corridor. "Pierre, where are you?"

Where was he? And, more importantly, where had he been when this happened?

Feeling nausea churn her insides again, Cassie wondered if she should be asking herself the same question. After all, she'd had that weird, unsettling dream where she'd seen a body. Was it possible she could have sleepwalked into Pierre's bedroom and looked over the balcony without realizing it? Although since it would have been totally dark, she couldn't have seen anything so far below.

In that case, though, why had the memory of pushing Jacqui over the edge of the ravine been so vivid?

Cassie called again for Pierre, and bedroom doors swung open. She saw Antoinette, dressed in her peach nightgown, standing in her doorway with guarded curiosity in her eyes. Marc shot from his room like a bullet, clutching a toy dinosaur.

"Where is Papa?" he shouted. "Papa, Cassie is looking for you!"

He thundered past her but she managed to grab him before he could run downstairs. Cassie turned back to Antoinette.

"Please, Antoinette, will you and Marc go back into your bedrooms and stay there. It's important and very serious. Don't leave your rooms. I'll explain why in a minute."

Luckily, the urgency of her tone was enough to convince Marc, and he returned to his room without argument.

Cassie went down the stairs, clutching the banister and stumbling as she ran.

She arrived in the kitchen, breathless, and the maid taking a tray from the oven looked up curiously.

"Where is Marnie?" Cassie was sobbing, tears blurring her eyes. There was Marnie, rushing over to her in concern, putting down the basket she was carrying to grasp Cassie by the shoulders as she swayed.

"What is it?" she asked. "What has happened, Cassie?"

"Call the ambulance, call the police, quickly," Cassie choked. "Margot is lying outside. She must have fallen from the balcony and I think she's dead."

"Oh my God," Marnie said. She closed her eyes briefly. Cassie saw she had turned very pale.

"Where is Pierre?" she asked.

"I don't know. He wasn't in the bedroom. He must have gone out somewhere."

Marnie nodded. "All right. Show me where she has fallen."

Cassie didn't want to go anywhere near that sprawled body, but she knew it had to be done.

Summoning all her strength of will, she walked with Marnie out of the kitchen. They went through the scullery door and around the back of the chateau, descending two more flights of outer stairs.

It was only now that Cassie realized what a steep slope the home was built on. That incredible vista from the master bedroom's balcony meant there was a three – or four-story drop to the paving below.

Marnie caught her breath when she saw the sprawled body on the ornate flagstones. She approached hesitantly, with Cassie close behind.

Cassie felt her bile rising and wanted to throw up again, even though there was nothing left in her stomach. She could see this was undoubtedly death. Margot's mouth was open, her eyes staring sightlessly upward. The pool of blood behind her head had spread and congealed on the silver-gray stones. Her skin was blue-white, and Cassie saw in horror that this made the livid bruising around her exposed neck even more visible. She could clearly see the finger marks in each purple stain.

Cassie thought Marnie muttered a prayer as she knelt and grasped the woman's outflung wrist.

"No pulse," Marnie confirmed, a tremble in her voice. "I will call the police; there is no need for an ambulance. Please can you stay with the children for now? It will be best if they remain upstairs until the police have done their work. I think you should go back to them quickly, as they may become curious."

Cassie nodded and hurried back the way she had come. She arrived upstairs just in time, because Ella was already heading down the passage toward Pierre's room, her hair mussed with sleep, calling, "Papa?"

"Ella, come back."

Cassie picked Ella up and carried her back to the little girl's bedroom, deciding it would be safer if all three children could stay together in one room.

"Please wait there, Ella," she said firmly, before going to fetch Antoinette and Marc. A few minutes later, they were all gathered in Ella's bedroom.

Cassie found she had no words. She stared at their expectant faces in silence. They had seen Margot's abusive behavior and the fight last night. That would be their last memory of Margot.

Cassie remembered how she'd grabbed hold of the long wooden mask when Margot attacked her, and how she'd thrown it at her, aiming for her face. She'd wanted to hurt Margot, because she'd thought maybe pain would make her see reason. In fact, she'd wanted to hurt Margot for what she'd said, even though she'd justified it as self-defense.

She recalled how she'd run up behind Margot with rage boiling inside her, those taunting words seared into her mind. She'd known that in those heels Margot was tall enough and the parapet was low enough, so she had shoved her hard. She thought Margot had tried to scream, but she'd managed no more than a whimper as she'd toppled and fallen into the emptiness below.

"No!" Cassie said aloud.

That hadn't happened. She was confusing the memory with her dream. After so much stress and accidentally overdosing on the wrong meds, it was no wonder the boundaries between imagination and reality felt blurred today.

She remembered how Antoinette had aimed and viciously swiped at the back of Margot's knee. When she broke the news to them, she must be sure to watch Antoinette.

"There has been an accident," she told them.

"What has happened? Is Papa all right?" Ella asked anxiously.

Antoinette said nothing.

"It's Margot. She fell last night." Cassie swallowed.

Was it her imagination or was Antoinette hiding a smile?

"Did she hurt herself?" Marc asked.

"She—she went over the balcony. She did not survive the fall. She is dead. We have to wait here until the police arrive."

She stared at the children's faces.

Ella burst into tears at the news, but in contrast, Antoinette showed no emotion whatsoever. She stared calmly back at Cassie.

Marc frowned. "What will the police do?" he asked.

"They will examine Margot and take her away," Cassie said.

Her knowledge of such matters was too sketchy to offer anything further. A knot of dread tightened in her stomach. What exactly had happened last night? The overdose of meds had left her memory fuzzy and there were gaps she couldn't fill. She barely remembered packing her bags. She thought she had gone to Ella's bedroom—or had that been the previous night? Had she really sleepwalked, or had that been part of her dream?

Cassie knew she had better try her hardest to piece together a coherent picture of the night before, because the police would undoubtedly question everyone. After all, the stone balcony was waist-high, and it would have been impossible for Margot to fall over it accidentally.

"I hear Papa," Marc said, brightening.

Cassie opened the bedroom door and picked up a babble of voices from below. Pierre's was indeed among them.

"Can I go to Papa?" Ella asked, climbing off the bed.

"No, no, definitely not. Not now." Cassie closed the door again. "He'll be very busy for the next while. I am sure the police will arrive any minute."

"Can we have breakfast, Cassie?" Antoinette asked. "I am rather hungry."

Cassie stared at her in shock. Food had been the last thing on her mind, and she'd assumed the children would be too upset to want to eat. But clearly, the news of Margot's recent demise had not affected Antoinette's appetite in the slightest.

Or else, she thought suddenly, the request for food might be a ploy to get Cassie out of the room, if Antoinette was dreaming up some mischief.

"Can you wait a little while?" she asked.

Antoinette sighed. "I suppose so."

Cassie heard the front door bang again and a fresh chorus of voices. The police must have arrived. If she'd been in her own room, she would have seen the cars approaching, but the children's bedrooms overlooked the gardens and fields at the back of the house.

Footsteps tramped up the stairs and then passed by, heading for the main bedroom. The police must be inspecting the scene, to see where Margot had fallen from. Perhaps they were also looking for clues within the bedroom itself, which would tell them what had happened.

She must remember to mention that she'd picked up the fallen chair on the balcony.

"Shall I read you a story?" she asked the children, trying to sound cheerful.

They agreed reluctantly, and Cassie chose a book she hadn't read to Ella before—it was a fairytale that she hoped would appeal to the other children as well, and keep their minds occupied. Distracted and unsettled, she found herself stumbling over the words, suddenly unable to understand the basic French that was usually like everyday language to her. Antoinette was clearly not concentrating on the story, and stricken-faced Ella was trying to listen to what was happening outside.

About half an hour later, Marnie knocked on the door.

"The police want to talk to you," she said, and Cassie saw a lean, sandy-haired man, dressed in a suit and tie, standing behind her. He looked serious and not in the least sympathetic.

Marnie was carrying a basket of snacks, and she handed out fruit and pastries to the children. Cassie wondered if she should eat something—she wasn't hungry at all, but her dizziness was getting worse, and she thought food might help to settle it.

There wasn't time, she decided reluctantly. The police officer was already walking downstairs. Following him, Cassie saw the dining room was being used as the interview room. It was only after stepping inside and closing the door that the police detective introduced himself.

"I am Detective Granger, and this is my colleague, Detective Bisset." He spoke in excellent English.

Cassie smiled nervously at the young woman in a navy blue trouser suit who was setting up a tape recorder.

"We have interviewed your employer, Mr. Pierre Dubois," Detective Granger explained. "We would like to hear your version of what occurred last night and this morning. Do you prefer the interview to be conducted in French or English?"

"French is fine," Cassie said in French, hoping that it would win her some favor with the two stern-looking officers. Although she guessed that Pierre must be the primary suspect—and she was certain he had committed this crime—she guessed she was under suspicion, too. The gaps in her memory were distressing, and they were making her feel very nervous. She didn't want to say the wrong thing, or appear to be hiding anything.

"Good. So now we begin. Take a seat here, opposite Detective Bisset. And tell me your name, date of birth, and home address for the record, please."

The first few questions were routine. Where she was from, the agency who had hired her, how long she had been with the family. Cassie noticed that Detective Bisset looked surprised when she said she had arrived only three days ago.

They talked her through what had happened that morning, asking her what she'd found when she had entered the bedroom. Cassie mentioned the knocked over chair on the balcony, and that she'd righted it and then noticed the body below.

"And why did you go into the bedroom?" Detective Granger asked.

"I wanted to ask if I could use the phone. It's in the study," Cassie said.

She didn't want to mention she'd been going to call a cab with the intention of leaving. That would surely seem suspicious. Then she realized that early morning in France would be midnight in the States, so she couldn't say she was trying to call anyone back home. Perhaps she could say she was trying to contact Jess, the au pair she'd met on the plane.

Luckily, the police didn't ask her any more about the phone call. She was relieved, but not for very long, because the questioning soon took another, more difficult, turn.

"Tell us what you have observed about the relationship between Mr. Dubois and Mme. Fabron," Detective Granger asked.

"I only knew her as Margot," Cassie said. "I didn't know her last name."

How much should she say? She found herself worrying at the tablecloth with her fingers and hastily stopped, in case this would be interpreted as a sign of guilt.

She could speak about the violent strangulation she'd seen play out in their bedroom, and the bondage equipment in the secret drawer, but that would mean explaining how she'd found it, and might lead down a dangerous road. The police would rightly ask why she'd been trespassing in her employers' private rooms. The story of the stolen passport sounded farfetched, and could only be confirmed by Ella, whom she wanted to protect.

It was all so complicated and she felt suddenly nauseous again.

"Could I have some water, please?" she asked. "I'm sorry, I threw up after seeing the body. I'm feeling very dizzy still."

"Of course."

Detective Bisset got up from her seat and brought Cassie a glass of water, and also a cup of black coffee.

Cassie spooned three sugars into the coffee and sipped it, grateful for the sweetness.

"They seemed to have a volatile relationship," she said. "Pierre and Margot, I mean. There was always an undercurrent of conflict in the house. I heard them arguing a few times when I got up to use the bathroom at night."

"Please continue," Detective Bisset encouraged her. She sounded so understanding that Cassie found herself saying more.

"Pierre is very controlling, but he doesn't seem to have a close emotional bond with the children," she said. "On the other hand, Margot appeared to be very insecure. Possessions and status seemed important to her. She reacted terribly to criticism."

"Did you like her?" The question came from Detective Granger.

Cassie hesitated. "No, I didn't dislike her, but we weren't friendly. I mean, I was only there to do a job, not to be her friend."

"I see you have a bruise on your face. And is that a graze on your arm?" Detective Granger leaned forward. "How did those injuries happen?"

"I—I can't remember," Cassie said, deciding to play it safe although she felt her heart accelerate. "I'm rather accident prone."

"We were told that you had a fight with Margot last night," Detective Granger said, and Cassie realized that the easy part of the questioning was over. She was in dangerous territory now because Pierre had already told the police his version of events.

"Yes. I had to go and do some business in town. I was late coming back because I got lost, and Margot had been drinking. She was angry that she'd been left alone with the children, because Pierre had also gone out for a while."

"Pierre said it was serious. You physically attacked each other."

"She slapped my face because she was frustrated, but the fight only lasted a moment or two. Then Margot tripped over her heels and broke a shelf," Cassie said, but she felt her face start to burn and knew the detectives must be noticing.

"When we looked in your bedroom earlier, we noticed that your bags were packed. Were you intending to leave today?"

Cassie stared at Detective Granger, horrified, wishing she'd had the presence of mind to unpack after this disaster happened. She should have realized they would check all the rooms.

"I was going to leave this morning," she confessed. "That's why I went to the bedroom, to tell Pierre I was quitting, and to call a cab."

"Are you depressed, Cassie?" Detective Bisset spoke now.

"No, I'm not depressed. I do suffer from anxiety though."

"Do you take any medication for it?"

They knew what she took already, she could tell.

"Yes, I'm on a few different pills. It's nothing unusual, I mean, lots of people are able to cope better if their anxiety is controlled," she said defensively.

Cassie was sure that the doctor had informed Pierre about the meds she was on. Or would the police have gone through her luggage? Perhaps they had.

She realized with a prickle of fear that the dispensing date was on the packets, and the police would have been able to see immediately that she'd exceeded the recommended dosage. This, too, they probably knew already.

"We understand that after your fight with Margot last night, you were sent to your room. Did you leave your room during the night, Cassie?" Granger stared at her intently.

"No," she said. "I was there all night."

And then, with a jolt, she remembered she wasn't. She had sleepwalked and had that vivid dream. She'd woken with her hand on the brass doorknob of Pierre's bedroom. There was no way she could tell the police that. She would be admitting to them that she was at the scene of the crime, without any memory of what had really happened. She didn't even know the real facts herself.

"Are you sure you didn't leave your room?" Granger asked.

Cassie grasped at another fragment of memory. Earlier that night, she'd heard Ella crying. She'd gone to comfort her and seen the bruise on her neck, and had felt uncontrollably angry about it.

"Wait, I'm sorry, I did go out during the night," she gabbled, seeing the detectives exchange a glance and Granger begin scribbling on his notepad.

"Ella, the youngest child, was having a nightmare and I went to comfort her. That was last night, of course. I've been so confused with all this stress. For a minute I thought it was the previous night. She's had them more than once."

"More than once in three days?" Granger asked, but he didn't sound disbelieving, just curious.

"Yes. It's part of the reason I decided I was going to leave," Cassie said. "I didn't think I was coping with the children well enough. On the first night I was here, Margot—"

She stopped herself hurriedly. Explaining how Margot had confronted her, abused her, and slapped her face for not attending to Ella fast enough, would only convince the police that there had been serious animosity between them.

But Detective Granger, his eyebrows raised, was waiting for her to continue.

"On the first night, Margot told me I must always go to the children. As quickly as possible, no matter how tired I was," she amended. "So even though I was told to stay in my room last night, I still went to Ella when I heard her crying."

The questions were starting to panic Cassie. She remembered Pierre's threats to her. How he had promised that if she didn't play his game, he would tell the police she'd been searching his room, and they would arrest her.

She was seriously worried that he might have told the police about that already, in an effort to paint a picture of her as unreliable and dishonest. Or, an even worse scenario, that Pierre didn't need to do that because he had a "good friend" in the local constabulary, just as the community's doctor was his "good friend."

It was obvious to Cassie what must have happened. Pierre and Margot had been fighting last night. She'd been drunk and aggressive beyond reason, and must have provoked him to violence, which he'd taken too far. They'd fought, and he'd pushed her over the balcony in a fit of rage. Then he had left in a hurry, so that he could prove he hadn't been home at the time.

Pierre was wealthy and powerful, and Cassie knew that he had no scruples about using his wealth and power to get what he wanted. He had a huge amount of influence within his community; it seemed that even those people who spoke badly of him were reluctant to discuss the facts openly, and were afraid of repercussions.

If Pierre had created an alibi for himself, Cassie knew he would need an alternative suspect, because somebody had to be accused of the crime.

If the police hadn't already arrested Pierre, that meant he was pointing them in another direction. Cassie could see already, from what he'd told the detectives, how his mind was working, and she felt sick with fear as she started to understand his plans.

Who better to take the blame for this crime than the new arrival in the community—the unstable, insignificant, and entirely dispensable au pair?

CHAPTER TWENTY ONE

Cassie sat opposite the detectives, staring down at her clasped hands with their torn and bitten cuticles. She knew how badly she'd messed up the interview. Pieced together, the evidence painted a bleak picture. The fight she'd had with Margot, and her packed bags, told a story all on their own. Her excessive use of medication, and forgetting basic facts that a responsible au pair should have remembered, would convince the police she was unreliable and untrustworthy.

She couldn't have chosen a worse time to overdose on the incorrect meds. The gaps in her memory were incriminating her, and if the police learned about the disturbing dream she had—if it was a dream at all—it would add to the weight of evidence against her.

She sensed that the writing was on the wall and she couldn't think of a way to counteract the evidence stacked up against her.

Her fears were confirmed by Granger.

"We will need to interview you again, after speaking to the children. Please remain in the bedroom with them when you go upstairs."

The questioning of the children seemed like a mere formality, a box to tick before the processes swung inexorably into action. She could picture what would happen next. She wondered whether or not they'd handcuff her, and prayed they wouldn't. She knew she wouldn't be able to handle that without breaking down completely, and if Ella saw, she would be traumatized.

As Cassie stood up, a reckless idea came to her, along with a sudden surge of hope. Perhaps she could simply run away. Would there be time? Could she leave the chalet, maybe even make it to the airport, before they noticed she had gone?

As if he'd read her mind, Detective Granger cleared his throat.

"We will require you to hand over your passport now."

Cassie's right hand dropped automatically to her jacket pocket, where it was safely zipped in.

She saw the detective had noticed her gesture. He knew she had the document on her. She couldn't buy another minute of time.

"For how long will you need it?" she asked.

Her final flicker of optimism, that perhaps they just had to make a copy of the document, was snuffed out by his brusque response.

"We'll hold it until we have concluded the investigation."

Despair sitting cold in her stomach, Cassie handed it over, hoping she would get an official receipt for it, but that didn't seem to be part of the protocol. Granger simply took it. That made her doubly nervous. She had no proof now that she was in the country legally, and also no idea where the passport would be kept. What if they lost it or it just disappeared?

Granger accompanied her back to Ella's room. Marnie, who had been supervising the children, saw Cassie's stricken face. She gave her a sympathetic smile and squeezed her hand supportively as she left. The unexpected gesture of friendship had Cassie blinking tears away.

"The crime scene team is still working in the house, so do not leave the room. Please would you come with me, mademoiselle."

Granger nodded to Antoinette.

As Antoinette followed the detective out, Cassie wondered if the forensic team would take fingerprints in the bedroom. If so they would find plenty of hers there. She'd touched many surfaces in the frantic search for her passport. The presence of those fingerprints would confirm their opinion of her as dishonest.

Even though she was shaky with hunger, she felt more nauseous than ever. She picked up the plate of food, but looking at the cream cheese croissants, fruit, and pain au chocolat that Marnie had brought made her want to throw up. She pushed the plate away.

Marc was engrossed in a comic book, but Ella was watching her curiously.

"Cassie, are you upset?" she asked.

Cassie sighed. She wanted to protect Ella from the outcome that was likely to occur, but there was going to be no way of shielding her from the truth when Cassie was escorted to the police car.

"Yes," she said. "The detectives don't know where I was last night. So that means I'm what is called a 'suspect,' and I might to go away with them just now. If I do, I don't know when I'll come back."

Ella's forehead creased and her lower lip wobbled, but to Cassie's relief she didn't burst into tears.

"Have a strawberry," Cassie said, offering her the plate.

She hoped the food would cheer Ella up or at least provide a distraction. Ella seemed calmer as she nibbled on the strawberry, but the frown didn't leave her face.

A few minutes later, Antoinette was back, and Granger marched downstairs again with Marc in tow.

Antoinette looked poised and smug, as if the questioning had been a test that she'd easily passed. Looking at her complacent face, Cassie was jolted by the memory of Antoinette saying, "I could kill her." That had been just a couple of days ago, after Margot had verbally attacked her during dinner.

Cassie knew how vicious the blonde-haired woman could be. She hadn't hesitated to say terrible things to Antoinette, even when others were present. What had she said last night, to reduce Antoinette to tears?

Cassie wondered if a twelve-year-old could push a grown woman over a waist-high balcony. She didn't think that Antoinette would have managed if Margot had fought back, but perhaps she hadn't.

She had a vision of Margot, alone on the balcony, leaning on the rail. Doing what? Perhaps throwing up, or smoking a cigarette, or maybe just pondering her life.

A determined shove from behind could have sent a drunken woman headfirst over the parapet, especially if she wasn't expecting it.

It would have been a lucky coincidence, but Cassie knew all too well about Antoinette's knack for taking advantage of a situation.

Given this ability, she was sure Antoinette would have told the police all about the fight between Cassie and Margot. Antoinette might even have exaggerated how serious it had been, which would cast further doubt on Cassie's version.

"What did the detectives ask you?" she said to Antoinette.

"Not too much."

Antoinette gave her a secretive smile, as if she sensed Cassie's anxiety. Clearly, she wasn't going to reassure her at all.

Ten minutes later, Marc arrived back and it was Ella's turn. She followed Granger obediently downstairs and Marc returned to his comic book, untroubled by his experience. Cassie guessed that they'd simply confirmed that he was in bed and asleep at the time.

They had to wait awhile before Ella's interview was concluded. Cassie wondered if she had become tearful while being questioned. She hoped that they had been sympathetic to the young girl, and not tried to bully answers out of her.

When she heard Granger's footsteps, nervousness uncoiled inside her. She took a deep breath, trying to prepare herself for what lay ahead.

To her surprise, the detective was alone. She'd expected him to bring Ella upstairs.

"Please come with me," he said to Cassie. "The scene has been cleared, and the forensics team has finished their work, so the other children can go back to their rooms now."

Cassie wanted to warn Antoinette and Marc about what might happen, but her mouth felt dry and she couldn't think of the right words. She couldn't even ask Antoinette to look after Ella and make sure she didn't peek out the window, because she had no idea where Ella had gone.

When they walked into the dining room, Cassie saw that Ella was still there. She was sitting next to Detective Bisset, holding her hand tightly.

Granger indicated to Cassie to take a seat, while he paged through his interview notes.

"Cassie, Ella Dubois has told us that you attended to her last night, as she was crying, and that you slept the rest of the night in her bedroom. Is that correct?"

Dumbfounded, Cassie stared at Ella, who innocently returned her gaze.

Cassie couldn't believe what she had heard.

This was an unexpected lifeline. Although the testimony of a five-year-old was not likely to hold up in court, for the time being it gave her an alibi and also corroborated her account of what had happened the previous night. Perhaps it had helped to redeem her in the eyes of the police. After the way she'd messed up the interview, she needed all the help she could get.

Because her account of the previous night had been so fragmented, she hadn't actually told the police that she'd gone back to her room after attending to Ella. That omission would work in her favor. She'd just have to be careful what she said now, and how she phrased it.

"Didn't I tell you that?" she asked, sounding surprised. "Ella gets very upset by her nightmares. She's terrified of them recurring. I found out on the first night I was here that the only way she could go to sleep again was if I stayed with her."

"Do you know what time you went to Ella's room?" Granger asked.

"I finished packing at about nine p.m. Then I got into bed, and as I was about to go to sleep, I thought I heard someone outside my room. I opened the door to see if one of the children needed me. There was nobody there, but I heard Pierre and Margot arguing in their bedroom," Cassie said slowly. "Then I got back into bed. I was upset by the argument and I kept listening out for the children. After all, if I had heard the shouting, they might have, too, and it would have been distressing for them."

She saw Bisset nodding and felt a flicker of encouragement as she continued.

"I remember wondering when I went to Ella's room, whether the angry voices might even have caused her nightmare. I know when I was younger I used to have nightmares after I overheard family fights. It's very disturbing on a deep level, especially for a younger child, as it erodes your sense of security."

Now Bisset was regarding her with definite sympathy.

"The timeline. Do you have an idea when Ella's nightmare happened?" Granger reminded her.

Even though the edge of accusation had gone from his voice, and he sounded carefully neutral, Cassie was sure he was waiting and watching for her to slip up. She was certain he didn't trust her account of events.

"Sorry, sorry, I got sidetracked. The timing—well, I was about to fall asleep when Ella screamed. So it wasn't too long after I got back into bed."

Granger sighed. "You didn't notice a clock? Or look at your phone?"

Cassie was about to say she hadn't when with a flash, another memory came to her.

"Wait!" she said sharply, and both detectives looked at her with sudden interest.

"The moon."

Cassie closed her eyes, trying to summon the details.

"I only remembered it now. Ella wanted air. She had been buried under the blankets and she was sweltering, so hot I thought she might have been feverish. Anyway, she had been battling to breathe so I opened her window a crack, and when I did that, I noticed that the moon was just above the horizon—almost touching the hills. I don't know if it was rising or setting. If I hadn't been so stressed about Ella, I would have spent some time watching, because it was beautiful. I should have told you earlier but it slipped my mind."

She remembered now that the moon had looked rather eerie, as well. Thinking of it made her want to shiver without quite knowing why.

Granger nodded. "That's helpful," he said. "It's not exact, but that does give us an approximate time."

He was scribbling notes furiously and Cassie guessed he would put together a timeline. She had no idea what time Pierre would have left the chateau—or claimed that he had left—or even how accurately the time of Margot's death could be determined. But Ella's testimony seemed to have saved her for now. The detectives exchanged a glance and the tight knot in Cassie's stomach eased just a little as Bisset gave a small nod.

"We will not need you to come in for further questioning at this time," Granger said decisively and Cassie felt like bursting into tears with relief.

"However, you must remain on the premises. We will still keep your passport, at least for a few more days. And we may need to interview you again."

"I'm worried about my passport. It went missing from my room once already, and I was super-stressed until I found it," Cassie pleaded. "Is there any way I could have it back?"

Before Granger spoke, Cassie could see from his face this was not an option.

"This is standard procedure we follow for every person of interest in an investigation who is not a French citizen. However, you need not worry. It will be kept safe, and we will remain in frequent contact."

Cassie guessed that was all the reassurance she was going to get. But at least, thanks to Ella, she was free to leave the room—if not the country.

Before she left, Granger handed her a business card with his name, phone number, and email. The email was useless to her in the chateau, but at least she could call the detective if she remembered anything else important.

Then Cassie took Ella's hand, and they walked out of the dining room together. She felt weak with relief as she left the room. The door had barely closed before she heard Granger and Bisset conferring in lowered voices.

Now that she was no longer worried about her imminent arrest, Cassie had another concern.

"Ella," she said gently, as they walked upstairs.

"Yes?" Ella looked trustingly up at her.

"Why did you say I was in your room all night?"

Ella shrugged, seemingly untroubled by what she'd done.

"I thought you were," she said simply. "You said you wouldn't leave me, didn't you?"

Cassie frowned, feeling uneasy at Ella's response. Did the young girl genuinely think she had stayed with her all night? Perhaps she was creating a more comforting reality for herself, where people she loved did not suddenly disappear. Or, more disturbingly, she had deliberately lied to the detectives to keep Cassie with her.

Either way, although she was still a suspect, Ella's words had given the police enough reasonable doubt not to arrest her on the spot.

That meant, surely, that the police would focus on Pierre again.

Cassie was certain that he would be asked to accompany the detectives for further questioning. As she unpacked some dolls for Ella to play with, she wondered what she should tell the children. It might be better to leave the details and just say Pierre had gone out.

Cassie helped Ella arrange the dolls in a circle, balancing them on wooden chairs. They were having a tea party. Ella chatted happily to herself as she pretended to pour the tea. She seemed unfazed by her encounter with the police, and Cassie wondered again whether she'd purposely lied.

When she heard voices in the hallway, Cassie jumped up and ran to her bedroom, where she had the best view of what was happening outside the front door.

Peering through the window, she saw the two detectives heading toward a white Citroen. Bisset put on a pair of dark glasses and climbed into the driver's seat. Granger, who was carrying a large briefcase, opened the trunk and stowed it inside, before hurrying to the passenger side, tugging his jacket closed against the chilly, gusting drizzle.

Pierre wasn't with them, so they couldn't be questioning him again. Where did that leave the investigation? Cassie pressed her lips together, wondering whether Pierre really did have the local police in his pocket as she'd feared. And if so, what that meant for her.

As she watched the unmarked sedan depart, Cassie considered her own situation.

With her passport unavailable to her, she was a prisoner in Pierre's house. He knew his efforts to pin the blame for Margot's death on Cassie had failed. She wondered if Pierre would be angry about that, or whether he would try to resolve the situation another way.

As the Citroen drove off, Cassie's arms prickled with gooseflesh as she thought about what another way might mean.

Realizing her breath had misted up the bedroom window, she moved back. There was no point in staring through the foggy glass. The police had gone, leaving her in a house where a suspicious death had occurred, without any means of escaping.

Cassie tried to calm herself by applying logical thought.

She was sure that if there had been enough evidence, the police would have arrested Pierre, or at least taken him in for further questioning. Perhaps that meant there were factors at play that she didn't know about. Somebody else could be a suspect or the police might even think it had been accidental. For all she knew, Pierre had last seen Margot dancing crazily on the balcony with a bottle of vodka in her hand.

If she could find out more, she'd know if she was in danger or not.

Unfortunately, Pierre was the only person who could give her that information.

Cassie would have preferred to avoid Pierre altogether. The thought of speaking to him about this made her palms start to sweat.

She would need to make sure he didn't become suspicious. She would have to ask innocent questions, while implying that she didn't think he had been involved. If she was able to walk that tightrope without triggering his temper, then her mission would be successful.

Cassie decided she'd better look for him now, before she lost her nerve.

CHAPTER TWENTY TWO

Although she would rather not have gone anywhere near the master bedroom, Cassie knew she had to check it, and since it was the closest place that Pierre might be, she should look there first. She headed down the corridor, hoping that Pierre was somewhere else, and that she wouldn't have to go inside.

As soon as she rounded the corner, she saw the door was open.

Cassie approached hesitantly, realizing that this was her chance to see how thoroughly the police had examined the room.

She peeked inside, and saw to her relief that it looked exactly as she had seen it earlier. She couldn't spot any signs of fingerprint dust. Although she'd never seen it in real life, she knew from books she'd read that it was dark gray and supposed to be very messy. There was no sign of any dark gray powder in the room, which hopefully meant the police hadn't thought it necessary to take fingerprints at all.

Cassie wondered if the open door meant Pierre might be in the study. She called his name softly, but there was no response.

She had already turned away when a sound stopped her in her tracks.

It was the loud, persistent peal of the telephone.

The phone rang and rang. Three rings, four, five.

There must be an answering machine, Cassie thought, or another phone elsewhere in the house, which would be answered at any moment.

Even so, she found herself tiptoeing into the bedroom, across the ornate carpet, and into the study.

It could be Detective Granger, calling to warn her about something. It could even be Zane, continuing to harass her.

The thought of Zane gave her the courage to pick up the phone.

"Hello," she said hesitantly.

There was a short silence and then a man's voice spoke.

"Margot?" he said. "Is that Margot?"

Spooked by hearing the name, Cassie nearly dropped the phone.

"No!"

The word came out louder than she'd meant. She paused, wondering what to say next, and how to break the news to this caller.

"She's—"

Cassie was going to tell him, "She's dead."

But as she started to speak, there was a click, and the caller disconnected.

Cassie replaced the phone carefully on its stand and left Pierre's study, wondering who could have been calling, and why. She had meant to say more after she'd gotten over the shock of hearing him ask for Margot, but the man hadn't given her the chance to say anything at all.

He'd obviously not known Margot had died. The police would have notified her family by now, so it must have been someone else. Margot's hairdresser, her jeweler, her fashion designer? Ideas, limited by her basic knowledge of the blonde woman, flitted through her mind but she rejected them all for the same reason—surely an innocent caller would have listened to what Cassie had to say? This man hadn't listened. He'd hung up in a rush.

What else had she picked up from that brief conversation?

He hadn't known Margot well enough to recognize her voice. And there had been background noise—as he'd said "Margot," Cassie had heard another phone ringing in the distance, which meant he could have been calling from an office.

More than that, Cassie couldn't say, but she decided it would be wiser not to tell Pierre about this strange call. It would be more sensible to inform Detective Granger when they spoke again.

❖   ❖   ❖

Before Cassie went downstairs, she checked the children's rooms to see if they needed her.

Ella was still contentedly occupied with her dolls, but Marc's bedroom was empty. Cassie hoped she would find him while looking for Pierre. She knew what destruction Marc was capable of causing, if left unsupervised for any amount of time.

Antoinette answered her knock with a polite, "Come in."

Cassie was struck, once again, by how calm and composed Antoinette appeared to be. She was lying on her bed reading, with a cup of cocoa on the bedside table, as if she hadn't a care in the world.

"Are you all right? Can I bring you anything?" Cassie asked.

"Perhaps later," Antoinette replied coolly. "I am enjoying my book now, thank you."

Cassie headed downstairs, deciding her first stop would be the garage, so she could check if Pierre was home or if he'd gone out.

She headed out of the front door and into the gray, breezy freshness of the early afternoon. The wind was chilly, slicing through her light jacket, and she wrapped her arms around herself for warmth as she hurried to the garage, where a quick glance confirmed that all the cars were in their places.

As she left the garage, Cassie heard a loud explosion from the nearby greenhouse. She jumped at the sound, her heart accelerating, realizing how fragmented her nerves were. The slightest stress was sending her over the edge.

The noise had sounded like smashing glass. Frowning in concern, she detoured to the greenhouse.

Marc had found his way to the back of the greenhouse and was picking up stones from the orchard, hurling them at the big glass panes. He'd already smashed three of them, and as Cassie hurried over to him, he scored a perfect hit on a fourth with a fist-sized rock. It punched through the pane, leaving a splintered gap.

"Marc, come here, you mustn't do that," Cassie cried, horrified by the extent of the destruction. "Your father will be angry."

Seeing that this wasn't having the desired effect on him, Cassie tried again.

"And the plants will get cold. You don't want the poor plants to get cold, Marc, do you?"

Thankfully, the welfare of the plants proved to be a more persuasive argument, and Marc abandoned the pile of rocks he'd carefully gathered and sprinted over to her.

"Cassie, I am hungry. I went to the kitchen to ask Marnie for food, but she wasn't there."

"OK, come with me. Let's see if we can find you something."

She retraced her steps around the front of the house again, rather than taking the shortcut round the back, because that would lead past the place where she'd seen Margot's body.

Walking into the kitchen, Cassie realized that this was the first time she had seen it empty. Pierre obviously hadn't wanted the staff to watch while the police collected Margot's body, and she guessed he had given them the rest of the day off.

Opening the fridge, she saw a large, covered plate of sandwiches and a big pot of beef stew. She packed some of the sandwiches into a container.

"Why don't you take these upstairs, Marc, and see if your sisters would like to share them? I'll be there in a minute, and I'd love to play soldiers with you."

His eyes widened as he took the container.

"But Cassie, there are only enough sandwiches here for me!"

Chortling victoriously, he sped upstairs, and as he disappeared, Cassie heard the crunch of gravel and voices outside.

A moment later, the front door opened and Pierre walked in. He was wearing a warm jacket and a scarf. Behind him, she saw a golf cart with the winery's logo driving away, and realized he had been inspecting the vineyards.

Nervousness boiled inside her as she remembered how cautiously she would have to tread.

"I'm so sorry about Margot. This has been such a huge shock," she said in a wobbly voice.

Pierre seemed preoccupied, as if he wasn't really focused on her, which suited Cassie fine.

"Yes. It is a tragedy," he agreed, taking a bunch of keys from the dish on the hall table.

"Do you know why the police didn't make an arrest?"

Cassie forced the question out, her voice high and squeaky with fright.

"The investigation will take some time to conclude." Now Pierre looked directly at her, and she saw his hair was ruffled from the breeze, his face etched into deep, stern lines.

"It is perfectly obvious what happened, though," he continued. "Margot committed suicide. So it is doubtful any arrests will be made."

Cassie stared back at him, struggling not to show her incredulity at Pierre's words.

"Margot committed suicide?" she repeated.

All she could think of was that dizzying drop down to the marble flagstones far, far below. What would it have taken for Margot—for anyone—to climb over the balcony and launch herself into that void, to feel the rush of icy air as she plummeted down, knowing that her body would be smashed and broken by the fall?

Cassie couldn't believe it was possible, but Pierre nodded distractedly.

"She was depressed. She was—unstable. You saw how she behaved. She was drinking heavily. Her death is most certainly a catastrophe, but the decision to end her life was hers alone."

He walked to the front door.

"I am going out now. I will be back later this evening. There is food in the kitchen, I believe. Will you be capable to heat the food, serve supper to the children, and put them to bed?"

Cassie nodded wordlessly, and Pierre strode out, closing the door behind him.

She stood in the hallway for a few minutes, trying to take in what Pierre had said.

Suicide? Margot?

Had the viciousness and hatred she showed to the world been a reflection of her own self-loathing?

Cassie shook her head hard. Margot had everything. She was a pampered princess. If she was depressed, she could have afforded any medication she needed; she was sure Pierre's doctor would unhesitatingly have prescribed whatever was necessary.

And that death? For someone so vain? Why not an overdose of pills, or a razor cut in the bath? Why choose that terrifying leap into darkness? It made Cassie's hands sweat just to think of what it would have taken to do it.

She walked upstairs slowly, deciding that Pierre must be lying, because there was no way this version could be true.

He had made it up to protect himself and Cassie didn't believe him at all.

The day's events had taken their toll on the children, who were all tired and sulky at supper and didn't resist an early bedtime. Emotionally frazzled and exhausted, Cassie unpacked her bags—which had clearly been searched by the police, even though her belongings had been replaced.

Then she went to bed after locking her door and making sure that she took the recommended dosage of her medication, even though she was tempted to take an extra tablet to ensure a dreamless sleep.

Once again, she was haunted by nightmares.

The first, vivid dream was of Jacqui. Her sister was facing her, her shiny hair blowing in the wind. In the dream, it was a bright, light blonde. Behind her was the ravine, deeper and more deadly than Cassie remembered it. Its steep sides fell away into a bottomless void.

Jacqui was holding onto a twisted tree trunk as she taunted Cassie.

"You're nothing better than a cheap slut. You deserve the miserable life you have. I have a better one. And I'm laughing at you, now, you pathetic, sad little loser."

Cassie felt her lips curl back in rage. She rushed at Jacqui, and her sister's taunts turned to screams. Her long, red fingernails clutched the tree, clawing at the bark, but Cassie saw its roots were weak and loose, and she knew what she needed to do.

She shoved the stunted, shriveled tree as hard as she could, and Jacqui screamed in terror, flailing her arms as the tree toppled over the ravine, taking her with it. Her screams went on and on, and Cassie realized she was screaming too.

"It's not real! It's not real," she shouted, and her terrified cries yanked her out of the dream and into comforting reality, back in the chateau.

But she wasn't in bed. She was wrapped in her dressing gown, looking at the moon again. It was a familiar sight, just as she remembered it, exactly as she'd told the police. The moon was almost full, low on the horizon. Its reddish glow illuminated the scattered clouds around it and the dark hills below. The sight was hypnotic, spooky, and beautiful. Chilly air blew toward her; the night was cold as ice.

Cassie knew for certain this was more of a memory than a dream.

But as she looked around, she realized she had plunged into a new nightmare, a more disturbing and terrifying one than she'd left behind. Dread filled her, because she wasn't in Ella's bedroom in this dream; she wasn't there at all, she'd gone somewhere else—perhaps while sleepwalking, but again, maybe not.

She was watching the moon from the ornate stone parapet of Pierre's balcony.

CHAPTER TWENTY THREE

Detective Granger poured himself a refill of coffee from the jug in the kitchenette before making his way back to his compact office. Here, the air conditioning rattled on its warmest setting—everyone joked that Granger was born cold-blooded—and the blinds were open just enough to give him a view of the Marne River. He loved this sight, enjoyed being able to look down at nature, to see happy people going about their lives, even when, like today, it was gray and rainy.

He placed the coffee on a side table where it wouldn't be accidentally knocked over, and turned his attention back to the files and papers spread out in front of him, representing his newest case.

The death of Margot Fabron.

Granger picked up his pen and unplugged his cell phone from the charger. What a relief to have a signal; it had felt stifling to be unable to call or message while at the chateau. Certainly, it complicated this case, because cell phone location and triangulation, the timing of messages sent and received, often played an important part in confirming alibis.

That facility would certainly have been helpful here. As it was, Pierre Dubois had told the police he kept his personal cell phone in his office in Champigny-sur-Marne, due to the lack of signal at home. He hadn't known where Margot's phone was, but had said she seldom used it for the same reason.

Granger had asked Pierre to hand his own phone in, and had requested a call log from Margot's phone as well as from the landline that appeared to be the chateau's only means of communication with the outside world.

In the meantime, he reread his interview notes.

Monsieur Dubois claimed that he had left the chateau sometime after nine-thirty p.m. last night. He said that Margot Fabron had been drunk and quarrelsome, and he had not wanted to get involved in an argument. He had told Margot he would spend the night in the "chalet"—a small, luxury cottage located near the estate's vineyards that was occasionally used to accommodate visiting journalists. Pierre had said he would be back in the morning and they could discuss things when she had calmed down and sobered up.

In fact, Pierre had gone nowhere near the chalet, but had instead headed out to visit his mistress, a young divorced woman who lived in Valenton. It was there he had spent the night. Her home had security cameras, and when the police visited yesterday afternoon, she had confirmed the story and even provided camera footage with time stamps that showed Pierre's car arriving at the gate at ten-fifteen p.m. and leaving the following morning, at six-thirty a.m.

The autopsy would be taking place today, and Granger hoped the report, or at least the initial findings, would be available by late afternoon. He didn't know how accurately the time of death could be confirmed. It might be a game-changer, or completely inconclusive.

Pierre's status as a well-known businessman was a complicating factor. Despite the fact he was an adulterer and a liar, the man had power, prestige, and influence in the area. That meant the police had to tread carefully. A wrongful arrest would be a catastrophe.

Margot's family, on the other hand, were not locals. Her parents were divorced; her mother lived in Normandy, and her father in Occitanie, in the south of France. They had been shocked to hear of their daughter's death, but neither of them had been close to her since she left home, and Margot had been an only child.

Interestingly, Granger got the impression that Margot's family was not wealthy. Her mother told Granger that Margot had worked as a model in Paris until she was twenty-two, and in the course of her work, had met Pierre. She had given up modeling and managed one of his art galleries for a couple of years, before moving in with him after the death of Pierre's wife last year.

Granger was convinced that their relationship had probably started much earlier, probably around the time of Margot's career change.

His thoughts were interrupted by a tap on his door. Bisset walked in carrying a sheaf of notes which she placed on the desk. She looked around the office and then, in a meaningful way, at the air conditioning dial.

"It is very hot in here," she observed.

Granger shrugged apologetically. "I do not enjoy the cold. Turn it down if you like."

"For a few minutes, I think I can survive." Bisset pulled up a chair and sat opposite him.

"Background checks for the au pair are confirmed," she said. "Cassie Vale was hired by the agency as she stated, no previous convictions, no criminal record."

Granger shook his head.

"She is a terrible witness. It is difficult to believe anything she says. Her story changes like the wind." He moved his hand to illustrate.

Bisset nodded in agreement.

"Her description of the moon sounds accurate, though," she said. "I checked the times. The bedrooms on that side of the house face southwest, so she would have seen the setting moon, and opened Ella's bedroom window somewhere between nine-thirty and ten p.m."

Granger frowned. "I just pray we do not have to put her on the witness stand. Under questioning, I am sure she would surprise us all with new information. Most probably, she would even surprise herself."

"I agree," Bisset said. "And the testimony of a five-year-old child is not going to hold up in any court. But if Margot's death was suicide, as Pierre Dubois claims, that would clear her."

"If it was"—Granger emphasized the word "if"—"Margot and Pierre were living together for a year, and probably lovers for much longer than that. She arrives, and suddenly there is a death."

"Yes, the timing is coincidental. I was also wondering…" Bisset stared thoughtfully down at her notes.

"Go on?" Granger reached for his coffee.

"She's a pretty girl. The au pair, I mean. And Monsieur Dubois is, from his own account, an adulterer. The relationship with the fiancée was stormy. Then along comes somebody new. Could he and Cassie have colluded to murder Margot Fabron?"

Granger nodded. "It's a possibility. But she'd been there only three days. How much of a whirlwind romance can you have within three days?"

Bisset smiled. "Celebrities have met, married, and divorced in a shorter time."

"True. So we don't rule that out. But I strongly feel there's more to the story, and it is not as simple as we think. Some facts are missing."

"We should know more after the coroner's report," Bisset said. "They've just emailed me and said it will be completed within the next few hours."

She looked out the window, admiring the view.

"Look, the rain is stopping. I think I will take some time off now and go for a nice stroll by the river to cool down."

Granger, to his surprise, found himself laughing along with her.

"You should be so lucky, to have the chance to do that today."

As soon as the report was submitted, Granger and Bisset met again.

This time, as it was going to be a longer meeting, Granger brought his files through to the conference room. Here, there was more space, which pleased him, and the air conditioning was set a few degrees cooler, which satisfied Bisset.

Granger printed out two copies of the report, controlling the surge of excitement he always felt when hoping the body itself would reveal secrets that the living were hiding. He reminded himself sternly to have no expectations, to make no assumptions, but simply to interpret what the evidence said.

He handed a copy to Bisset, and for some minutes they paged through, reading carefully.

"There are some interesting details here," Granger said eventually.

The biggest and most shocking revelation, the one that jumped out at him, was the fact that Margot Fabron had fresh strangulation marks on her neck, no more than two days old. The bruising was significant, the coroner reported, and there was still some minor swelling in her throat. That was compelling evidence that her relationship with Pierre Dubois had been neither normal nor happy and that detail caused Granger a flare of excitement.

In addition, her blood alcohol level was just below 0.20. At the time of her death, she was seriously intoxicated and in addition, the report showed the presence of antidepressant drugs and sleeping tablets in her bloodstream.

"The strangulation is a significant detail," Bisset said. "But it's a shame the time of death can't be more accurately calculated."

Granger nodded. That was the biggest disappointment in the report. The coroner stated that from her body temperature, Mme. Fabron had died somewhere between ten p.m. and midnight. As Granger had expected, it was impossible to tell from the angle of the fall whether she had in fact jumped or been pushed. The overturned chair that the au pair had mentioned could point to evidence of a struggle, or simply mean that Fabron had used it to climb onto the parapet and knocked it over in the process.

"So, what is our next step?" Bisset asked.

"Serial womanizing, violent tendencies," Granger said. "We need to investigate Pierre Dubois's background in more detail.

Find out about previous partners and affairs. This can't be his first or only mistress. Where are the others? What can they tell us? Also, Dubois said his wife passed away a year ago in a car accident. Let's get the details regarding that."

Bisset nodded.

"One other item for the list," she said. "Pierre mentioned he'd fetched Margot from the hairdresser earlier that day. I'd like to find out who that person is and speak to him or her. Women talk to their hairdressers and often disclose personal details—if there was anything going on in Margot's life, any personal conflicts or situations she felt uneasy about, the hairdresser might be able to tell us more. Especially since that visit was shortly before she died."

"Good idea. Will you contact the hairdresser, then?"

Granger closed the folder, frustrated that the evidence was not conclusive, but hopeful that they had new avenues to explore.

He himself had come from poor parents who had battled to afford a better life for their children. He knew what it was like to have to struggle to make something of yourself, and what an enormous handicap poverty could be. He had seen the advantage family wealth conferred, and how far ahead of the pack it placed you.

Because of this, Granger had an innate dislike for Pierre. He sensed arrogance in him, and a belief that he was above the law. Pierre knew he held all the aces, and would use them as he pleased to ensure the minimal personal or reputational damage.

Even so, Granger knew he had to separate emotion from logic. If any foul play had occurred, the nervous au pair, with her vacillating story and flimsy alibi, was far more likely to have been involved. After all, Pierre wasn't the only man ever to have indulged in an affair, and his otherwise good reputation in the area would have been earned over many years.

Perhaps Bisset was right, and the two had conspired together. Or else, jealousy could have played a role. Margot was not much older than Cassie. After seeing what the other woman had, following a bitter fight between them, it could have pushed Cassie to commit a hot-blooded crime.

Granger sighed. He'd have to put his own personal prejudice against Pierre aside, follow protocol, interview witnesses, and let the evidence speak for itself.

Even if Pierre held all the aces, Granger suspected that the unreliable au pair would probably end up being the joker in the pack.

Chapter Twenty Four

Cassie shifted uncomfortably on the cold, hard church pew. Ella sat statue-still on her left, while Marc fidgeted nonstop on her right. Despite the cold, rainy weather, there must have been close to a hundred people gathered in the historic chapel for Margot's funeral service.

The interior was cold and drafty, and the gas heaters placed throughout did little to dispel the chill. Looking at the chapel's ancient stone walls which seemed imbued with the smell of incense, and the exquisitely crafted stained-glass windows, Cassie guessed it was centuries old, and must have seen thousands of similar events in the past.

She had never imagined that less than a week after arriving in France, she would be attending the funeral of one of the family she worked for, and still less, that the death would have taken place under such suspicious circumstances.

Pierre, clad in an impeccably cut black suit, his hair perfectly styled, was sitting in the front row, flanked by Margot's parents. His head was bowed. From time to time, he took a pristine white handkerchief from his pocket and dabbed his eyes.

He was playing the part of the bereaved fiancé to perfection, and though it was a stellar performance, Cassie simply didn't buy it. Why did nobody else suspect him? The unanimous opinion seemed to be that Margot's death was a suicide. Even the priest, in his sermon, referred to "the tragic act" Margot had committed, and how "our all-forgiving God" would welcome and absolve her regardless.

What if somebody else was to blame, Cassie thought, staring at the priest fiercely, as if her gaze could force him to admit there might be another reason for Margot's death.

As the service drew to a close, the priest invited the congregation to accompany him to the nearby graveyard, where Margot's ashes would be laid to rest.

Trying to keep hold of an outsized umbrella and two children—one of whom wanted to run laps round the graveyard's neat gravel paths, and the other who was lagging behind and complaining about the rain, Cassie didn't have a chance to notice very much until they had reached the graveside.

Scanning the crowds, she saw Marnie and a few other staff from the chateau, and she noticed with surprise that Bisset was also attending, wearing a black dress and smart gray coat. Although she stood still with her head lowered, Cassie noticed the detective's eyes were alert and her gaze was constantly on the move. It reassured her to know that she wasn't the only one who had suspicions about Margot's death. The police, too, were hopefully there to observe.

Realizing that Bisset was staring directly at her, Cassie dropped her gaze hurriedly.

"We therefore commit her body to the ground," the priest said loudly, bringing Cassie's attention back to the service. "Earth to earth, ashes to ashes, dust to dust."

As the finality of the words rang out, Cassie heard sobs and cries from all around her. Pierre embraced Margot's mother, his head bowed and his shoulders shaking. Margot's father buried his face in his hands. Ella, after an astonished look at everybody else crying, burst into loud sobs herself, and even Marc, sensing the solemnity of the moment, stood quietly.

Looking across the gravesite, through the drizzling rain, Cassie saw there was only one person entirely unaffected by the emotion of the moment, and as she watched, her suspicions flared up again, this time in a different direction.

Antoinette, her head high, her eyes dry, and her dark blue beret arranged at a perky angle, was watching the urn being lowered with a small, secretive smile.

Cassie drove back to the chateau in a convoy of cars. She hadn't realized so many people would be attending the wake. It seemed as if every person who had been at the funeral was heading back for food and drinks.

"Can we go and play in the orchard?" Marc asked, as she parked the Peugeot.

"No, not yet," Cassie said firmly. Marc's smart black shoes were already covered in mud from the trip through the graveyard—despite her best efforts, he'd detoured off the main pathway. She could only imagine what mischief he would get up to in just a few unsupervised minutes, showing off for the guests.

Of course, as soon as she unlocked the car, he darted out, and Cassie was forced to hunt him down in the muddy, leaf-strewn orchard. By the time she'd caught up with him, grabbed him, and gone back to collect Ella, her boots were also mud-spattered and she'd snagged her black suede jacket on a branch and torn a hole in it.

Cassie hesitated at the front door, taking in the crowd of mourners inside. A dark-clad violinist was playing in the hallway, and the formal lounge and dining room had been opened up. A fire burned in the fireplace, and the long dining room table had been loaded with food of every kind. Crystal glasses were set out on the sideboard, along with a selection of wines, sherries, beers, and brandies. Cassie tightened her hold on Marc's arm, knowing she couldn't leave him alone for a moment with so many breakable items in plain sight.

As more and more people arrived, Cassie found her stress levels rising. Antoinette, still icily composed, was seated on an ottoman sipping a small glass of sherry which Cassie prayed she was allowed, because she hadn't poured it for her.

Ella and Marc demanded two plates of food each, which kept them busy for a while, but when the lure of the food table wore off, they started becoming bored and unmanageable. Cassie found it impossible to keep hold of Marc, comfort Ella, and politely interact with the other guests. In addition, she was starving, and hadn't had the chance to get any food for herself. She felt trapped in her role, and was suddenly desperate to get out of this claustrophobic space.

"Are you the au pair?"

Yet another black-clad mourner greeted her, just after she had settled Ella down on the ottoman next to Antoinette.

"Yes." Cassie forced a polite smile.

"Isn't it a tragedy? Did you know Margot was so depressed?"

Cassie guessed this woman, like many of the others, must be connected to Pierre. She wore a pearl choker and diamond earrings, with a fur stole draped over her shoulders. In contrast, Cassie had noticed Margot's parents were more plainly dressed and her mother didn't seem to be wearing any jewelry at all.

"I'd only been there three days when it happened," Cassie said, trying to maintain eye contact while hanging on for grim death as Marc, who had refused to sit down with the others, used the opportunity to make a serious break for freedom.

"Ah, you arrived so recently?"

"Yes. I'm still settling in and finding my feet. It was a terrible shock. And of course, it's been stressful for the children."

Cassie's smile had become a rictus. Sensing her distraction, with a twist of his arm, Marc pulled free and vanished into the throng.

"Yes, poor things, I remember it was this time last year their mother passed away, although I couldn't attend her funeral as I was abroad. She crashed her car, you know, late at night, on the main road going toward Guignes."

Lowering her voice, the woman elaborated, "It left the road, rolled multiple times, and burst into flames. I don't think they ever found out the cause of the accident. What a tragic year Pierre has had."

"Nobody should have to deal with so much loss in such a short time. If you'll excuse me, I must just keep an eye on Marc," Cassie said, before turning away.

Where had the boy gone? Her first stop was the dining room, but thankfully he wasn't there. She took the opportunity to grab three sausage rolls, stuffing them into her mouth and turning her face to the wall so she could chew and swallow quickly, without anyone talking to her.

Marc must have headed outside to burn off his energy after eating all those cakes, pies, and pastries. Cassie weaved her way back through the lounge and took a detour to the left, just in case he'd found his way into the music room.

Thankfully, he hadn't, and the room was empty. Cassie pushed the door closed and slumped down on the piano seat, unable to face the crowds for the moment.

The bejeweled woman she'd just spoken to had dropped another bombshell. Cassie found it deeply troubling that Pierre's wife had died under such mysterious circumstances. Where had she been going late at night? What had caused the car to lose control so badly? It sounded as if it had been a single-vehicle accident. And now, another tragic death had occurred. Why was nobody questioning all of this? Cassie wanted to scream.

She buried her head in her arms, wishing she was anywhere other than here.

In the darkness, she relived the fight she'd had with Margot.

How she'd fought her off, twisting away from those lethal spiked heels. How Margot's screamed insults had assaulted her, piercing deep into her soul.

"Bitch! Whore!"

She'd hated Margot for her viciousness, her entitlement, her complete lack of empathy or even recognition of Cassie as another human being. How did you get to be so aggressively self-obsessed, believing you were better than everybody else and could treat them exactly as you pleased?

One thing was for sure, even if you weren't supposed to speak badly of the dead, Cassie thought she'd deserved what she had gotten.

She remembered how she'd looked down from the parapet and seen Margot vanish into the darkness below, limbs flailing, under the cold light of that serene moon.

"No!" Cassie shouted aloud.

She opened her eyes wide, breathing deeply, staring down at the richly patterned carpet. It hadn't happened. It hadn't. It was her own fantasy, intermingled with the nightmares she'd been having about Jacqui, and the view of the moon from Ella's room. She hadn't really done that. She couldn't have.

"Are you all right?"

Cassie jumped, realizing Pierre had walked into the room and was closing the door behind him. He must have heard her shout. He could never know what she'd been thinking.

She scrambled hurriedly to her feet.

"Yes, I'm fine. I'm so sorry, I've been with the children the whole time but Marc went outside, and I was just taking a minute to gather myself before I looked for him. It's been such an emotional day."

She made to leave, but he stopped her, his hand heavy on her shoulder.

"It has indeed been an emotional time. For me, worst of all. I am feeling very alone, Cassie. At times like this, we realize how vulnerable we are, how fragile life is. Come here, hold me, let us comfort each other for a moment."

The last thing she wanted was mutual comfort from Pierre. The idea made her skin crawl, but since a refusal at this time would be heartless, she stepped reluctantly into his arms. He drew her tightly into his embrace while her arms clasped loosely round his waist. Her cheek was crushed against the perfectly stitched woolen lapel of his suit.

"Ah, Cassie. You are so young, so beautiful, so alive. I think you do not know your own beauty."

Too late, she realized she was trapped in his grip. His breathing had changed and roughened. His hands roamed down, to her waist, to her hips. He pressed her into him, cupping her buttocks with his right hand, kneading and squeezing them while his left hand pinned her close. He bent his head to hers, his breath tickling her ear.

"We shall console each other. Not tonight; I have other obligations as some guests are staying over. But soon, I will come to your room, or maybe I will bring you to mine, so that the children do not hear us. I see how caring you are to them, how concerned. But you cannot think of pleasing them all day and all night. You must think of your employer, too, no? You must please the man who has given you this job."

"No," Cassie cried, but her face was pressed into the smothering wool and her voice was muffled.

Shell-shocked by what was happening, Cassie wondered if she should just grit her teeth and endure the experience, violating as it was. With so many people next door, surely this was just a grope taken too far, and he would stop at any moment?

But then she realized this was Pierre. His home, his rules. He would stop whenever he felt like it, and probably not at all. Worse still, every moment she spent in his arms would be seen as passive consent, giving him the entitlement to continue.

"No!" she shouted, louder this time, and she knew he had heard her but he didn't stop.

She tried to push him away, but his arm clamped like a vise around her. As she struggled in his grasp, he found the gap between her skirt and top and his hand slipped inside, into her clothing, under her panties—his fingers splayed out, hot against her bare flesh.

Panic flooded Cassie. She did not consent to this, not at all, not to any part of it, and she wasn't going to let Pierre fool himself into thinking so.

In any case, this was his fiancée's funeral, for crying out loud—could there ever be a more inappropriate time for him to force himself on her?

The outrage provoked by that thought gave Cassie the courage to act. She twisted to the right, just far enough to grab the only item that she could see out of the corner of her eye. It was one of a set of old, hard-covered encyclopedias in a shelf next to the piano.

She lifted the book and slammed it as hard as she could into Pierre's head.

The heavy volume caught him on his left temple. It was no more than a glancing blow, but it was painful and unexpected, and it was enough to make him let go of her.

Adrenaline gave her wings as she squirmed away and dodged past him, heading for the door. She snatched it open, hearing his cry of rage as she escaped, not daring to look back but knowing his face would be set in a thunderous frown, flushed dark with anger.

Then she was out, her heart pounding, her hair in disarray, her blouse pulled loose from her skirt and its top button missing. But she'd escaped him, and was back in the safety of the crowds.

Totally shaken by what had just occurred, Cassie decided to give up on the search for Marc. She needed to go to her room, get herself tidied up, and try her best to regain enough composure to get through the rest of this endless afternoon, even though she felt like lying on her bed and sobbing in hysterical reaction at the horror of Pierre's assault.

But when she headed that way, she saw Bisset standing at the foot of the staircase. As she approached, she noticed the detective was looking at her curiously.

Cassie turned away immediately and walked outside, worried that her disheveled appearance would make Bisset suspicious. If any questions were asked, it would only be her word against Pierre's. The police would eventually leave, and she'd be on her own, faced with Pierre's fury. The consequences for her would be unthinkable.

With coldness tightening around her heart, Cassie realized the consequences already were.

Pierre had said there were guests at the chalet tonight, but they would leave tomorrow.

She knew Pierre would not be discouraged. She had bought herself a couple of days' grace at the most. He'd be coming after her again—angrier this time, more determined than ever, and prepared for anything she might do.

There was nobody who could protect her from this, and without her passport, she was imprisoned here.

Suddenly, Cassie wondered if Margot, too, had been a prisoner in her seemingly perfect life, and if her death had been the punishment for trying to escape.

CHAPTER TWENTY FIVE

Cassie barely slept that night. Her mind was buzzing with ideas as she tried to think of workable ways that she might escape her situation. She'd come up with plenty of plans for how to get away, as well as ways she could protect herself while she was at the chateau, but every single one was impractical, or simply impossible.

Near the end of the seemingly endless night, she finally dozed off and started to dream. Desperate for a good outcome, her subconscious invented a brilliant solution to her problems—a logical, step-by-step process that she could follow to be safe from Pierre, get her passport back, and leave.

On waking, the dream dissolved, and so did the feeling of incredible relief that had filled her, knowing that everything would be OK.

There was no solution. Her moment of comfort was snatched away from her by the cold morning light, leaving her feeling vulnerable and alone.

Cassie went to the bathroom and had a long, hot shower. The running water was comforting, and it helped to kick-start her brain. She resolved that her next step would be to call the au pair agency and explain the entire situation to Maureen. Maureen would know how to handle this. She could advise her on what to do, and at least somebody else would be aware of the predicament she was in, because at the moment she was utterly alone.

Returning to her room, she walked to the outlet where her cell phone was charging.

It wasn't there.

Cassie looked down at the place where she was sure it had been. The cable was lying on the floor and she frowned in consternation as she realized her phone was not in the room at all.

When was the last time she had seen it? Cassie tried to think back over the whole of the previous, chaotic day. She'd wanted to take the phone with her to the church, just in case she was able to get signal there. She'd picked it up—and then she'd thought, correctly as it turned out, that she wouldn't have any time to spare during the funeral service.

Even so, she'd considered taking it and now she couldn't remember if she had.

If that phone had ended up in her jacket pocket, there was a good chance she'd dropped it somewhere or it had fallen out, and there was a very long list of places where that could have happened. The church, somewhere in the graveyard, the parking lot as she'd wrestled the reluctant Marc back into the car. It could have dropped out while chasing him through the orchard, or even in the music room.

Cassie bit her lip as she recalled what had happened in that room yesterday. She wouldn't have noticed if she'd lost her phone while she was trying to escape Pierre's advances, and if he'd picked it up, he wasn't likely to give it back after what had happened.

She'd left her bedroom door unlocked while she'd showered, and also the previous evening while the children had been having supper. So someone could have taken it.

Cassie decided she wasn't even going to go down that road. It was far more likely she'd dropped it, and in that case she'd lost all her contacts, all her downloaded messages, and all her emails. She didn't even have a hard copy of the agency's phone number. The mails, the calls, the messages, the screenshot of the contract—everything had been on her phone.

She wasn't sure if it would be possible to get a new sim card here in France. This was a complete disaster. Her only means of communication with the outside world, with people who knew her, had gone.

Cassie turned away from the depressing sight of the empty charger, desperate for a new plan, but unable to think what it could be.

As she took the children down to breakfast, Cassie distractedly wondered what kind of blithe optimism she'd had when signing up with the agency, believing she would end up in a normal house, with ordinary, likeable people. Instead, she was stuck in a hellish situation that was spiraling further out of control with every hour that passed.

She didn't know what she would say to Pierre at breakfast. She guessed she would have to act as if everything was normal, because those were the rules of the grotesque game he'd forced her into playing. She could step out of the game and confront him, but she knew how risky that would be. And if she did it in front of the children, it would be hurtful and cruel to them.

The tables that had been set out for the funeral service had been tidied away, but the large, framed photos of Margot were still displayed on the hall table. There were three of them—a head shot, a full-length photo of her in an evening gown, and a portrait of her and Pierre standing in front of the chateau. The one of Margot and Pierre looked like it had been taken during a formal shoot, and Cassie thought the other two must be studio pictures, because Margot looked like she was modeling the clothing and jewelry she wore.

Cassie had noticed when she'd first seen them, and was reminded again now, that Margot wasn't smiling in any of the photos.

To her relief, there was no sign of Pierre at breakfast, and when Marnie brought coffee and orange juice, she confirmed he had other plans.

"It is a fine day, so Monsieur Dubois will be taking his guests on a tour of the estate and the winery at eight, and we are setting up breakfast for them at nine, on the verandah overlooking the vineyards," she explained, giving Cassie a warm smile as if she sensed Pierre's absence was good news.

"Will the guests be spending another night here?" Cassie hoped that this meant she'd be safe for longer, but fear prickled her spine when Marnie shook her head.

"They are leaving after breakfast," she said.

"Is there anything the children or I need to do today?" Cassie asked.

"The holidays are over now, and school will be starting on Monday. Could you check that the children's school bags are ready, and that they have all the supplies of notebooks and textbooks they need? Whatever is required, you can buy in town tomorrow."

"I'll do that," Cassie said.

She poured herself a cup of coffee, realizing her hands were trembling and hoping the children wouldn't notice. Ella was busy spreading Nutella on her toast, and Marc was picking all the strawberries out of the fruit bowl, but Antoinette seemed to sense her worry. As soon as Marnie had left the room, she struck up a conversation, in the sugary voice that Cassie had learned to be wary of.

"Did you go to your sister's funeral, Cassie?" she asked.

Cassie spilled some of the cream she was pouring. It splashed across the blue saucer and onto the tablecloth, and she hurriedly grabbed a napkin.

"What are you talking about?" she asked. "My sister didn't have a funeral."

The memory of her dream surfaced again. Jacqui's taunting words, and the way she'd pushed Cassie over the edge mentally, so that in turn, Cassie had shoved her physically into the ravine.

She wished she could speak to somebody about that dream and find out what it meant, what fears she needed to address, and how she could work through them. She was sure a therapist could help her, but she couldn't use anyone local. After what had happened to Margot, she would only incriminate herself by sharing it.

"Did they not bury her?" Antoinette asked, sounding deliberately shocked.

"She didn't die." Cassie spoke cautiously, worried about where this was heading.

"You said she was dead," Antoinette shot back, but she said it more in a matter-of-fact way than tauntingly.

"I never said such a thing!" Cassie could hear the defensiveness in her own voice.

"But you did. When we were talking in the car, on the way to the funeral yesterday. Didn't she say that, Marc?"

Antoinette looked across the table at Marc, who had finished the strawberries and was now picking out the mandarin segments.

"You said your sister was lost in the woods!" Marc said loudly, and Cassie froze as Antoinette nodded vigorously.

"Yes, that's what you said. She was lost in the woods and you were worried she had died."

Cassie felt sick. She put down her cup without drinking any of the coffee. Surely it couldn't be possible for both children to confirm a completely fictitious story. Also, their mention of the woods was deeply disturbing because it had formed part of that terrible dream. She had never intended to share those details with any of the family, ever. Now the children were telling her she had.

Struggling for perspective on the situation, Cassie guessed it was possible that Marc was remembering back to when Ella had been lost in the woods—thinking of his own sister, rather than hers, and simply playing along with Antoinette.

She'd been nervous driving to the funeral. She'd felt stressed and unsettled. In the car, she'd chatted without really thinking about what she was saying, preoccupied by the need to find the church and get everyone there in plenty of time. She'd been fielding Antoinette's probing questions, which always put her on the defensive, and she'd been trying to keep an eye on the back seat where Marc had been undoing his seatbelt and sticking his head out the window.

So, given the amount of distraction she'd had to cope with, it was possible that she'd said something, especially seeing both children were certain of it.

Cassie felt like crying. She couldn't trust herself anymore. The gaps in her memory were terrifying her. She could so easily have said something to the children that would implicate her, and perhaps she had. If she'd mentioned the woods, she could have taken the conversation further, and spoken about that haunting, vivid dream.

After breakfast, Antoinette went to the music room to practice her piano, and Cassie decided to make a start on the school supplies. She found herself longing for Monday to arrive, so that she could have some time to herself each day, and the children could hopefully have more structure and discipline in their lives.

"Marc, could you and Ella show me your school bags and tell me what you need?" Cassie asked, hoping it wouldn't take too long, and she would be finished by the time Antoinette was ready to help her.

But Marc shouted, "No, I don't want to help. We're going outside to play hide and seek."

Grabbing Ella's hand, he charged out of the dining room. Cassie ran to the door and shouted after them.

"Marc, please! Wait a minute. I'll come out and play with you later but we need to get this done. Ella, come back!"

Both children ignored her completely and raced outside.

The thought of chasing them down in the huge garden, or the orchard, or the greenhouse, filled Cassie with exhaustion. She'd do the damned school bags on her own. Let the children blow off some steam; there was surely a limit to the damage they could do in the half hour it would take to go through their belongings and make a list.

She felt deeply relieved to have some quiet time. The constant presence of all three was claustrophobic, and their nonstop questions and demands fragmented her concentration. It was giving her no chance to straighten out her muddled mind. She longed for a day of silence to collect her thoughts, and a week of sleep to banish the exhaustion that was making every move an effort.

She trudged upstairs to check through the bedrooms, realizing that since Marnie hadn't given her any details about what the children needed, and they weren't cooperating, it would be down to her own common sense and guesswork.

She decided to start by looking through their school bags, making sure that the bags themselves weren't broken and that no surprises, such as two-week-old sandwiches, were lurking inside. Then she'd just have to work out what, if anything, was missing.

Checking the bags felt like a Herculean task. Ella's contained very little equipment, but how much did a five-year-old need for school? She had pencils, crayons, a sharpener, and two notebooks.

Marc's bag was a chaotic mess. His pencil case had been left open, and it had spilled out into the bag. Pencil shavings, markers with their lids off, toy animals, and leaking pens were cluttered on the ink-stained bottom of the bag. His notebooks had pages torn out and the covers were bent.

By the time she'd finished organizing it, Cassie had made a long list of what would need replacing, starting with the bag itself. It was a mess; one of the straps was broken, and he'd drawn a rude picture on the outside of the bag, of a short woman with wild hair and a frowning face. Cassie guessed the artwork might be of his teacher.

His room was as untidy as his bag, and she spent some time straightening it out. Model soldiers were strewn in every corner and there was a pile of them under the bed. She couldn't believe the mess Marc was capable of creating in no time at all.

Walking out of Marc's room, Cassie listened for piano music, but it had stopped. Since Antoinette hadn't come upstairs, she decided to push ahead and finish the job on her own. She hoped that Antoinette's bag would be in order, because she didn't have the energy to repeat what she'd just done with Marc.

Antoinette's turquoise satchel was neatly packed, as she'd hoped, and everything she needed seemed to be there. Cassie checked through the geometry set, thinking back to the equipment she remembered from school. It all seemed correct. Even the small pencil for the compass was sharpened.

Cassie put the bag back where she'd found it, but as she bent down she caught a glimpse of something else far back on the wooden shelf, something that seemed weirdly familiar to her exhausted and befuddled mind.

She pulled the bag out and took a closer look, drawing in a sharp breath as she saw what was there.

It was her cell phone. Its distinctive cover, gleaming with silver holograms, had caught her eye in the darkness.

Cassie pulled it out and turned it on, noticing her hands were shaking more badly than ever, but this time from shock, rather than stress.

It was in one piece, and in working order. She wasn't going crazy, she hadn't dropped it or mislaid it. She clutched the phone to her chest, closing her eyes in utter relief that it was back in her possession.

It took a few moments for relief to evaporate and sheer, blind fury to take its place.

Antoinette must have gone into her room, pulled the phone from the charger, stolen it, and hidden it away where Cassie had only found it by the luckiest chance. Antoinette had acted deliberately and maliciously. Cassie was sure she hadn't intended to give it back until she'd seen her suffer—if she'd planned to return it at all.

As a twelve-year-old, Antoinette had no excuse for what she'd done; she was old enough to know better. This was theft, pure and simple.

Cassie realized that in terms of her emotional reserves, she'd just hit rock bottom.

She was out of patience—it was all gone. She was sick of the children's mind games, their agendas, their defiant rejection of her authority, and their refusal to understand the basic concepts of right and wrong. She couldn't deal with it anymore.

Cassie imagined grabbing Antoinette by her slender shoulders and shaking her until her teeth rattled. She imagined lifting her hand and slapping her smug face, seeing her head snap sideways, that superior expression vanishing.

She took a vicious joy in thinking about exactly how much force she could put into that blow.

Cassie shoved the school bag back onto the shelf and marched out of the bedroom, banging the door behind her.

Priorities first, she decided. With her phone back in her possession, she could at least look up the agency's number. It was already a quarter past ten. That meant it was still very early in the States; too early to use Pierre's landline to call the agency. They opened at eight a.m. By the time they were open, Pierre might be back from breakfast. If he was around, she couldn't exactly march into his room to make an important, confidential call for help.

Cassie let out a frustrated sigh. Was there seriously nowhere in this godforsaken place where a person could make a cell phone call? Now that she had prepaid minutes loaded, perhaps she should check. The estate was huge. Surely there must be somewhere that offered enough signal to allow for a phone call, even if there wasn't enough to enable data. A sliver of signal would be adequate. One bar might do it.

Holding her phone in front of her, Cassie stepped outside and went hunting.

The front of the house yielded nothing. Cradled in between the hills, Cassie guessed there was simply no line of sight to an available tower—and if there was signal elsewhere, the stone bulk of the chateau itself would prevent it from reaching through to this side.

She was more hopeful about the back of the house, where that beautiful, dizzying view stretched for miles. Even the tiniest trace of signal from a faraway tower might be enough. In addition, today was clear, dry, and still, which meant a better chance of success. Cassie remembered Zane, of all people, telling her that bad weather affected cell signal. Heavy clouds, rain, and even high winds tamped down the signal. He'd learned that from his older brother, who was involved in maintaining cell towers.

Cassie rounded the corner and headed along the paved walkway, with the chateau's high stone wall on her right. She kept her phone turned slightly to the open vista on the left, not knowing if that would help, but feeling it couldn't hurt. She walked slowly, keeping her gaze fixed on the screen, where that frustrating "No Signal" logo was refusing to budge.

With all her attention focused on her phone, Cassie didn't see the gutter ahead of her, a deep trench in the stone. Her foot caught in it and she almost fell, diving forward to save herself and her phone.

As she did so, she sensed, rather than saw, something heavy falling behind her—she heard the swift breath of sound as it fell, and felt it as a sudden chill of air.

A heartbeat later, the huge object crashed to the ground.

Cassie spun round, shouting in panic. Her heart hammered in her throat as she stared incredulously down at the heavy stone bust. It had fallen directly behind her, no more than a step away from where she was standing, and she realized in horror that her stumble had only just saved her, because if she hadn't tripped and dived forward to save herself, it would have fallen directly onto her.

The marble head and shoulders were bigger than life-sized. It must weigh hundreds of pounds. Its solid form looked to be undamaged by the fall, but the large flagstone where it landed had shattered.

Weak with shock, Cassie stepped back to get a better view of the balcony, far above.

The statue on the left pillar of the balustrade was still in place. The one on the right had fallen. The balcony itself was empty, and she could see no movement there.

Had somebody seen her walking past, and pushed it?

She didn't want to believe it, but it had been close—so impossibly close. She'd only just escaped being crushed.

Opportunistic, yes, but she had to face the reality that somebody genuinely could have been trying to kill her.

The only question was who.

Chapter Twenty Six

As Cassie stood, frozen by the realization that the statue could have been aimed deliberately at her, she heard a shout.

"What is happening? What was that?"

Pierre rounded the corner at a run, sprinting up to where she was standing.

Cassie saw genuine astonishment in his face as he stared at her, then up at the balcony, breathing hard.

All she could think at that moment was that it hadn't been Pierre who pushed that bust over the edge. It would have been impossible for him to have run all the way from that upper balcony, down the staircase, out of the front door, and around the side of the house in such a short time.

"It fell as I was passing," she said, her voice high and shaky. "It almost hit me."

"It fell? That statue could not simply fall. It has been in place for centuries." Pierre stepped back to get a better view.

"Look, you can see the podium where it rested."

He squatted down and scrutinized the statue carefully.

"Unbroken, although we will need to replace the flagstone," he said. "I will go and tell the vineyard manager to organize for it to be put back in its place."

"It almost killed me," Cassie said. Her head was swimming now from delayed reaction. Half a second slower, and she wouldn't have had a chance.

Pierre frowned at her and Cassie knew that after what had happened between them yesterday, sympathy would not be forthcoming. In fact, she shouldn't even have mentioned her near-escape from death. She didn't want to be the focus of Pierre's attention for any reason. It was better when his gaze passed over her dismissively, as if she was insignificant in his life, and her problems not his concern.

"You are hurt?" he asked, in a tone that told her he knew she wasn't.

"No, I'm not hurt, I'm fine," she said defensively.

"If furniture was moved out of the room while it was being cleaned, one of the household staff could have knocked it over by accident," he said.

Or one of the children, Cassie thought with a shiver, and if so, maybe it wasn't an accident at all.

Pierre headed for the garage and climbed into the golf cart before driving down the sandy track in the direction of the vineyard.

Cassie decided to see if she could find out for herself who had been there.

The balcony belonged to one of the guest suites, in the wing of the house that was standing empty. She supposed a few of the rooms would have been occupied last night by the funeral guests, but didn't know which ones. When she went upstairs, she found all the rooms were unlocked, with their doors closed. She went into the wrong room first by mistake. The inside of the house looked different, and seemed bigger, than the outside.

The next room was the right one. It was immaculate, with a four-poster bed neatly made with burgundy pillows and a cream bedspread. The door to the balcony was open, but there was nobody outside. She walked onto the balcony and looked down, her stomach churning as she surveyed the drop. Uneasy, she checked behind her and moved quickly away from the railing. She wondered if she would ever be able to look down from a height again without remembering the jolting shock she'd felt, and the sick dizziness that had filled her, when she had seen Margot's body.

She gave the remaining bust a tentative wiggle. With its narrow base, wide shoulders, and large, imposing head, it was top-heavy and unstable. It wouldn't have taken much force to push it off. Physically, even Ella could have done it.

One thing was for sure—there were no housekeeping staff in this room, or even in this wing. They must have finished their work earlier.

Pierre hadn't even mentioned the possibility that it could have been one of the children, even though it was obvious that apart from the staff, they were the only ones who could have done it. Cassie wondered if it genuinely hadn't occurred to Pierre, or more likely, whether he simply wasn't allowing himself to consider the possibility.

She guessed this was an extension of his belief that the family name must remain squeaky clean, and untainted by scandal, at all costs.

Having narrowly escaped death, she was still none the wiser about who had done it, and the incident had only drawn Pierre's attention to her again. On top of it all, she was convinced that there was no cell phone signal anywhere in the area. There hadn't been the slightest trace downstairs, and when she checked her phone on the balcony, the stubborn "No Signal" sign refused to budge.

Frustrated, Cassie realized she'd have to wait until Pierre went out. Perhaps he would do so later, and then she'd use the landline to contact the agency, and damn the consequences if he found out.

Everything she'd tried to do that day had ended in disaster, and when Cassie thought of it from that perspective, it made her want to burst into tears. Antoinette had stolen her phone. Someone had tried to kill her. Everyone seemed to hate her apart from Marnie, the only friendly face in the whole chateau.

She left the room and, remembering her responsibilities, searched for the children. Ella was in her bedroom, and Antoinette was in the library. She was curled up in an armchair reading, smiling at Cassie innocently when she walked in.

Cassie bit back the urge to scream at her that she was a thief, and possibly a would-be murderer, too. If the statue had been pushed off its stand deliberately, she knew which child was the most likely culprit. It took all the remaining fragments of her self-control to ask her if she knew where Marc was, and when Antoinette shrugged dismissively, Cassie was tempted to grab her shiny ponytail and pull it until she screamed.

Marc was in the kitchen. He'd raided the fridge and found a plate with some iced cakes. He'd dropped one on the floor, and was marching triumphantly out of the scullery with another, when Cassie arrived.

She managed to catch up with him as he was heading for the orchard, having eaten half the cake on the run and thrown the other half down onto the immaculate paving in a shower of crumbs.

"It's almost lunchtime, Marc, you must come in now," she entreated.

"I'm not hungry," he shouted gleefully, and she had to chase him again, all the way to the greenhouse with its broken panes. Cassie supposed she should tell someone about them but she didn't have the energy, and if she told, she'd have to explain that Marc had done it while unsupervised.

It seemed better just to leave it be.

Her only tenuous link to sanity was the key to her bedroom. She could feel its reassuring shape in her pocket. When it was night-time, she would lock her room, and nobody could get to her. She clung to that fact like a life raft. It felt like the only thing she still had control of.

Pierre joined them for lunch, which surprised and dismayed Cassie. Still more disconcerting was the cheerfulness of his mood.

"May I serve you some roast chicken, Cassie?" he asked genially, and she forced a polite smile.

"Marnie prepared this herself before she left. I feel it is one of her most accomplished dishes. Roast chicken, ratatouille, and gravy. Simple and classic. Do you like it, Antoinette?"

Antoinette smiled coquettishly, clearly delighted to be her father's main focus of attention.

"It's delicious," she agreed.

"Margot never used to eat gravy," Ella observed. "I don't think she liked it."

Nobody responded to this observation and there was a short silence after her words. Marc glanced at Margot's empty chair before returning his attention to his meal.

"Where has Marnie gone?" Cassie asked, worried. She'd hoped to be able to speak to her this afternoon and find out if there was another phone she could use.

"She asked for the rest of the day off; she had an errand to run. She has had a few days off recently, but she is a hard worker. We cannot begrudge hard workers their leisure time, especially when they perform so well. After all, those who put their hearts into the job are the ones who are well rewarded. It's always important to please your employer."

His gaze met Cassie's over the table and he gave her a meaningful glance. She had no difficulty in picking up the innuendo. The fact that Pierre was saying this in front of the children, the day after Margot's funeral, made her want to vomit.

With a superhuman effort she kept her expression neutral and forced the food down, hoping that keeping quiet might help her to become invisible to him again.

"I am going into town this afternoon on business," Pierre announced as the plates were cleared.

"When will you be back, Papa?" Antoinette asked.

"By early evening."

"Can we play a game?" She smiled again.

"Perhaps we can. You know how much I enjoy games." But as he spoke, Pierre was looking at Cassie, not at his daughter.

She thought he'd been about to say something else, but at that moment, there was a knock at the front door.

Pierre stood up.

"I will answer it. I am on my way out anyway," he said.

Cassie stood up too, feeling as if her nerves had been put through the shredder. She walked out of the dining room, overhearing Pierre's brusque conversation with the visitor at the front door.

"Madame, there is nothing to see here. Margot's funeral service was yesterday, and I am leaving the house now. If you wish to spend some time remembering her, let me direct you to the churchyard where her ashes are buried."

He paused.

"You are a reporter? Then you may contact my office for a copy of her formal obituary. Some information on her life, together with excellent photos, is available. Here is my business card with the relevant details. I am still grieving and have nothing to say to you."

Pierre closed the door firmly behind him, and a few minutes later she heard his car leaving.

Now was the time to act, Cassie decided. She wasn't going to wait another minute.

She marched up the stairs and along the corridor to Pierre's bedroom. Taking her cell phone out of her jacket pocket, she scrolled through until she found the agency's number. Then, lifting her chin determinedly, she turned the door handle.

It was locked.

The reality hit her like a punch to the stomach.

She tried it again, rattling the handle. This door had never been locked, and now it unmistakably was.

There was no way she could access the landline now. She could make no calls this afternoon and receive no good advice. Her only means of communication was gone.

Cassie turned away from the door, shattered. This must be her punishment for rejecting him yesterday.

How had he even known she'd come into his room that first time? Clearly, he'd guessed it or sensed it, and she'd been found out. And now he was telling her that he knew, and he was going to stop her, because this was part of the sick power game he was playing.

Thinking of that, thinking of his odd satisfaction during lunch, Cassie had another premonition of disaster.

She'd left her bedroom unlocked that morning, as Marnie had asked her to do, because she and the children had been at home and housekeeping needed to clean.

Cassie went back down the corridor, took the key out of her pocket, and closed the bedroom door. Then she tried to lock it.

This time, though, the key wouldn't go in properly. It wouldn't fit at all, and she couldn't make it turn. She wiggled it, jiggled it, pushed and pulled. She twisted it with all her might until she stopped, because she knew if she kept trying, the slim metal shaft would simply snap off in the lock.

She took it out and put it back in again and tried a second time in case the lock had developed a glitch, or there was a flake of rust in the way, or her own panic had just meant that she'd done it wrong.

It was the same no matter how many times she tried. She couldn't turn the key and she couldn't lock the door.

Pierre had found out she'd been locking it for her safety.

Tonight, he was making sure she couldn't.

CHAPTER TWENTY SEVEN

Cassie threw the useless key across her bedroom as hard as she could. It hit the wall and jangled down onto the floor. She didn't bother picking it up. She turned her back on it and slammed the door as she left.

The low-grade fear that she realized she'd been living with ever since Margot died was erupting into full-blown terror.

She told herself that this was just Pierre playing mind games with her and punishing her for fighting him off yesterday. She tried to reassure herself that she still had options open to her and could sleep in Ella's bedroom if she had to.

But she couldn't do that all night, every night. She had no idea when her passport would be returned, and she couldn't call anybody to ask for help.

Cassie breathed in deeply. She had never felt more trapped or defeated. She was sharing the house with an adulterer who'd set his sights on her, and with a suspected murderer. She had no idea if these were one and the same person, or whether they were two different people. Who had pushed Margot over the balcony? And who had shoved that statue off the pedestal, sending it crashing to the ground as she passed?

Why, oh why, had she overdosed so badly on her meds on that night of all nights, resulting in confusion and nightmares and muddled memories that meant that not even she knew what had really happened, or what role she herself had played in all of this?

She plodded downstairs and went to the kitchen, wondering where Marnie had gone. For all she knew, Marnie had actually quit her job. She couldn't believe anything she was told anymore.

One of the other kitchen staff was working in the scullery but the kitchen itself was empty.

In the food preparation section there was a big wooden block where the chopping and carving knives were stored. They were all in their place, their handles jutting out from the block, waiting to be used.

Cassie inspected all the knives pushed into that wooden block. She picked out what she hoped was the deadliest weapon of them all—a medium-length one with a hard, shiny silver blade that tapered to a wicked point. Its beveled edge was lethally sharp.

She imagined grabbing it and stabbing it into somebody, point first. Or using that razor edge to slice across flesh, opening a deep gash in her attacker's throat.

Holding the knife, she felt as if she was at a crossroads. Would she be able to use it?

Cassie shook her head. Tempting as it was to have the protection that knife offered, it was too deadly a weapon and that meant she might freeze instead of using it, because its ability to seriously hurt or kill terrified her. There was also the possibility that it could be taken from her. Then she might end up being the victim, and Pierre could truthfully say he had used it in self-defense.

She needed something less lethal, that would still be an effective deterrent. Pepper spray would have been ideal, but she was sure there was none in the chateau. Would plain pepper work?

Cassie rejected this idea, too. It wouldn't be practical to use. Then the solution came to her.

Insecticide. She needed a can of powerful bug spray. The poison would temporarily blind or choke Pierre, it would be easy to use, and the can itself could also be used as a self-defense weapon if she smacked it into his face.

In a chateau that was hundreds of years old, there must surely be plenty of bugs, and therefore, spray. She guessed it would be kept in the scullery or broom cupboard.

Cassie waited another few minutes for the maid to leave, and then looked in the scullery, where she found an almost-full can of a toxic-looking insecticide used for cockroaches and other kitchen pests.

She sprayed a test squirt into the air, waited a few seconds, then fanned it toward her. The fumes were choking and eye-watering.

"Come and get me, Pierre," she whispered, clutching the can with her finger tight on the nozzle. "See how well it goes for you."

Despite the bravado of her words, her feeling of terror hadn't budged. In fact, it had worsened. Preparing her defense was forcing her to acknowledge the reality of what she guessed he was planning.

She took the spray up to her bedroom and hid it under her pillow. Then she closed her bedroom door and went in search of the children.

She searched fruitlessly for nearly half an hour, getting more and more worried about where they were and what disaster they might have caused, before the shriek of a car's engine alerted her, and she rushed to the garage.

Marc had stolen the keys from the dish in the hallway and had unlocked the Peugeot. He'd managed to get the car started, and was perched on the edge of the driver's seat, gripping the steering wheel tightly, with his foot flat on the accelerator. The engine was howling in protest and the air was thick with fumes.

Antoinette had brought Ella along to watch the spectacle, and was standing outside the garage, screaming with laughter.

"Stop it now!" Cassie shouted, but over the roar of the car, nobody heard her.

She dashed into the garage, coughing as she breathed in the cloud of choking fumes. She wrenched at the door handle and pulled it open, wondering why it felt sticky to the touch.

"Out, now!" she ordered.

Marc grabbed the wheel tightly, shouting in protest. Looking inside, Cassie saw to her horror that he'd brought a cup of cocoa and a honey sandwich into the car with him. The cocoa had, predictably, spilled all over the passenger seat. Marc's face and hands, together with the car's steering wheel, the indicator stick, and most of the knobs on the dashboard, were smeared in honey.

Cassie suddenly wondered how complicit Antoinette might have been in all of this. She could imagine her handing Marc the cocoa and sandwich, and suggesting that he go for a drive.

"Out," Cassie yelled. The garage air was thick with fumes. She grabbed Marc's arm and hauled him out of the car, before reaching in and turning off the ignition. The key was sticky, too. Every possible surface was thick with honey.

"Marc, what the hell is this? You know you're not allowed to go into the garage," she screamed, dragging him outside where the air was, thankfully, clearer. She turned on Antoinette, not caring that the older girl could see exactly how furious she was.

"You were watching the whole time! Why did you let him do that?"

Antoinette just shrugged rudely and spread her arms. The gesture, and in fact her entire demeanor, indicated nothing but contempt for Cassie.

Ella turned away, as if she couldn't be bothered to continue with her manipulative behavior now that Cassie was trying to enforce discipline. So, Cassie decided, Ella didn't really like her. She just capitalized on her weakness, and the fact Cassie was putty in her hands.

Her brain felt overloaded. She could almost feel the neurons burning out, one by one.

"Inside," she snapped. How was she going to make the children realize how destructive, how downright dangerous, this had been? If Marc had gotten the car in gear, he could have run Ella over.

"I don't want to go inside," Marc began, and Cassie yelled at him with all her might, bending down so that her mouth was only inches from his ear.

"You are going! Now!"

She marched them inside. Marc dragged his feet in sulky silence, Ella kicking the gravel and whining. Antoinette was still giggling, as if she found the entire situation, including Cassie's loss of control, too hilariously funny for words.

"Come with me," she said, and headed upstairs, but at the top of the staircase she turned toward the guest wing. She hustled Marc in front of her, with Ella whimpering behind, and slamming her hands on the doors as she passed. Cassie could hear Antoinette's silvery laughter bringing up the rear.

She punched the door open, stomped into the bedroom, and pointed through the glass sliding door to the empty podium on the balcony where the statue had been.

"Which one of you pushed that statue off there? Tell me. Now. Because I was walking underneath the balcony when it fell, and it came within inches of killing me."

She scanned their faces. Ella mutinous, Marc defiant, Antoinette smug.

She expected it would take a while for anyone to confess, and that she might have to watch their body language for signs of guilt. But Marc shouted out immediately, as if he was proud of what he'd done.

"It was me! I was hiding there, because we were playing hide and seek. It looked wobbly so I pushed it. I'm so strong! Look, I can make the other one fall, too."

He rushed toward the glass doors as Antoinette squealed with mirth.

Cassie dived after him, remembering that Pierre had said a crew would be replacing the statue during the course of the afternoon, which meant there could well be people underneath.

"No," she shouted. "It's dangerous, and you could hurt someone."

"I don't care!" Marc yelled. He kicked her shins, his toes hammering her painfully in his efforts to make her let go, and as she struggled with the insubordinate youngster, his fingers still sticky with honey, Cassie felt herself consumed by a raw, violent rage.

She dragged him away from the door. He screamed in anger, his face crimson, and his grasping hands left giant smears on the glass.

"You have to stop acting like this! You have to start listening," she shrieked at him.

"I won't, I won't," he shouted back.

Before she could think about the consequences of her actions, Cassie picked the young boy up bodily and hauled him across the room to the large mahogany wardrobe. She opened the door, forced him inside, and banged it shut, leaning against it for good measure.

"Now stay in there and think about what you have done!" she yelled.

For a moment there was a shocked silence, as everyone took in what had just happened.

Then Marc began screaming, terrified and hysterical.

"Let me out! Let me out!"

He hammered on the door, fists drumming against the wood, but Cassie only pushed back against it harder. She was breathing fast, her heart pounding and adrenaline surging through her. She was not letting him out; she was not.

Marc started to cry.

"I'm scared of the dark. Please let me out, please!"

Clenching her teeth, Cassie stood firm against the door. She could hear the raw fear in his tone and knew how scared he must be, but her anger was more powerful than the inner voice which was telling her she was being unfair to him.

Ella started sobbing.

"He's scared in there! Marc's scared!"

"I was scared when that statue crashed down behind me. Marc needs to learn to think before he acts," Cassie shouted. "And not deliberately do things when he knows they're naughty and destructive."

Marc's crying had quieted down. His sobs were forlorn now.

"I'm so scared," he whimpered. "Please let me out."

Antoinette marched up to Cassie, contempt in her eyes.

"Let him out," she demanded. "You're being cruel."

"I'm being cruel?" Cassie raised her eyebrows, a fresh wave of anger surging inside her. "Maybe you should be pointing that finger at yourself, not me."

Antoinette was furious at being defied. She stepped forward with her face set in a scowl and tried to physically push Cassie away from the door.

Cassie did what her fingers had been itching to do the whole day. She lifted her hand and slapped Antoinette hard across her face.

Antoinette recoiled, dropping to her knees and doubling over, cradling her face in her hands, whimpering in agonized tones.

"Ow, ow, ow."

Ella ran over and knelt beside her, sobbing as she helped Antoinette rub her face. From inside the wardrobe, Marc's cries had become nothing more than hoarse, desperate whispers.

"Let me out. Please, please let me out."

Listening to the fear in his voice, Cassie found that memories were surging inside her. She was having flashbacks to a forgotten experience, one she'd buried deeply.

She suddenly had the weird feeling that she was on the inside of that closet. She knew exactly how it felt in there. How the tiny sliver of light narrowed and then disappeared completely as the door was closed, leaving her in oppressive, airless darkness. How the cupboard space suddenly seemed too small to contain herself and her panic, but no matter how loudly she screamed, she hadn't thought it would reach outside that solid door.

She knew her father was standing outside that door because she could hear him shouting, even though she couldn't make out exactly what he was saying. It didn't matter. He was angry and she had been bad, and that was why he had dragged her upstairs and shoved her into that big, dark cupboard and bolted the door closed.

He'd gone away, Cassie remembered. She'd waited in there for what felt like hours, until her throat was raw from screaming and her heels were bruised from kicking the door, in her desperation to force it open. It was airless and hot, and every breath she took felt like a struggle.

Her father hadn't let her out. Eventually, it had been Jacqui who came upstairs and freed her.

Suddenly unable to continue with the punishment, Cassie moved away from the wardrobe and opened the door.

Marc was lying prone on the floor, just as she had done. He crawled out, blinking in the light, and Cassie remembered how light it had been after the suffocating darkness. It had been painful, and she could hardly open her eyes for a while.

Marc's face was swollen and wet with tears and he seemed more subdued than she'd ever believed he could be.

As he stumbled past Cassie he muttered something that she couldn't quite make out.

Antoinette scrambled to her feet and tried to put her arms around him but Marc pushed her away and trailed out of the room, turning in the direction of his bedroom.

Antoinette and the still-sobbing Ella followed him silently out.

In her terror and trauma, Cassie remembered she'd pushed her sister away, too.

She'd pushed her hard, and Jacqui had screamed as she'd fallen, down into the dark.

Cassie shook her head violently. She was confusing memories with dreams again. That hadn't happened. She'd pushed Jacqui, but it had only been a weak, gentle shove. She hadn't been standing on the brink of a ravine. She hadn't tried to save herself, her red-nailed hands clutching at empty air as she'd fallen.

Cassie closed the cupboard door and as she did so, she found her earlier rage had evaporated. Instead, she was filled with guilt.

She tried to tell herself that her actions had been justified, that these children had been running so wild that they had needed a serious dose of discipline. That no harm would come to Marc from a few minutes spent inside a cupboard and that Antoinette had more than deserved that slap.

It didn't stop her from acknowledging what she felt inside, even though she cringed away from the reality.

She'd behaved in exactly the same way as her abusive father.

She had spent years trying to escape him and turn her back on him. She had firmly believed that she was a better person and in any case had been the victim, not the oppressor. None of it had helped her.

She had to face the truth, which was that she had ended up becoming him.

CHAPTER TWENTY EIGHT

After they had left the room, Cassie expected the children to run wild through the house in defiance. She was surprised when they meekly walked back to their rooms. They were so quiet and compliant that she guessed the incident had traumatized everyone.

She headed downstairs and searched the scullery for cleaning materials. Then she tried her best to fix up the car, wiping every surface and getting as much of the spilled cocoa off the leather seat as she could. She was glad of the activity, as it gave her an escape route from her shattered emotions.

She'd crossed the line with the children. She'd become their abuser instead of their protector.

She tried her best to replay the incident in her mind so that she could get some perspective on it, and decide how unacceptable her behavior really had been, and whether she could somehow make amends for it. Thinking back, she found she couldn't remember exactly what had happened in that guest room.

She couldn't recall all the details. How had the situation escalated? What had Marc said that she had reacted that way? She supposed she had taken them up to that bedroom to discipline them about what had happened in the car. When she tried to remember, she went back to being small and helpless, locked in the closet herself.

Then when she tried again, she found herself on the brink of that ravine, trapped in the nightmare of fighting her sister.

Cassie wondered if her mind was deliberately erasing memories to protect her from the overload of stress. She hoped the details would come back to her when she was better able to cope with them.

Meanwhile, she felt as if her thoughts were being tugged in a hundred different directions. She kept thinking of the phrase "torn apart by wild horses." That was exactly what she felt was happening to her sanity. There were too many uncontrollable worries, she had no support structure, and her biggest fear was that the worst was still to come.

She kept wanting to cry, and thinking she had been crying, but when she lifted a hand to her eyes she could feel they were dry. Outwardly she was showing nothing, but inside she was falling apart.

Checking the time on her phone, she realized it was late afternoon. The hours had slipped by as if she'd been in a dream. Seeing Marnie was not here, it was her responsibility to make sure that there was supper ready and get the children bathed and into their pajamas, assuming they were willing to speak to her. Gathering her thoughts into a semblance of normality, she headed downstairs.

The kitchen was empty. The maid who'd been washing up earlier had obviously knocked off for the day. Thanks to Marnie's unexpected disappearance, no plans for supper had been made.

Cassie checked the fridge, the freezer, and the enormous pantry. There was plenty of food of all kinds, including a six-pack of slimmer's shakes in the pantry which looked out of place compared to the other contents. She guessed they had been Margot's, and would now never be used.

As she took stock of what was available, a few dinner options occurred to her. Then she thought—why not ask the children? Perhaps she could mend her relationship with them and absolve some of the gnawing guilt she was feeling if she opened up the lines of communication herself.

She called them all into Antoinette's room.

They filed in obediently and stared up at her in silence. Cassie was struck again by the change in their behavior since she'd completely lost the plot.

"I want to tell you all that I'm sorry for shouting earlier," she said. "I lost my temper and behaved very badly. So I have to say I'm sorry. I was angry but I shouldn't have said and done what I did. It's not OK to do that ever, but if it happens, it's important to apologize afterwards. I know now that if I'm in the same situation again I must control my anger and not let it control me. That's what I've learned from this."

"I'm sorry, too," Antoinette said in a small voice. "I didn't try to stop Marc; in fact, I told him he should do it."

"And I'm sorry," Marc said, scuffling his feet on the tiles. "I know I was naughty. I was very bad."

To Cassie's surprise he sounded genuinely ashamed, rather than proud of his behavior.

Ella hugged her in silence, clinging to her legs.

"I thought I would ask you what we should have for supper," Cassie said. "Marnie's not here so I've got a couple of choices in mind. We could either have ham and cheese omelets, or we could have a beef and mushroom pie—there's one in the freezer—or we could have pancakes with sugar and cinnamon."

"I'd like pancakes," Ella said tentatively, and there was a chorus of "Me, too," from Antoinette and Marc.

"All right. If you like, you can help me make them now. We can keep them warm in the oven while you bathe and get changed."

Cassie went downstairs with the children, feeling a weird sense of separation from reality. As long as she lived in the moment, she was absolutely fine. As soon as she thought about what had happened earlier, or what was going to happen, her brain went into overload and she started to shake with fear.

She decided it would be better to stay in the moment, seeing it was safer and the right choice for her own sanity.

Down in the kitchen, the children genuinely seemed to enjoy the pancake making. Cassie guessed they didn't have much chance to cook, with so many staff in attendance so much of the time. After she'd mixed up the batter and the cinnamon-sugar topping, she gave them each a job to do. Antoinette was in charge of pouring the batter into the pan. Then, when Cassie had flipped the pancakes, Ella was responsible for sprinkling the cinnamon-sugar mixture. Standing on a low chair and leaning on the large wooden table in the center of the kitchen, she seemed proud and contented in her role.

Then, finally, Marc was in charge of rolling the pancakes up and arranging them on a plate.

Half an hour later, the plate was piled with pancakes, and Cassie covered it with tinfoil and put it in the oven's warming drawer.

She felt massive relief that she'd managed to redeem the day just a little, after its disastrous start. Now, she needed to get the children bathed and ready for supper.

Her thoughts strayed to what might happen later that evening, and Cassie shut them down. She wasn't going to go there. No matter how the night turned out, or what she ended up doing, at least the children could all remember the fun of the cooking afternoon they'd had.

"I like your hair decoration, Cassie," Ella said when she was in the bath.

"Thank you," Cassie said. She couldn't even remember what she'd put in her hair, or when. Perhaps she'd tied it back before starting to prepare the food, so it wouldn't get in the way.

She put a hand up to her ponytail and felt the gossamer touch of silk. Pulling her hair to the side, she saw a trailing end of emerald green.

Anxiety knotted her stomach as she realized that she had absolutely no memory of fastening the silk scarf Pierre had given her into her hair.

Once the children were bathed, dressed, and downstairs in the dining room, Cassie asked Antoinette to read them a story before dinner. Realizing her clothes were stained and dirty from the day's activities, she hurried back to shower and change before she joined them.

After pulling on clean jeans and a fresh sweater, Cassie headed back to her bedroom to put her dirty clothes in the laundry basket, and pick up the list of school supplies she'd made earlier that day. Now that the children were more cooperative, she could run through it with them over supper and see if anything was missing.

She put the clothes in the basket and picked up the list from the table. Then she turned back toward the door—and clapped her hand over her mouth to stifle a scream.

Pierre was sitting in the high-backed chair near her bed.

Staring at him in horror, Cassie felt her heart accelerate. He'd been a move ahead of her all along. He must have come home while she was showering, gone straight to her room, and waited for her.

Perhaps he'd expected that she would sleep in one of the children's bedrooms tonight and had made a preemptive move.

"Did I startle you?" he asked.

Too late, Cassie realized that she should never have smothered her scream. She needed to yell now, as much and as loudly as she could. If she could attract the children's attention, she would be safe.

If she couldn't, she was in a world of trouble.

But as she drew breath, Pierre put his finger over his lips.

"Quietly, now," he remonstrated. "Don't you know the rules? This evening's game is not to make a sound."

He stood up, advancing toward her as she backed in the direction of the bed.

"The children are happy downstairs," he said. "They are eating their pancakes and told me they have had a good day. They seem to be coping well after the tragedy we have so recently experienced. It would be a pity to spoil their contentment when the unfinished business we have is only between us two, no? Although even if you screamed, the dining room is so far away that they would probably not hear you."

Cassie sank down onto the bed, her legs weak with fear.

"No," she muttered. "Please, Pierre, no."

Pierre leaned over her. With his hand firm on her shoulder, he pushed her back. She heard the jingle of metal and realized, with a sense of unreality, that he was undoing his belt.

"I spoke to the police today," he whispered in her ear. "They told me you, unfortunately, are still very much under suspicion. There are several issues that concern them. They asked me if you were trustworthy. What was I to say, Cassie?"

She looked up at him in silence, horrified by his words and the way he was coercing her into silence. His brown eyes were staring into hers. She could see the shadow of stubble on his face.

"I requested a meeting with the detective tomorrow. So you see, it is up to you now. Are you going to play my game and keep quiet, as quiet as a mouse, not a sound from you? If so, I will tell the police tomorrow that you are reliable and trustworthy, that I can personally attest to your character. But if you do not play the game, I will not hesitate to say that I believe you have already stolen from me, and that I have photographic evidence of you snooping in my bedroom, opening drawers and searching through my possessions. Which decision will you make, Cassie? What will you choose?"

He bent over her. His hair tickled her face, his strong fingers pressing her into the mattress.

Cassie realized there was no point in begging or screaming. Pierre had considered every possible scenario, and all of them were checkmate for her.

Except one.

Reaching behind her head, scrabbling under the pillow, Cassie closed her fingers over the cold steel can of the poison spray she'd hidden there. Her finger found the plastic nozzle, and it felt solid and reassuring in her grasp as she slid it out from under her.

She knew which decision she would make, and what she would choose.

CHAPTER TWENTY NINE

Detective Granger sat with Estelle Bret in the small lounge, which was bright with low autumn sunshine. Estelle owned a modest apartment in Senlis, an hour's drive north of Paris, and she was the second of Pierre's ex-mistresses who had agreed to be interviewed by him that day.

"Pierre and I had an affair for the best part of a year," she said.

She fidgeted with a lock of her long, dark hair as she spoke. She was tall, slender, and very beautiful, perfectly made up and trendily dressed in ripped jeans and a fringed suede jacket.

"Please continue," Granger said. Reassuring her again, he added, "This is entirely confidential, madame. I am writing a few notes but this is not being recorded."

Granger had assumed that these interviews would be routine background research, just a box to tick in the investigation. The first interview had shocked him, and this one was heading the same way. Estelle had been very reluctant to talk. She had only agreed to the interview after he'd promised that it was for background only, and that what she said would not be disclosed to Pierre.

"I was married and living in the area. My husband traveled a lot and was away for long periods of time. I met Pierre in town; we were standing together in a bank line and he started conversing with me. He was flirtatious, attractive. He invited me to dinner. He told me he was married, but I was, too." She shrugged.

Granger looked down as he made a note on his pad.

"Most people in the area think he is wonderful," Estelle continued. "He is a prominent businessman who has been careful to protect his reputation. But there are a few who know otherwise, who have seen how he lies, and what he conceals. When I told a friend that we were seeing each other, she warned me about him. I should have listened, but I chose not to believe her. Instead, I listened to his promises."

She twirled a lock of hair tightly around her finger and stared through the sunny window at the bare tree branches nodding outside.

"What did he promise you?" Granger asked.

"He said he was in love with me, that he wanted me to leave my husband, that he would marry me. So, like a fool, I confessed to my husband that I was seeing someone else, and we separated. We divorced a year later. Meanwhile, Pierre continued as usual, seeing me once, twice a week. There were many compliments and many more promises. Eventually I realized he had no intention of leaving his wife. But I also started to see another side to him."

"What was that?"

Granger was scribbling furiously in his notebook to keep pace with her.

"He was into kinky things. Strangulation, bondage." Estelle looked down and Granger saw her cheeks were flushed.

"At first it was an adventure. He made it seem fun and exciting. Then, over time, he became more violent. He refused to stop when I asked. There were a few occasions where he really hurt me. Once, he strangled me so hard I actually lost consciousness for a while. I knew that for my own health—physical and emotional—I would have to end it with him. But that was easier said than done."

"How so?"

Granger made sure to keep a calm demeanor, despite his conviction that the puzzle pieces were starting to fit together.

"He was furious that I wanted to end it. We had a huge fight. He threatened me with all sorts of things. There were a few personal details I'd told him in confidence—he said he'd make sure the whole town knew. And when I threatened to tell everyone about him, he grabbed me and shook me, and then shoved me away so hard I fell. I had bruises on my jaw and shoulder."

"Did you take it further?" Granger asked.

"I went to the police and they asked me to get a physician's report on the injuries as soon as possible, in order that the correct charges could be laid."

Granger nodded.

"I went to the local doctor but I only found out afterwards that he was a friend of Pierre's. After I told him what had happened, he questioned me about my sporting activities, which included horse riding and gym. He examined me and said my injuries were not severe enough, and the circumstances were not conclusive enough, for him to be able to write a police report and that I could have incurred the bruises after a fall from my horse. Then Pierre phoned me the next day, threatening me that if I didn't drop the charges he would sue me for defamation, and that I was lying about everything."

She spread her hands.

"By then I wasn't sure if I even believed myself. I dropped the charges and moved away. I found a good job near here as an event organizer so I decided to restart my life completely. It was a horrific experience. It showed me how toxic a person he was, and how he'd stop at nothing to protect his so-called 'good name' in the area."

Granger nodded slowly. This was telling evidence. Before speaking to these women, he would never have believed that Pierre had such a dark side to him, and had clearly gone to extreme lengths to protect his reputation.

He concluded the interview and thanked her for her time.

As soon as he'd left her apartment, he called Bisset to update her. She sounded excited.

"I have just left Margot's hairdressing salon. Alex, her stylist, was extremely helpful."

"What did he say?" Granger asked.

"Margot was unhappy. She felt trapped. She wanted to leave Pierre but she was terrified of the consequences."

Granger felt a chill at the words.

"Did he explain why?"

"She was planning to go back to modeling; it was all she knew. Her involvement with Pierre had cut short a promising career. The problem is that it's a high-profile job. She would be in the public domain, and questions would be asked about her past. She told Alex that she was desperate to leave Pierre, but she knew how difficult he would make it. She was extremely depressed."

"My interview with Estelle went along similar lines," Granger confirmed.

"There's something more," Bisset said.

"What's that?"

He hoped she would be quick; his cell battery was running low, and he'd forgotten his charger cable at the police station.

"Technology. You know we complained there was a lack of it?"

"Yes."

"Well, Margot left her cell phone at the salon. Alex said she was using it throughout her appointment, and she forgot to take it with her when she left. He called her landline the next day, but another woman answered the phone. He decided it would be better to disconnect and wait for Margot to contact him. He wasn't aware at that stage she'd died."

"You think the cell phone might contain important information?"

"There's definitely proof that she was looking at restarting her career. Alex said she made a few calls to her modeling connections while she was in the salon, reestablishing contact with them."

"That's great. We'll follow up on those phone calls. Pierre has not been in touch?"

"Not at all," Bisset confirmed.

Granger disconnected and continued driving.

The previous interview, his first of the day, had told him a similar story. The relationship had begun with flowers, jewelry, seduction, and promises. Then it had deteriorated. Kinky sex had turned violent. Promises had become threats. Romance had soured, and ended with more threats.

The only difference was that in the first case, Pierre had broken off the relationship, but the same silencing methods had been used.

Granger noted that neither of these mistresses had high-profile jobs. As a well-known model, Margot's decision to leave could have represented more of a threat to Pierre.

Granger decided he pitied any woman who got herself involved with Pierre. Every relationship seemed to end in heartbreak or worse.

Pierre's wife, Diane, had been speeding when she'd lost control of the car and rolled it. She had been killed instantly and the car had caught fire in the horrific crash.

Granger doubted that the car had been tampered with, even though it had been destroyed to an extent where this could not be sure. But he had discovered that just two minutes earlier, Pierre had received a speeding ticket along the same road.

Diane had been following him, late at night, pursuing him along the main road that a few miles later, passed Coubert.

It might be just coincidence that Margot had, at the time, been residing in Coubert.

Granger sighed in frustration. Despite the amount of character evidence provided, they needed something more in order to make an arrest. What they had uncovered today was almost enough, but not quite.

He was three-quarters of the way home, and heading into afternoon traffic, when Bisset's next call came through.

"Granger!" She sounded excited.

"What is it? Talk quick; my phone's about to die."

"I've just got back. There's been a new development involving Pierre. You need to get here quickly. The woman working at the chateau—"

He lost the rest of her words as a truck driver next to him, stuck in the same traffic, blasted his horn impatiently.

"What is it?" he asked, feeling his pulse start racing, but he was speaking to a dead line. Which woman, and what had happened? Granger guessed this must somehow involve the au pair that he'd initially suspected. She had seemed to him to be emotionally unstable, on the point of snapping. Her extreme nervousness and her vague recall of recent events had got all his instincts prickling. He had no idea whether she always behaved this way, or whether the inner fragility he sensed had been exacerbated by severe stress.

Stress that could, of course, have been caused by the fact she'd played a role in Margot Fabron's murder.

With an empty battery, it would take another thirty frustrating minutes for him to get back to his headquarters and find out the latest twist in this complex case.

Half an hour later, Granger pulled into the parking lot and raced to the front door of the police station. Calling out a quick greeting to the officer on duty, he headed upstairs at a run. Scenarios were spinning through his head. For all he knew, they might have been heading off in entirely the wrong direction by investigating Pierre, despite the weight of evidence in that direction.

Bisset's office door was open.

"What's she done?" Granger asked, rather breathlessly.

"She came here earlier. She took the afternoon off work especially to come and see us."

Granger stepped inside and closed the door.

"Who? The au pair? Cassie Vale?"

He remembered again her frightened face, how her gaze had slid away from him when he'd tried to make eye contact and how she'd then hastily stared back at him, wide-eyed, as if realizing he'd noticed what she'd done. He recalled the nervous habit she had of digging her fingernails into her cuticles. The way she'd changed her story about whether she'd left her bedroom on the night of Margot's death. She'd seemed genuinely shaken by her own inability to recall what she'd done, and that made Granger wonder what else she might—intentionally or otherwise—have forgotten.

He expected Bisset to confirm his suspicions, but instead she shook her head.

"No, no. Not her. The housekeeper who works at the Dubois residence came to see us. Her name is Marnie Serrurier and she's waiting for you to interview her. She came to the station earlier and she brought us a piece of evidence she found."

"Important evidence?"

He could hear the excitement in Bisset's voice as she replied.

"Most definitely yes. I've spoken to her already. This changes everything, Granger. With the evidence and her testimony, I believe we have sufficient grounds to make an immediate arrest."

CHAPTER THIRTY

Cassie grabbed hold of the insecticide spray.

As Pierre's grip on her shoulder tightened, her shaking finger pressed down on the nozzle. She was going to do it. She was going to spray him with poison like a roach, and she didn't care if he choked on the fumes, or even if it blinded him.

Then, from downstairs, the door knocker banged, loudly and repeatedly.

For a moment, they both froze. Then Pierre's grasp eased, and Cassie lifted her finger off the nozzle.

Pierre stood up hurriedly, fastening his belt and swearing as he turned away from her. It was as if he'd forgotten her in an instant, thanks to this interruption. With no staff on duty tonight, there was nobody else to answer the door, and that meant she had been given a reprieve.

"Probably another damned journalist," he muttered.

He strode out of the room and Cassie climbed off the bed. She was shaking all over from delayed shock. He'd so nearly trapped her, and she felt sick when she thought about what could have happened.

She wasn't going to linger in the bedroom. This was her chance to escape downstairs and rejoin the children, and she resolved not to leave them again, no matter what. Their presence was her only protection now.

As she followed Pierre downstairs, keeping a wary distance from him, the knock sounded again. It was loud, authoritative, reverberating through the house.

"Papa?" Antoinette called, running out of the dining room. "There's someone at the door."

"I am on my way," Pierre snapped. "Get back to your dinner."

Cassie guessed he didn't want the children to overhear the tirade of abuse he was going to give whoever was waiting on the other side of the door. Even so, Antoinette was clearly curious. She headed back in the direction of the dining room but as soon as Pierre looked away, she stopped.

"What is it?"

Pierre flung open the front door, shouting the words angrily, and Cassie's heart leaped into her mouth as she saw the two police detectives standing there.

This was it. Pierre's earlier words to her hadn't just been threats. He must have told the detectives what she'd done, and how she'd searched his room, and now the evidence was pointing back to her.

Cassie's mouth felt so dry she wasn't sure if she could speak, but she decided she had to be completely honest with the detectives now. She had to disclose that she genuinely had no memory of what she might have done on the night of Margot's death, or whether her nightmare was rooted in reality, her imagination, or some place in between. She would promise to cooperate with them fully and tell them everything that had happened to her at this chateau, from the abuse to the attempted assault.

Perhaps if she cooperated, they would allow her to take her cell phone with her and she could at least look up the number of somebody she knew and explain what had happened.

Cassie stepped forward on quivering legs, wondering what they would tell her and how she would start her confession.

Then she realized what the police officers were saying and she stood still, her head whirling, not daring to believe what was happening.

"Monsieur Dubois, you are under arrest on suspicion of the murder of Margot Fabron. You have the right to remain silent, but it may harm your defense if you do not mention when questioned something which you later rely on in court."

"Wait! What the hell is this? What grounds do you have?" Pierre blustered.

"Monsieur, we will explain to you at the police station. Please, come with us." Detective Granger took his arm.

"I want to call my lawyer. Now! I had nothing to do with this."

Pierre jabbed his finger accusingly at Cassie.

"She is the guilty one; I'm telling you the truth. She was going into my bedroom while I was not at home. She was stealing from me. She was—"

Cassie braced herself for the probability that the detectives might want to take her with them after all. But Pierre's shouted words had no effect. Granger didn't even glance at her.

"You have the right to make a phone call as soon as we arrive at headquarters, and you may request legal representation. Now get into the car."

There was steel in the detective's voice and his words left no room for further argument. Swearing and threatening, Pierre was marched to the car.

How had this happened? Cassie wondered. What was the reason for Pierre's surprise arrest, and how long would he be gone for?

She heard a cry from behind her, and turning back, she saw that all three children were standing near the staircase and watching the scene in horror.

"Papa!" Antoinette called in a shrill voice, running to join Cassie at the front door.

"Where are you going? Why are the police taking you away?"

Pierre glowered in her direction.

"Get back inside!" he shouted.

Antoinette pushed past Cassie and dashed toward the car, followed by Ella, who had started to wail at the top of her voice.

"Come back," Antoinette pleaded.

Cassie got hold of Ella and picked her up, while Bisset caught Antoinette by her shoulders and turned her around, half-carrying her away from the waiting car.

"Your papa is not going to be home tonight, but you will be safe here. Come inside now," Bisset said.

The two of them shepherded the screaming children back inside, where they joined Marc, who was sucking his thumb and watching the spectacle wide-eyed from the hallway.

"We will call next of kin as soon as we arrive at headquarters," Bisset said, somewhat breathlessly. "Will you be able to stay with the children until a family member arrives?"

"Yes—yes, sure, of course," Cassie said. She was longing to ask Bisset what had happened, but she couldn't do so in front of the children and in any case, she didn't know if Bisset was allowed to tell her.

"You have access to the chateau's landline?" Bisset asked.

"Yes, I do." Cassie assumed Pierre had unlocked his bedroom door already, but even if he hadn't, he'd left his keys on the hall table.

"Please be ready to answer our call in the next half hour. We will update you as soon as we know who will be arriving to care for the children, and when."

"I'll be waiting."

Bisset ran back to the car. Cassie thought they were going to leave immediately, but instead Bisset took a manila envelope out of the car and jogged back to her.

She handed the envelope to Cassie.

"Your passport," she said. "We are returning it to you because you are no longer a person of interest in this case. Thank you for your cooperation throughout."

"My passport?"

Cassie took the envelope, pressing her fingers on the small, slim document inside, as relief flooded through her. It wasn't just the official confirmation that she was off the suspect list, but the fact she had her freedom back. She was no longer a prisoner here and could choose to leave at any time. She felt an enormous weight of worry slip off her shoulders, only realizing when it was gone how badly that fear had been crushing her.

Tears prickled her eyes and she blinked them away.

"Thank you so, so much," she whispered. "You don't know what it means to have this back, or how afraid I've felt without it."

She wanted to hug Bisset but felt it might not be appropriate, so she shook her hand instead, and to her surprise, Bisset clasped her hand warmly in both of hers.

"I'm glad we could give it back to you," she agreed.

Cassie remembered how the detective had stared curiously at her after she'd escaped from Pierre's clutches on the day of the funeral, rushing out of the music room in a panic with her clothing in disarray. She wondered if Bisset might have guessed what had happened, and if that was why she was so sympathetic now.

"We'll be in touch very soon," Bisset said in a reassuring tone. Then she turned away and hurried back to the waiting car.

After the police had left, Cassie found herself in charge of three hysterical children.

Antoinette was in floods of tears. Cassie had never seen the elder girl lose control so completely. She guessed that with Margot gone, Antoinette had hoped to become her father's favorite. Perhaps she had expected that at last, she would receive the love and attention she'd always craved from him but never received.

Cassie knew Antoinette was wrong in that regard but there was no way of telling her that now.

"Why?" she screamed, over and over.

"I don't know why," was all Cassie could say in response.

She was still in shock over what had taken place, unable to believe Pierre was really gone. She kept thinking that at any moment he might walk in again; that he would make an emergency call to his lawyer and force the police to turn around and bring him back. Or that the detectives might change their minds and arrest her after all. She found herself listening for the crunch of gravel on the driveway, and wished she knew what evidence had been used as grounds for Pierre's arrest.

"What will happen to us now?" Antoinette wailed.

This was another question that Cassie couldn't answer. What would happen to the children? Within a few short days, they had lost both of their parents and guardians. They must feel completely adrift in the world, and she couldn't find any way of reassuring them.

In fact, Cassie feared that if Pierre was released on bail, it would be back to business as usual in the chateau. She wondered whether Pierre's bail conditions would change his behavior to her, but she doubted it. That meant for her own safety, she'd have to leave as soon as she could, and turn her back on three extremely traumatized children from a fragmented family, who needed her more than ever.

She had no idea what the next few hours or days would bring, and felt so emotionally wrung out that she knew she wasn't capable of offering the calm, reasoned comfort the children needed. With a desperate effort, she tried to collect her thoughts and become the strong, responsible person they needed.

"We'll know more when the police contact us," she said, realizing as she spoke that this wasn't reassuring at all.

Ella was sobbing uncontrollably.

"Where has Papa gone?" she kept repeating, and Cassie remembered with a pang how she had been told that her mother had "gone" when she'd in fact died.

Marc was sullen and aggressive. Before Cassie could stop him, he grabbed one of Margot's framed photos from the hall table and threw it to the ground, cracking the glass. She couldn't find it in herself to chastise him, and decided just to say nothing about it at all.

"Let's go upstairs," she said, hoping that the bedtime ritual would calm them, and herself, down.

On the way upstairs, Marc kicked each stair hard and shouted in protest.

When she was halfway up the stairs, Cassie remembered with a jolt that she'd left her passport on the hall table. She'd put it there while comforting the children and forgotten to pick it up. Her most important item in the world, and she hadn't kept it with her. She felt like kicking the stairs too, out of sheer frustration at how fragmented and disorganized her thoughts were.

Her shoulder was bruised from where Pierre had grasped her and pushed her onto the bed, and she suddenly remembered how she'd breathed in the overpowering sandalwood scent of his cologne. She couldn't believe he was really gone. He'd been so furious at being arrested, and had tried so hard to force the police to take her instead.

Let him not come back, she prayed.

Eventually, the three children were congregated outside Antoinette's bedroom, and the girls' cries had quieted enough for Cassie to speak.

"I'll tell you what's happening as soon as I know."

She paused, clasping her hands together tightly so the children wouldn't see them shaking, wondering what the best way to console them would be, after their whole world had just fallen apart.

"Can we sleep together tonight?" Antoinette asked, and Ella and Marc nodded vigorously.

"That's a good idea," Cassie agreed.

"And can we have some milk, and cake?" Marc asked.

"I have to wait for the police to call. But after that, I'll bring you a treat," she promised.

Relieved they had suggested something positive to help them feel better, Cassie moved Ella's pillow, and a few of her stuffed animals, into Antoinette's bedroom. Marc carried the contents of his toy box into the room, and Cassie brought his mattress and bedding along in case they needed more sleeping space.

As she left their bedroom and closed the door gently behind her, Cassie remembered those muttered words Marc had spoken earlier, when she'd let him out of the closet and he had walked past her.

They hadn't made sense at the time, and she'd been too caught up in her own memories for her brain to decipher them. Now, as she walked down the passage to Pierre's bedroom to wait for the police to call, Cassie found herself shivering as the reality of what he'd said hit home.

The words Marc had spoken had been, "You are just like Papa."

CHAPTER THIRTY ONE

B ack at headquarters, Granger completed the paperwork on the case while Bisset made the necessary phone calls. They were ensconced in his overly warm office, but on this chilly evening, Bisset did not complain about the heat.

As she replaced the receiver after her final call, there was a loud knock at the door.

Captain Palomer, the station commander, marched in, visibly smoldering with anger.

"I have just been speaking with Pierre Dubois, who is in custody here. What is happening? This is unbelievable. Please explain your actions."

Granger exchanged a glance with Bisset, before replying politely.

"Evening, Captain. Yes, we arrested him an hour ago."

"Without my permission?"

The captain's face, always florid, had turned brick red with anger. He leaned on the desk, spreading his plump fingers out and glowering at Granger.

"You were unavailable so we consulted with the area commander."

Granger kept his tone calm. He was well aware that the captain's absence had been a stroke of luck for them. He was certain that if the captain had been available, he would have ordered them not to arrest Pierre. After all, the original artwork in Palomer's office had been gifted to him by one of Pierre's studios, and his wife headed up one of the marketing firms that Pierre used.

"This is crazy! We are arresting a community leader, someone who has an impeccable reputation."

"With all due respect, sir, Pierre's community involvement and reputation will be discussed during the trial, where people can make their own decisions about it, but that fact could not prevent his arrest."

"I order you to drop the charges against him. You have acted irresponsibly and have not followed due process. Send him home immediately."

Bisset cleared her throat and Granger saw she looked even angrier than Palomer.

"We followed due process every step of the way. That is why we made this arrest, sir. Not to make the arrest, with compelling evidence against this suspect, would have been a dereliction of our duty."

"Show me the paperwork," Palomer snapped. "Pierre informed me that he hired a foreign au pair a few days ago and that he suspects her of stealing, and other crimes. Why was she not arrested?"

"There was no evidence against her," Bisset insisted.

Despite Granger's own misgivings about the emotionally unstable au pair, he knew Bisset felt extremely sympathetic toward her. After Margot's funeral, Bisset had shared her fears that she believed the au pair was either being sexually assaulted, or pursued with sexual intent, by Pierre. Based on the testimonies from the other interviews, Granger couldn't help but agree this was likely, and he'd been relieved to return her passport to her. She was an innocent nobody who'd unwittingly been caught up in this situation, and could now go on her way and live her life—hopefully finding better emotional balance along the way.

"Please take a look at our dossier. And tell me, sir, if this was a poor man from the suburbs of Grigny, would you have arrested him? Based on the evidence, I think so. We cannot make an exception for those who are wealthy or well connected," Bisset insisted to Palomer.

She shoved the file across the desk.

Granger was sure Bisset wanted to add that making an exception would constitute corruption, but she didn't say it. The political tightrope was a careful balancing act that had to be respected, even when you knew you were doing the right thing.

"Pierre has an expert legal team at his disposal," he said quietly. "I am sure that they will do their best to counter the evidence against him, and enable the judge to make the best decision. However, we had to act according to our mandate as officers of the law."

As the arresting officer, Granger knew only he or the prosecutor could drop the charges, and he could see Palomer's evident frustration at the fact.

Granger personally didn't think that the charges would stick. He knew Pierre would hire the best lawyers money could buy, and would spend whatever it took to clear his name. But in a court of law, the outcome was never certain. Whatever the end result, he was confident that he and Bisset had acted as they should, and he couldn't help feeling satisfied as Palomer, now purple-faced, grabbed the folder and stalked out of the room.

"How far away from retirement is he?" Bisset murmured.

"Two years," Granger said. "Sooner, perhaps, if he suffers from medical issues. Hypertension can be exacerbated by frustration, I believe. We can see this one through."

He gave her a conspiratorial wink, and she smiled in return.

Cassie decided to wait in Pierre's study for the police to call. She pulled out the leather-upholstered chair, and as she perched on its edge, she thought about what Marc had said.

"You are just like Papa."

Marc's words had been a shock to her, but they had made her think about how the children had reacted after she'd lost the plot earlier that day. Instead of being upset by her behavior, like a normal child would be, they'd quieted suddenly, reined their unruliness in, and hunkered down, as if they were preparing to handle whatever might come.

Perhaps they had learned these coping mechanisms through experience, to protect themselves when a situation became violent and spiraled out of control.

Where had the violence come from? Margot?

Margot had only been there a year, and in any case, Pierre was clearly the head of the household, and would dictate their treatment as he chose.

Cassie was convinced that Pierre was an abusive father.

She was certain this wasn't the first time the three had been physically abused. They seemed to be familiar with it and, in fact, it was the only form of discipline they appeared to understand.

Cassie hugged herself, rocking back and forth on the chair as she thought about what the children must have endured, and what a toxic environment they were being raised in. She should have realized, from their consistent rebellion against discipline, what they were trying to tell her. But she'd been too slow on the uptake, she hadn't understood, and had ended up blaming their antisocial behavior on her own lack of skill.

Cassie jumped as the phone started ringing loudly. She snatched it up, relieved that the call was coming through earlier than she'd expected, and anxious to know what awaited the children.

She realized she should probably have had a pen and paper handy, because she might need to write down notes. She opened the desk drawer and rummaged through it while she answered, doing her best to sound calm and professional.

"Hello. Cassie speaking."

There was a short pause.

"Baby! I thought you weren't allowed to answer the phone or take calls."

Zane's tone managed to combine hurt, accusation, and triumph.

"Zane?" Cassie was too flabbergasted to do more than stammer out his name, but that gave him all the encouragement he needed to continue.

"I thought you were just blowing me off. I mean, there's no such thing as people not being allowed to take calls. That was a ridiculous excuse. I never believed it for a moment. But anyway, I wanted to tell you more about this job. They're keen to interview you, even if it's a Skype interview, so you can do it from where you are. If you can email your CV through they'll have a look in the meantime. And of course you can stay at my place when you come back. I don't hold any grudges after the way you treated me. I'll be glad to help you get back on your feet again. So, you want me to set you up with this?"

Cassie was so angry she found herself climbing to her feet. The words she wanted to say didn't feel right while she was sitting down.

She planted her feet on the tile floor and glowered at the opposite wall while she spoke.

"A few things," she said, pleased by how level her voice sounded. Zane's unacceptable behavior hadn't pushed her over the edge or been the last straw that reduced her to tears. On the contrary, she felt strong enough to fight back, and angry enough to tell Zane, at last, exactly what she thought of him.

"Firstly, how dare you doubt what I said? What gives you the right to accuse me of lying? Because that's exactly what you've done, and it isn't the first time you've done it, either. Do you even realize? Do you have any idea what it makes a person feel like inside, to be unfairly accused of being a liar? But that's how you conducted our entire relationship. You broke me down, time after time, with this kind of crappy emotional abuse. And I'm not taking it from you again. Because that's what you are, Zane, you're an abuser. Just like my father was. I went and chose him all over again when I met you."

"Baby! I'm no such thing! I was joking when I said that. I didn't mean it seriously. Please, you've misunderstood me completely and now you've got me on the back foot. I—"

Zane sounded outraged, but Cassie didn't give him the chance to speak any further.

"Secondly, you don't give a shit about me. I told you I'd get into trouble if you phoned. But you don't care about that. You're selfish, arrogant, and entitled. You do what you want and you don't care what the implications are for others. When I realized that, it opened my eyes to who you really were. I dated you because I thought you cared for me. First you ended up emotionally abusing me, then physically abusing me. Finally, you just showed me you don't care at all if I get into trouble with my employer and, in fact, you'll take action to make sure I do, because it suits your warped agenda to get me back so you can control me again. What kind of assholery is this? I had to put up with it for some of the worst months of my life, and the only thing I'm thankful for is that it showed me who you really were, and I managed to get away from you."

She was shouting now, screaming the words at the wall in anger, gripping the phone with all her

"Baby! I'm sorry. I didn't mean it that way. It was urgent because the applications close tomorrow, and I wanted you to have a chance."

Zane sounded panicked now, but yet again, Cassie overrode his protests.

"Thirdly, Zane, I'm the one who has to forgive you. I left because you hit me, and the only reason I didn't tell you earlier what a disgusting, cowardly act that was, is that you made me too scared of you. Do you like that? Is it fun for you to be in a relationship where the other person is trying to manage your awful, unacceptable, violent, antisocial behavior all the time? Does it make you feel big and good to know how much of an abuser you are? Are you looking forward to making your next girlfriend as 'happy' as you made me? I'm sure you are and all I can say is whoever she is, I pity her."

Cassie lowered her voice with an effort. Even though the children were in the furthest bedroom, they might still hear if she carried on shrieking out her rage.

"I took photos of that bruise and I still have those photos on my phone. I'll be delighted to go to the police if and when I'm back in the States, and lay a charge of harassment and physical abuse. Have you ever been arrested, Zane? The police don't like abusers who hit women. I believe they give them a hard time."

"Baby, please." Zane gabbled out the words. "I don't want to contradict you, I'm willing to accept what you say, but it's not true about that bruise. Please hear me out, I remember better than you, because you'd had too much to drink. I've told you this before and I promise you, my version won't change because it's the truth. We fought, but I didn't hit you. I tried to pull you out of the path of a car. The bruises were from that. You would have been knocked over for sure. Yes, I'm full of shit, I gave you a hard time, I wasn't the perfect boyfriend. All that I'm willing to admit, but I wouldn't hit you. Genuine. You created that in your own mind."

Doubt flickered inside Cassie, but she reminded herself to be strong. She wasn't going to fall for his gaslighting, or believe the alternative reality he was trying to create. Not this time.

"I know what happened. I was there. You don't forget or mis-remember when somebody hits you. So don't ever call me again, not ever in your life, or I'll come back to the States just to lay that charge."

"Please, believe what I say, baby. Please don't..."

Zane's voice was taut with tension.

Cassie didn't bother wasting her time listening. She stabbed the disconnect button as hard as she could and put the phone down.

She was still trembling with rage, but she felt utterly triumphant that, at last, she'd spoken her mind to Zane—in full, and without fear.

Why had it taken her so long? Cassie berated herself for not having had the courage to do this earlier. After all, needing to escape from Zane was the reason she'd ended up here. She could have avoided so much stress if she'd managed to stand up to him before leaving.

As the phone rang again, Cassie realized with a jolt that she couldn't have done it earlier, because the experiences she'd gone through here in France had given her the strength she needed to confront Zane.

Chapter Thirty Two

Cassie sat down again and let out a deep breath to calm the last of her rage before picking up the ringing phone. She guessed there was a small chance it was Zane calling back, but after the way he'd sounded by the end of their conversation, she doubted it.

The voice on the line was unfamiliar. The woman sounded pleasant, if rather stressed.

"Hello, is that the au pair?" she said.

"Yes, I'm Cassie, and I've been looking after the children."

"I am so glad you are there. My name is Josephine, and I am the sister of Diane, Pierre's late wife."

"It's great to speak to you," Cassie said, relieved that she wasn't speaking to a direct relative of Pierre's. After his recent arrest, his family was bound to be furious.

"I told the police I'd like to call you myself. I am shocked by this news and I'm sure you must be, too. I am coming to Paris immediately so that I can be with the children. I am traveling all the way from Bordeaux, but I'm on the way to the station now, and there is a train leaving in twenty minutes which I will hopefully be in time for, so you can expect me by about nine p.m."

"That's great," Cassie said. "Do you want me to tell the children? Should they wait up?"

"They must be exhausted. That choice is up to them, but please let them know that Aunt Josephine is on her way, and that I have missed them."

"I will do that," Cassie said.

She put the phone down, glad that a family member would be arriving that night, and encouraged that Josephine had called personally, rather than having the police phoning on her behalf.

Thinking about what Josephine had said, Cassie realized she obviously hadn't been to Margot's funeral. Her words had implied she hadn't seen the children for a while.

Cassie headed back down the passage to tell the children the news.

They were all huddled together in Antoinette's bed, and she was reading them a story. Ella was sucking her thumb and Marc looked to be almost asleep.

"Your aunt Josephine is arriving later," she said. "She asked me to tell you that she's missed you."

She'd wondered how the children would react, but hadn't been prepared for Antoinette's scream of joy.

"Hooray! Aunt Josephine! We love her so much. Marc, wake up. Aunt Josephine is coming tonight, to look after us."

Jumping out of bed, Antoinette ran over to Cassie and hugged her tightly.

"Thank you for telling us this."

"She's our favorite aunt!" Marc shouted, jumping up and down on the bed. A beaming Ella joined in.

Antoinette made a face at him.

"She's our only aunt, silly. But she likes to joke with us that she's our favorite aunt. She's so nice to us. Cassie, she's really kind and loving. We sometimes go on holidays to her house, it is so beautiful. She has a farm really close to the sea."

"There are animals on the farm," Marc said in between bounces. "She has sheep and cows and horses."

"And ponies. I rode a pony the last time I was there," Ella added.

"Do you think our cousins will be coming too?" Marc asked. "I like them a lot. Their names are Tomas and Nicolas, and Nicolas is the same age as me."

"I don't know, but it sounded as if she was traveling on her own," Cassie said.

"When will she be here?" Antoinette asked anxiously.

"She said by nine."

"We will wait up," Antoinette decided.

"I will come and call you as soon as she arrives," Cassie promised.

"Thank you so much, Cassie."

Antoinette hugged her again, squeezing her arms tightly around her, and to Cassie's surprise both Ella and Marc joined in, hugging her and thanking her.

She hugged them back, sniffing hard, amazed by how emotional this display of gratitude had made her.

"I love you all so much," she told the children. "I'm happy that your favorite aunt will be here soon. You deserve to be with someone who will be really kind to you."

Cassie couldn't believe how the atmosphere in the room had changed after she'd broken this news. The children were happy and positive now, as excited and expectant as if the summer holidays lay ahead.

Cassie wondered if Aunt Josephine reminded them of their mother, and this was partly why they were looking forward to being in her care—at least for now, because she had no idea what would happen in the longer term.

She headed downstairs to clear up the supper dishes, tidy the dining room, and find some snacks for the children. She made a mental note to put her passport away for safekeeping, and to pick up the photo which Marc had thrown to the floor. The glass had cracked but it hadn't shattered. If it wasn't too badly damaged, hopefully she could salvage it.

When Cassie reached the hallway, she saw the photo was back in its place. The crack in the glass had been pressed together so it was almost invisible. The envelope with her passport inside had been placed neatly on the corner of the table. She put it in her pocket and zipped it closed, wondering who was working tonight. She'd assumed she was the only one here apart from the children, and checked the front door was locked, just in case.

Going through to the dining room, she found the dishes had all been cleared away. Someone had definitely been helping her out.

Curious to see if whoever had done this might still be tidying up, she headed to the kitchen.

When she walked in, she saw Marnie was sweeping the kitchen floor.

Marnie jumped so hard when she saw Cassie that she dropped the broom and it fell to the floor with a clatter.

"Hey," Cassie said, surprised. "I thought you had the afternoon off, but thank you so much for helping."

Then she looked more closely at Marnie. She was sheet-white.

"Are you OK?" Cassie asked.

"Pierre has gone? Tell me he has gone, Cassie."

"He's been arrested," Cassie said. "The police arrived at about half past five. Why? Did you know about it?"

She felt as if her brain was starting to catch up with the reason for Marnie's odd behavior.

"I knew about it," Marnie confirmed. She spoke in a low voice, and Cassie found herself doing the same.

"Was that why you took the afternoon off? I assumed you were at a job interview. Was I wrong?"

Marnie nodded.

"I was at the police station."

"Why?"

Cassie looked again at her tense, frightened face.

"I think you should sit down and tell me what happened. Can I make you some tea?"

Cassie put the kettle on, and took cups and teabags from the cupboard where she'd seen them in her earlier search for dinner ingredients. There was a bottle of milk in the fridge so she took that out, thinking as she did that the detail-oriented Marnie would have poured it into a smaller jug and put everything on a tray.

Marnie sat down at the kitchen table. She lowered her head and let out a deep breath, looking down at her hands.

"I was so frightened that they would not arrest him, and he would find out where I had been, and I would be in more trouble than anyone could imagine. I know that could still happen, because yes, I was the reason Pierre was arrested today."

Cassie stared at her, taking a few moments to process what she was saying. Shock and relief chased each other around her mind.

"What did you do?" she asked.

She poured the tea and sat down next to Marnie.

"I was emptying the dustbin this morning. That one, over there."

Marnie pointed to the large bin where the compostable waste was thrown away.

"It was by pure chance that I saw it, because it was right at the bottom of the bag and covered in dirt. It was a cell phone. A simple, older type of phone, not a fancy smartphone. I had never seen it before."

"That's weird," Cassie agreed, wondering how the cell phone had incriminated Pierre.

"It was just after the funeral. I thought maybe a guest had dropped it, or else one of the children had gotten up to their tricks and thrown it away as a joke."

Cassie nodded, thinking these were good guesses.

"I decided to try and find out who it belonged to, because some-one was surely missing it. So I wiped it off and turned it on. There was still a little battery life remaining. I checked the recent call list and the contacts. There were no contacts. This phone had only made a few calls, and they were all to the same number. So I took the phone and drove down the road to the far side of the vineyard, where you can get a cell phone signal on fine days. There, I called the number."

"What happened then?"

"A woman answered almost immediately," Marnie said, cradling her cup in her hands.

Cassie stared at her, not daring to breathe, waiting for what Marnie was going to say.

"The woman said, 'Pierre, is everything all right? I thought you had thrown this phone away.'"

Cassie stared at Marnie, aghast, and for a while she had no words.

CHAPTER THIRTY THREE

Cassie felt stunned by the turn events had taken. The incriminating content of the mystery woman's words put everything in a completely different perspective. The fact that Pierre had been calling her on a secret phone, disposed of soon after Margot's death, was a bombshell.

"What did you do when you heard her speak?" she asked Marnie.

Cassie put a hand on the table, reassured by the solid feeling of the wood, which grounded her when everything else seemed dizzyingly uncertain.

"I disconnected the call. I knew instantly that if Pierre discovered I'd found the phone, I would be in serious trouble. I was tempted to throw it straight back in the trash and pretend I'd never found it. Then I thought to myself—do I want to do what is easy, or do I want to do what is right?"

"And you chose what was right?"

Cassie could imagine how difficult that decision must have been.

"I did. I knew I had to take it to the police. But at the same time I could not just abscond with it. So I went to Pierre immediately, praying that this woman would not already have called him back."

"I don't think she ever did," Cassie said. "Maybe she realized she'd made a mistake and decided to keep quiet."

"Yes, I think that is what may have happened. Anyway I asked Pierre for the afternoon off. I said I had a few urgent errands to run. He granted it to me, and I drove straight to the police station. I had to wait a while for the detectives to return as both of them were out. When they returned they examined the phone and interviewed me. That was when I found out that the evidence wasn't just incriminating, but grounds for arrest."

Cassie refilled Marnie's teacup and waited for her to continue.

"They said the calls had been made to Helene, Pierre's mistress, who he visited on the night of Margot's death. The timing was significant. The phone had only been used five times. Calls were made the morning before Margot died, later that afternoon, and late in the evening, and then another two calls were made the following morning."

The pieces were falling into place for Cassie.

"So they used a different phone to communicate over that short time? Then Pierre threw it away?"

"Yes. Pierre never disclosed that phone to the police, and they said the phone together with the calls indicated preplanning."

"I'm so proud of you, Marnie," Cassie said. "What you did was very brave."

"I was beside myself with worry. Pierre has a violent temper, and I have seen its effects. I'm not staying here anymore."

"You couldn't, after doing that. Has the other job offer been confirmed?"

"It has, but I am leaving France. The company who employed me is based in London and they have two hotels there. I asked if I could work in one of those, and they agreed. I don't want to be in Paris, or even in the country, with Pierre's trial under way. He is a vindictive man, and his influence is far reaching."

"I understand," Cassie replied soberly.

Marnie's words made her think about her own situation, and the threats that Pierre had directed at her. She felt more uneasy than ever about her predicament, and wondered what she would say to Josephine and how much she should try to explain.

After she and Marnie had said goodnight and exchanged phone numbers, Cassie took some chocolate milk and biscuits up to the children, and then waited in her bedroom until she heard the cab arrive. She hurried to open the front door for Josephine.

A slender, dark-haired woman climbed out of the cab, walked straight up to Cassie, and gave her a warm hug.

"You poor thing," she said. "What a terrible situation to have to cope with. Are the children all right? I came here as quickly as I could."

"They're all right. They were very upset, but they handled it well and supported each other. And they cheered up hugely when they heard you were coming. They're having biscuits and milk in bed now," Cassie said.

But they weren't. Cassie heard running footsteps on the stairs and saw Marc was leading the charge to the front door, with Antoinette and Ella following close behind.

"Aunt Josephine is here!" he yelled.

Placing her bag hastily on the floor, Josephine gathered the three children into her arms and hugged them tightly.

"It's so wonderful to see all of you—how you have grown! Cassie has told me how brave you have been. I am so proud of you all."

Cassie realized Josephine was crying. She took a tissue out of her pocket and wiped her eyes before turning back to the children.

"What's going to happen now, Aunt Josephine?" Antoinette asked.

"Right now? We are all going to go to bed and get some rest."

"And tomorrow?" Ella jumped up and down impatiently.

"Tomorrow, we have decided you will come home with me and live in the farmhouse in Bordeaux."

"Really?" Antoinette asked, and there were tears in her eyes, too.

"Yes," Josephine said gently.

Marc and Ella screamed in delight, dancing around Josephine, while Antoinette wrapped her arms tightly around her aunt and cried harder.

"I'm happy. I really am," she said when she could speak. "I'm crying from happiness."

Josephine smoothed her hair.

"It's always good to cry, whether you're happy or sad. But I'm glad you will be happy to come and live with me. I have spoken to your papa, and he sends his love and says he is fine. He is excited you will be living in the farmhouse. Now come on, you sleepy heads, you need to rest. We have a lot to do tomorrow. We have to get all your bags packed up, ready for our train journey back to Bordeaux."

Cassie followed the family upstairs and helped Josephine put the children to bed. Not that she needed very much help, Cassie noticed. The children genuinely adored her, and were on their best behavior.

Within a few minutes, all of them were tucked up in bed.

"Let us have a little talk downstairs," Josephine suggested to Cassie.

They headed to the dining room where Josephine poured them each a glass of claret.

"I find a glass of wine at night helps me sleep well," she confided. "And after the craziness of this afternoon, I need something to calm me down. I'm sure you do, too."

"Thank you," Cassie said, sipping the rich, red claret and thinking how lucky the children were. Josephine was so kind, so down to earth, and genuinely friendly.

Josephine took a deep breath.

"I cannot thank you enough for helping to look after the children. I know how troubled they must have been with all this happening and I am sure you have not had an easy time."

"It's been OK," Cassie said, but Josephine shook her head.

"Things have been very difficult these past few years. First, there were problems between Pierre and Diane in their marriage and I know Diane was tremendously unhappy for a long time. When she died, I suggested I should take over the children's care but Pierre refused to allow it. Margot moved in almost immediately, and he told me Margot would cope perfectly, and that my interfering was unnecessary."

"That must have been so hurtful," Cassie said.

Josephine tilted her glass, gently swirling the red wine.

"I have not been welcome at the chateau for a long time. Pierre and I never got along, and our relationship worsened over the years, despite Diane trying to smooth things over between us. She and Pierre were fighting so badly, so much of the time, that it only worsened the conflict between us all. I ended up staying away and inviting the children to come to me for holidays. Then when Margot moved in, Pierre refused to allow that to happen. The children and I haven't seen each other for over a year."

"They must have missed you terribly," Cassie said.

"I think they did. Their life here was not happy, and I doubt it improved during this past year," Josephine agreed.

She took another sip of wine.

"The police said, when they called me, that there is compelling evidence against him. I asked if I could speak to Pierre and to my surprise, they allowed him to call me while I was on the train. He blustered and swore and blamed everyone except himself. He said that he had recently used a different phone to call his mistress after Margot grew suspicious. He disposed of it after her death because he didn't want the police to know about it, and that because of this, they suspect collusion and preplanning."

"That doesn't sound good, surely?"

"He kept shouting that he was innocent and would clear his name, but even he acknowledged it might not be quick or easy. That was when I asked him again if I could take over the children's custody. He had no choice but to agree. After all, with his future being so uncertain and even his release from prison not yet confirmed, there is no place in his life for children and I also pointed out that they would suffer from the rumors and accusations which will circulate in the community."

"Yes, without a doubt," Cassie said, wondering how many of Pierre's supposed friends would switch sides when the news came out.

"We agreed that he will officially sign the children's care over to me. I am more than happy to do this. My husband and I love the time we spend with them, and they get on well with our two boys."

"It sounds like the perfect move for them. I am so relieved that it's turned out this way," Cassie agreed.

"I am sure you are wondering where this leaves you," Josephine said.

Cassie realized, to her enormous relief, that now the children would be starting a new life, there would be no place for her at the chateau.

She nodded politely, clasping her hands tightly as Josephine continued.

"Please let me have your banking details. First thing tomorrow, I will transfer the amount due to you, together with a bonus for the stress and unpleasantness you have had to endure."

"Thank you so much," Cassie said. "I've got the contract saved on my phone, so I can check what my November salary is."

Josephine shook her head firmly. "My husband and I both agree in this case, your full annual salary is due to you, together with a bonus as a thank-you. In return, all we ask is that you do not speak about what has happened—to the press, or to anyone who might be curious. For the children's sake, we'd like to try and limit any damaging information as much as possible."

"I understand," Cassie said. "I wouldn't have said anything, even without the bonus and the full salary, which is extremely kind of you."

Josephine set her glass down. "Thank you so very much. If you or the children need me, I will be in the first bedroom on the right, in the guest wing. Sleep well."

Cassie watched her go upstairs, her mind whirling.

She couldn't believe the surprise ending to this dreadful day.

She realized how worried she'd been about the children, who had seemed to be stuck in this dysfunctional situation with no way out. Now they had a way. They had an aunt who loved them, a safe place to go, and a stable home life ahead of them, and she was relieved beyond measure about this.

And her circumstances had done an about-face, too. From living in fear, under a cloud of suspicion, she was free to leave and had some spending money—far more than she'd expected.

She set down her empty glass and headed to the front door to lock up for the night, but before she did that, she stepped outside.

She gazed up at the imposing stone frontage of the chateau, the pale stone seeming to glow in the darkness. A cool breeze made her shiver.

She wasn't entirely free. Although Josephine hadn't said so directly, she was certain Pierre had mentioned her name during his blustering. She was sure he would follow through on his threats to have her arrested for stealing and that might lead to her being accused of other crimes.

If Marnie was leaving the country, perhaps she should do the same, at least until his trial was over. After all, Pierre was a wealthy and vindictive man whose influence was far-reaching, and although the police had believed her story and let her go, Cassie feared that others might not. And who knew when Pierre might be freed on bail? With all of his influence, maybe he could be let out as soon as tomorrow. And return to the chateau.

A shudder went down her spine. There could be no time to spare.

Yes, leaving France was exactly what she should do.

And she would do so first thing in the morning.

CHAPTER THIRTY FOUR

Morning light streamed into the chateau as Cassie helped the children carry their bags downstairs. Marc's bag contained some clothes, as well as all the toys that could possibly fit into the large travel case. Marnie was carrying Ella's bag and a spare rucksack, while Josephine and Antoinette rolled Antoinette's enormous suitcase across the hallway.

"Shall we call a cab?" Josephine asked.

"No, no, let me drive you to the station," Cassie insisted.

Marnie fetched Pierre's SUV, the most spacious of the cars available, and brought it around to the front of the house, opening all the doors while Cassie started loading it up.

It was a beautiful day—cool, breezy, and clear. The crisp autumn wind ruffled Cassie's hair and she felt hopeful about what lay ahead of her. After she'd dropped the family at the station, she could drive back here, return the car, and then pack her own bags and call a cab. She decided she would then head back to the very same station and take the Eurostar to London. In just a few hours, she could be across the Channel and in a brand new country—one she'd always wanted to explore.

Marnie was also ready to leave, and had loaded her belongings into her own car. Cassie hugged her, sad to say goodbye to someone who'd become such a good friend, even though she hoped that if they were both in London, they'd be able to see each other again soon.

"We will stay in touch," Marnie whispered. "My new workplace has a signal, and I love messaging. Good luck."

Then it was time to head for the station with the children, excited about the journey, singing in a tuneless chorus in the back of the car. Once there, Cassie helped Josephine load a trolley with all the bags and wheel it to the platform where the train to Bordeaux was already waiting.

Cassie looked at the sleek, shiny train and felt suddenly bereft. She wished she didn't have to say goodbye.

One by one, she hugged the children.

"Antoinette, I am so glad for you. I know you're going to have the most amazing time with Josephine, and you're such a strong person."

"Thank you. You are too, Cassie. I was so hateful to you because I was unhappy, even though I wanted to be your friend," Antoinette whispered.

Marc strutted up to her and held out his hand. Cassie took it, and nearly started to cry when she found Marc had given her one of his prized toy bulls.

"Will you come and visit us, Cassie?" he asked.

"I will. I promise."

Ella approached shyly, and gave Cassie a folded piece of paper.

"I made you a drawing," she said. "It's of the sun, because whenever I think of you, I think about sunshine. Thank you for looking after us."

Cassie blinked tears away while hugging Ella.

"I will always remember you," she said to Ella with a smile.

After all the goodbyes, the family boarded the train, and Cassie watched, waving frantically as they waved back, until the train had disappeared from sight.

Cassie headed back to the SUV, thinking of her plans, but as she climbed inside, she picked up the trace of a familiar scent that made her go cold all over.

It was the sharp sandalwood tang of Pierre's cologne. As she breathed it in, Cassie felt her skin pucker into gooseflesh.

She remembered how Pierre had pushed her down onto her bed, his fingers gripping her shoulder, whispering threats into her ear to force her to stay quiet.

With shaking fingers, Cassie buzzed open the window and let the breeze blow through, wishing the memories would leave as easily, but they had never been more vivid and she felt as if she was reliving the awful scene.

He'd been so confident, so calculating. His expression of triumph at her helplessness had sickened her. In her terror, she'd blanked out all the details of what he'd said, but now his words came flooding back. He'd told her that he knew she'd been in his room, and that he had photographic evidence of her snooping and searching and opening drawers.

Photographic evidence?

Cassie pressed her forehead on the steering wheel, thinking about what he had threatened, and realizing the enormity of what those words actually meant.

She didn't think they were empty threats. The certainty in his voice, combined with the fact he'd basically described her actions, pointed to another alternative—that Pierre had a hidden camera in his room and he'd caught her on it.

It would be impossible for Cassie to plead innocence if it existed. She had only one chance left to find it and if she could, she had to destroy it. Otherwise, she was sure Pierre would follow through on his threats and use the footage to incriminate her as soon as he had a chance.

She sat there, debating.

On the one hand, she had to leave the country before Pierre was freed.

On the other, she had to see if there was any real evidence against her.

Finally, she turned the wheel and hit the gas.

Leaving the country would have to wait.

She had to take one last trip back to the hated chateau.

CHAPTER THIRTY FIVE

There were two housemaids working in the kitchen, but the upper floor of the chateau was quiet, and Cassie couldn't hear any sounds from the guest wing, or the children's bedrooms, as she made her way to Pierre's bedroom.

You have to do this, she told herself. *You have to find what's there before he uses it against you, because he will.*

She looked around the room, butterflies fluttering in her stomach, hoping that if Pierre had a system set up, it would be easy to find. She didn't know how much time she had. Pierre could already have briefed a private investigator on what to do and where to look. The investigator could even be on his way.

Her first idea, that there were CCTV security cameras set up in the room, was wrong. There were no visible cameras.

What about hidden ones, though?

Cassie scanned the walls, wishing she had a better idea of what the cameras might look like, or how high up they would need to be placed. Pacing round the room, nerves churning inside her, she tried to approach the situation logically.

The camera, if there was one, would have filmed her searching the secret drawer. So it had to be mounted on a wall, with a view of the bed.

Turning to stare at the bed, Cassie started to wonder whether the camera's main function had been security at all, or whether it had been there for another reason.

Perhaps Pierre had enjoyed filming his kinky exploits, so that he could relive those scenes over and over again.

In that case, the walls on either side of the massive bed would be the best place to hide a camera.

Looking closely at the magnificent oil painting on the right hand wall, Cassie noticed a darker patch in the midnight-blue pool in the center of the artwork. Light reflected off it, the way it might shine off a glass lens.

Cassie lifted the oil painting off the wall, noticing it was easy to remove, and that there were two gaps in its canvas.

Cassie leaned closer, her heart hammering as she saw the alcove in the wall. The video camera behind it was a small, state of the art model. The bigger gap in the canvas accommodated its lens, but there was a tiny gap, the size of a fingertip, that allowed access to the Record button.

"He used this for his sexploits," she said aloud, horrified by the thought. She wondered if Margot had known. What footage was on here? Well, she was going to find out.

She removed the camera carefully from its alcove. Its battery was dead, but there were two spares in the alcove with it, and the second one she tried had some charge left. So this was not a permanent surveillance camera. The footage would be based on the battery life, which she guessed would be a couple of hours at most.

How did it work?

Sitting down on the bed, Cassie unfolded the view screen and turned the camera on. She navigated to the menu and found the stored videos.

There were four films loaded on the memory card.

Cassie started with the fourth and oldest one, and as the crystal-clear footage began playing, she gave a cry of surprise.

Pierre was moving away from the camera, smiling. He must have just turned it on. And on the bed, with a black blindfold over her eyes and her hands tied together behind her back, was a curvaceous woman with porcelain skin and long, red hair.

"When was this taken?" Cassie asked aloud.

She could hear the incredulity in her own voice. Pierre had brought another woman into his bedroom. Was this redhead his mistress, Helene?

She didn't want to watch any more of that video. Instead, she checked the date and raised her eyebrows in surprise as she saw it had been filmed just a week ago. Margot must have gone out, and Pierre had sneaked the redhead in here.

He must have taken the opportunity to do this before Cassie had arrived. After all, having an au pair in residence meant another person in that bedroom wing, which would make it more difficult to smuggle anyone in.

Cassie moved on to the next video, grimacing as she found herself watching the awful strangulation scene she'd spied through the keyhole. The crystal clear screen showed every detail of Margot's struggles and to her shock, she realized it also recorded very accurate sound.

Shaking her head, she stopped the video. She didn't want to watch another moment of this footage.

The third video was of her.

Cassie saw herself walking in, looking nervously around, and proceeding to search the room. She looked terrified and furtive, and as she lifted out the bondage equipment, she faced the camera and there was a clear picture of her shocked face.

She was sure Pierre had gotten a cheap thrill from it, and it had certainly provided him with the information he needed. He could have shown these photos to the police and they would have compromised her badly.

Cassie watched right through to the end and then she firmly pressed the Delete button. No matter what happened, there would be more opportunity for blackmail. The evidence of herself in this room had been erased.

With the third video deleted, the fourth image sprang onto the screen, and Cassie tensed as she looked down at it.

It was of Margot.

Margot was dressed in the turquoise coat she'd worn when she died. She was sitting on the bed and staring directly at the camera.

"What the hell?" Cassie whispered to herself.

This was the most recent footage on the camera, and it must have been taken on the night Margot died.

She was saying something. Carefully, Cassie turned up the sound, not daring to breathe as Margot's angry voice filled the room.

"You bastard," Margot slurred, staring at the painting with narrowed eyes.

"You didn't think I knew this camera was here, did you? Of course I did, I'm not as stupid as you think I am. I don't believe what you tell me, either. Gone to the chalet for the night? Oh, I don't think so. You're with one of your girlfriends, I know all about them. Perhaps you've taken Cassie somewhere, if you didn't get your fill of her earlier. Or maybe this time, you've gone to Helene. Don't pretend to me you've stopped seeing her. You're still calling her, I'm sure. You're a lying, cheating bastard, Pierre, and I regret the day I met you."

At that moment, Margot stopped her rambling and turned to stare at the bedroom door, as if she'd been interrupted by a sound.

Dread sent icy fingers down Cassie's spine.

This was where she would walk into the picture. She was certain the door would open and she'd be standing there. Memories churned in her brain. Fragments of a fight, and the way Jacqui had felt in her dream as she'd shoved her. The scream she remembered, as sharp and shrill as if she'd heard it while she was awake, and the uncontrollable feeling of her own anger.

The boundaries between reality and imagination had been blurred for Cassie, but the camera would have recorded every detail in sharp focus.

Cassie steeled herself to watch, wondering if she would be able to handle seeing herself commit a murder.

Chapter Thirty Six

Cassie watched the screen, clutching the camera with cold hands, fearing the worst as the seconds ticked by.

The bedroom door remained closed and she let out a slow, trembling breath as Margot turned her attention back to the camera.

Margot must have heard Cassie when she'd sleepwalked to the door, but she hadn't come into the bedroom and that filled her with sick relief.

Margot continued with her diatribe.

"I know you'll never let me leave. Your massive ego won't allow it. You'll never let me be successful again in my career. I'm so sick of you, and your lies, and your desperate need to control everything in your life. I'm tired of all of this."

Margot stood up, swaying slightly.

"I can't be bothered to fight you. So I'm going to end it, and guess what?"

Margot stabbed her finger at the camera.

"It's your fault. You're to blame. And I hope you feel guilty knowing you were responsible."

Cassie's heart hammered in her throat.

"No, Margot, please don't. Don't do it," she pleaded, even though she knew it was already too late.

"Goodbye, Pierre," Margot said.

Cassie clapped her hand over her mouth in horror as the blonde woman stumbled out of the bedroom and climbed onto a balcony chair. She balanced on the railing, swaying for an endless moment, and then fell, diving down into the darkness and disappearing from the picture.

"Oh, no, oh my God, no, I can't believe this," Cassie muttered.

She put the camera down and rubbed her eyes furiously, pressing her hands over them, wishing she could erase the vivid imagery from her memory. The resigned fury in Margot's demeanor and the desperation in her voice were chilling.

Margot had killed herself, and filmed it, to exact a twisted revenge on Pierre. And he had never found out about it. There hadn't been a chance for him to view the latest footage stored on the camera; he hadn't known that last recording had been made at all.

Cassie's eyes opened wide again as she realized this recording proved Pierre's innocence.

It proved, beyond any doubt whatsoever, that Margot had in fact committed suicide, and that cleared Pierre of all suspicion.

She remembered what Marnie had said earlier. You could do the easy thing, or you could do the right thing.

The easy thing would be to put this camera back behind the painting and pretend she'd never known it was there.

The right thing would be to take it to the police.

Then Cassie started wondering about what would happen if she did.

Pierre had been reluctant to sign the children over to their aunt, even with the charges against him. If he was cleared of all charges, Cassie was certain he would renege on the agreement and carry on with his life. The children's happy future with Josephine would be cut short and they would return to the chateau. Helene would move in and the toxic cycle would repeat itself. For Pierre, it was all about power. The children gave him status as a family man in the community and their presence back home would help him to rebuild his reputation after being unfairly accused of the crime.

Cassie had seen how scarred, how damaged the three were. This was their only chance at a better life, in a more stable home, with an aunt who loved them dearly.

She could do what was easy, or what was right.

But perhaps there was a third choice, the hardest one of all, which would be to do what was best for everyone, and that would be to erase this footage.

To delete it from the camera, and remove the memory card so that no backup could possibly remain. To dispose of the card somewhere else, to drop it into a dustbin at a shopping center or flush it down a toilet so that it disappeared forever and no trace of it was found.

Cassie found she couldn't breathe as she considered the implications.

If she did that, Pierre would have to face his charges, even though he was innocent of them. He might well be found guilty of a crime he never committed. He could spend a long time in prison—a life sentence, at worst, and he would have signed his children into someone else's care.

And Cassie would be committing a crime herself by destroying this evidence. She could certainly go to jail.

Cassie's lips tightened as she remembered how Pierre had almost raped her, how he'd threatened and assaulted her, the helpless fear she'd felt in his presence knowing that he could, and would, do as he pleased. She thought about the threats he had made to others and how scared they were of him, and how even people in the community were frightened of speaking badly about him, though they had reason to.

The way that the chateau staff tried desperately to be invisible around him because he felt entitled to do as he pleased and take what he wanted. How he'd been cheating on Margot and had made her so miserable that she couldn't see a way out. He'd abused her emotionally and she had killed herself, seeing no other way to escape. She'd wanted Pierre to pay for what he'd done to her but the ironic twist to her actions was that if he knew about this footage, he'd be getting off scot-free. That wasn't what Margot had intended, and it wasn't even fair.

Then, most importantly, there were the children to consider. They had certainly suffered abuse at his hands. They were being brought up in a toxic environment that was all about control, rather than love. Now they had the chance to make a new life, a brand new start. They could heal, they could move forward, they could learn to function as normal, happy family members again.

Cassie would have to take the responsibility, and bear the guilt, for this decision for the rest of her life.

Could she do it?

Cassie hesitated for a while, wondering at the circumstances that had led her to this undiscovered footage, which had the power to change the course of so many lives in so many ways. She thought about imagination and reality, and how blurred their boundaries had become in her world.

"Decision time," she said aloud, and she was suddenly sure what the right course of action would be.

Quickly, before she could debate it with herself any further, she pressed the Delete button and erased the footage from the camera.

With that single touch, Margot's last words were erased forever, her secrets locked in the past.

Cassie found the memory card and removed it, shoving it deep in her pocket. She'd throw it out someplace where it would never be found, when she was far away from here.

She replaced the camera in the alcove, hung the painting back in its place, and smoothed the bedspread where she'd sat so that it looked as if she'd never been there at all. Then she walked out of the room.

She'd feared that she would feel tormented by guilt after what she'd done, but she felt strangely peaceful, as if justice had been achieved.

As she turned around, she thought she saw a flash of turquoise—but looking again, perhaps it had been a reflection of light in the window.

"Goodbye," she whispered, and closed the door.

Now Available for Pre-Order!

ALMOST LOST
(The Au Pair—Book Two)

ALMOST LOST (THE AU PAIR—BOOK #2) is the second book in a new psychological thriller series by debut author Blake Pierce.

When a divorcee vacationing in the British countryside puts out an ad for an au pair, Cassandra Vale, 23, broke, still reeling from the ruins of her last placement in France, takes the job without hesitation. Wealthy, handsome and generous, with two sweet children, she feels nothing can go wrong.

But can it?

Treated to the best England has to offer, and with France out of sight, Cassandra dares to believe she finally has a moment to catch her breath—until a startling revelation forces her to question the truths of her tumultuous past, her employer, and her very own sanity.

A riveting mystery replete with complex characters, layers of secrets, dramatic twists and turns and heart-pounding suspense, ALMOST LOST is book #2 in a psychological suspense series that will have you turning pages late into the night.

Book #3 in the series—ALMOST DEAD—is available for pre-order!

ALMOST LOST
(The Au Pair—Book Two)